OUTSTANDING PRAISE FOR

SHIRLEY ROUSSEAU MURPHY'S

JOE GREY SERIES . . .

"This is delightful entertainment. It would be a true cat-tastrophe if you let it pass you by."
Todd David Schwartz, CBS Radio, Four Stars
(Highest Rating)

THE CAT, THE DEVIL, AND LEE FONTANA

"This is excellent reading, whether you believe or not. Not to be missed!"
Armchair Detective

By Shirley Rousseau Murphy

By Shirley Rousseau Murphy and Pat J.J. Murphy

SHIRLEY ROUSSEAU MURPHY

CAT SHOUT FOR JOY

A JOE GREY MYSTERY

wm

WILLIAM MORROW

An Imprint of HarperCollinsPublishers

First William Morrow mass market printing: November 2016
First William Morrow hardcover printing: February 2016

ISBN 978-0-06240350-6

William Morrow® and HarperCollins® is a registered trademark of HarperCollins Publishers.

16 17 18 19 20 QGM 10 9 8 7 6 5 4 3 2 1

For 99, a fine, bossy tomcat, and for Joanne, who allowed him to leave this earth with dignity, allowed him not to suffer.

For the cat is cryptic,
And close to strange things
That men cannot see.

—H. P. LOVECRAFT, "The Cats of Ulthar"

Prologue

EVENING DREW DOWN quicker than the old woman liked. She hurried up the wooded hill with her grocery bags; she wanted to be in the house before dark. She didn't like living alone since her nephew and his wife moved out, and this evening she had lingered too long chatting with a friend at the village market. Around her now there was only silence; nothing stirred on the narrow, shadowed street or in the overgrown yards.

Suddenly she was struck from behind, a hard blow across her shoulders that knocked her sprawling. Pain shocked through her, her hands ground into asphalt where she tried to catch herself; grocery bags flew from her arms, apples bounced away, cans of soup and beans rolled into the gutter. Flailing, trying to right herself, she heard racing footsteps, soft-soled shoes running, and then silence;

a dark figure vanished among the dusky trees, blending with the shadows and then gone.

Terrified, she slowly got to her feet, nearly falling again when she put weight on her throbbing leg. She found a tissue in her pocket and wiped at the blood, staring up and down the darkening street and into the neighbors' yards: tangled trees and bushes, no one there that she could see, no one to threaten her now. And no one to help her. Nervously she studied the unlit houses and empty driveways. Every window was black, folks not home yet from work. A few part-time summer cottages still closed up since winter. She shivered, weak and shaken, cold with shock at the cruel prank.

What else could it be but a prank? She hadn't been robbed: her purse still hung from her arm, the leather scarred in long scratches where she'd fallen. She'd read about an earlier attack or two, had seen news clips on TV, had thought they were flukes, that such a thing wouldn't happen again, not in their cozy village. Surely not in this quiet neighborhood, though she was always careful. She wanted to get home. Wanted to be safe inside her own house where she could call the police. Still frightened but growing angry now, she picked up what groceries she could find and hurried uphill toward her own empty house.

1

SPRING FOG," JOE Grey said, shivering, lifting a wet paw and licking irritably at his sleek fur. "May is supposed to be sunny, warm." Though the gray tomcat knew better, he knew as well as Dulcie that Molena Point weather, this time of year, was always unpredictable. The morning fog, in fact, pleased him well enough; the shielding mist was perfect for the hunt as they prowled the jagged rooftops. Their quarry wasn't pigeons or roof rats but human prey, their attention on the village streets below, on the narrow, fog-shrouded sidewalks. The cozy shops were still closed this early in the morning, the wares in their windows indistinct behind the shifting mist. Here, the hint of a doorway, the vague outline of a cypress or pine; there the corner of a window ledge, a half-seen pot of flowers. Only an occasional pedestrian passed, bundled up against the chill, wool scarf tucked into a down jacket, a warm cap pulled low; each passed into the damp haze and was gone again, the streets empty once more.

In the pearly light, trotting up and down from peak to peak, Dulcie gleamed rich with dark stripes; but the gray tomcat seemed nearly lost in the gloom. Only his white paws and the white stripe down his nose shone out flashing as he dropped from a gable into a hollow between overlapping roofs. Together they slipped along the edge of the shingles, peering over, scanning one street and then the next, their noses and ears nearly frozen. Their warm breakfast of pancakes and eggs seemed a very long time past.

On the fog-wet streets the tires of an occasional vehicle hushed by, then again silence. They watched a lone woman leave her motel, strolling idly, wrapped in a heavy sweater, looking in the shop windows, watched until she disappeared inside a steamy café; the few tourists who had remained after the weekend, maybe hoping for better weather, would still be abed or drinking coffee beside a warm fire. Or the hardiest ones already off running the beach, smug and righteous in their exertion, sweating despite the chill.

But as the cats prowled the roofs alert for the human predator, their moods were deeply mixed. Their urgency to spot the assailant, to pass his description to the cops and help put an end to this cruelty, ran crosswise to their distaste at having to witness such an attack, the brutal terrorizing of innocent citizens, most of them frail or elderly. What was his purpose? The victims were never robbed. This wanton cruelty was the dark side of humanity that the cats hated—the flip side to the love and kindness with which their own human friends embraced them.

But another sadness filled the cats as well. A distress that had nothing to do with the street prowler, one that no amount of their own effort could change. A mourning filled them for the old yellow tomcat: Misto was failing; his debilitating illness would soon take him.

His pain had begun suddenly, the cancer progressing rapidly. Already this morning, just at dawn, Joe and Dulcie had sat with him as he drifted in and out of sleep; as, off in the kitchen of the Firetti cottage, Mary washed up the breakfast dishes, and Dr. John Firetti was across the garden seeing overnight patients in his veterinary clinic. Quietly the cats had tried to ease Misto, to love him. They had left him only when Misto himself hissed and sent them away. Tucked up among the pillows in the big double bed, the fragile yellow tom wanted simply to nap. Joe and Dulcie had gone, looking back wistfully. They were not as resigned to his fate as was Misto himself. He was weak and tired, yet he seemed quite content, facing these last days of his long and adventurous life.

"You can't change what is," he had told them. "You can do nothing about my illness. I'm lucky to be among those I love. I'm happy to end up here, where I was born, after my life's long journey. *This* life," he'd said, "this life is not the end." He'd yawned and pawed at the pillows. "I have known more lives than this one, and I will know more yet to come.

"But right now," he'd said, flipping his thin tail, "now I need sleep. Go, my dears," he'd said, extending a gentle paw. "Come back when I'm rested, when the pain meds have kicked in for the day."

As Joe and Dulcie turned away, Misto had given Dulcie a secret and conspiratorial smile. Joe, catching his look, continued even now to puzzle over it, though he had asked no question. He'd trotted away beside Dulcie in silence as the old yellow tomcat rolled over and started to snore.

Joe had waited for Dulcie to explain, yet she'd said nothing. What secret was this? What could be so urgent that his lady would keep it from him? While Misto's malaise left both cats steeped in sadness, Dulcie had shared her deepest conscience, her most private thoughts, only with the old yellow tom.

EARLIER THAT MORNING before Joe arrived at Misto's cottage, when Dulcie and the old cat were alone together, he'd given her a deep, steady look. "Life and death hang in balance, now, Dulcie. My life is ending. But you alone guard new lives."

How could he know that? She had looked at him, shocked, her green eyes wide.

But then she smiled. Of course Misto would know her most private secret. How often did the old cat know what was in another cat's mind, what lay hidden in the past or even ahead, in the future. How often did Misto divine secrets Dulcie could never dream.

"As the end of my days draws near," he'd said, "three bright new lives have begun for you, my dear. Oh, yes," he'd said, twitching a whisker. "Three dear little lives snuggled safe and warm in *your* most secret world. And," Misto had said, studying her, "you have not yet told Joe Grey."

She had told no one. Except her human housemate, because how could she *not* tell Wilma, when Dulcie threw up her breakfast every morning?

But yet Misto knew, with those same powers that let him remember ages long past and let him see into the future. "Three kittens, three tiny mites," he'd said, "snuggled within, secret and warm and happy." And he had known more than that about her unborn kits; he had said, with a faint and ragged purr, "Three strong babies waiting eagerly to be born, two boy kits, and a calico girl.

"And," he had told her, "there is an amazement about the calico kitten. She . . ." But he began to yawn, and before he could continue, the old cat had drifted into sleep, as was often the way since his illness. Maybe it was the medication sending him dozing, or maybe he thought he had said enough. Dulcie only knew that now, prowling the roofs in the cold fog, she fidgeted with unanswered questions. What had Misto started to tell her? What *about* her girl kitten, *what* amazement?

And, though she longed to tell Joe Grey about the kittens, still she didn't know how to tell him. What would Joe say when he learned that new little lives waited within the dark of her sheltering body? Would he *want* kittens, this tomcat whose very existence was committed to the exciting dangers of tracking human criminals? To the uncertainties of helping the law, of apprehending evil? Would fatherhood hold him back from what he was born to do? Would rallying around helpless babies, while burning to chase after human scum, only make him restless and cross? Joe Grey was not an ordinary tomcat to casually father a litter and then disappear. Would the innate commitment, the very responsibilities of kittens, *his* kittens, only distress him?

And, she wondered, if she told Joe about the kittens now, would that news make Misto's impending death seem even more cruel by comparison? As if the inestimable powers of the universe meant to take Misto's life in exchange for the three new lives soon to be?

She knew that made no sense. But would such an idea strike Joe, as he grieved for their dying friend? Would such thoughts make him turn away from her joyous secret?

Or was the intention of the greater powers not to exchange life for life, but instead to fill the emptiness, once their friend had departed? To bring new happiness into their world through these young, fledgling spirits?

No matter how she pondered the question, she didn't know how to tell Joe. And she didn't know *when* to tell him. Now, as they watched the foggy streets, still she kept her own counsel; though she was amused that Joe hadn't already guessed, by the look of her.

She liked to think she was still svelte and sleek, that no one would see her condition. But when at home she posed before Wilma's full-length mirror, looking at herself sideways, she could see the gentle curve of the babies that waited safe beneath her tabby-striped fur.

Well, she was just as fast as ever at the hunt. Or nearly as fast. Maybe it took a little more effort to outrun a rat and take him down; maybe she was a bit slow keeping up with Joe, was too often the last to rise after resting in the grassy fields. So far Joe had said nothing about the changes. He was either being polite or was too occupied with the crimes that had beset the village and with Misto's illness to think much about a lazy partner.

And, Dulcie worried, what would happen to Misto's spirit when he'd left them? *Would* the old cat step into a new life, as he said would happen? Into the bright realm where, he told them, all souls journeyed after this world? *Were* Misto's tales of multiple lives true or were his stories of a long and varied past, before this life, only fabrications, the yellow tom's imaginative fancies?

Yet what he'd told them of those past lives was linked to facts in the present, to photographs of a long-ago child Misto had known, to the cache of hidden money the cats had found, to so much that was very real, that they could do no less than believe him. But now, as the old cat grew thinner and his life faded, now when Misto asked for his son, Pan, they knew he was reaching his last days. The old cat was weak, indeed, if he had forgotten that just a few days earlier, before Misto grew ill, Pan had left the village. That the red tom would already be too far away from Molena Point for anyone to ever find him—Pan and tortoiseshell Kit were off on an adventure of which they had only dreamed; they had set out for a world where perhaps no sensible feline would venture. They wandered, now, on a journey they would not have begun had they guessed that Pan's father soon would die.

If, when they departed, Misto had already divined his own illness, he didn't tell Pan. He had wanted them to pursue their journey free and happy, perhaps the greatest adventure, in *this* world, that any cat could know.

But then later Misto, caught in the haze of pain medication, would forget they were away, traveling, and would ask for Pan. And then, remembering, the old cat would drop his ears, embarrassed. But then he would look at Dulcie and remember she was expecting kittens and the old cat would smile. In illness, his moods and the clarity of his thinking swung alarmingly, frightening Dulcie, and saddening Joe Grey.

Now on the foggy rooftops Joe and Dulcie dropped down from a high peak to a shingled slope, moving on toward Ocean Avenue, toward the village's main street. Pausing sometimes, they looked idly into the second-floor windows of scattered penthouses where residents had left their shades up. Folks glancing out while showering or brushing their teeth knew there was nobody up on the roofs to see them—only gliding seagulls, and a pair of prowling cats peering in. They had no idea how their morning rituals amused the two feline observers. But at last the pair moved on, watching the streets and listening—and suddenly they leaped to the roof's edge.

Paws in the roof gutter, they cocked their ears to a sound barely heard. They caught an elusive aroma drifting on the mist. Every sense alert, they stood seeking through the fog, keen to spot the attacker, hoping they might alert some unwary would-be victim.

But it was only a dowdy woman walking her three leashed beagles, only the hush of her footsteps and of their paws and the faint jingling of their collars.

So far neither the cats nor the cops had any clue to the

street prowler. He left footprints that the police photographed or picked up electronically or captured in casts, but they had nothing to match them to. They'd detained no suspect, had found no matching footprints from another crime scene, no shoes tossed into a Dumpster, yet the prints at each attack were different.

Even more puzzling to the cats, the attacker left no scent for them to follow. Always some mélange of competing smells got in their way: diesel exhaust, the heavy aroma of fresh bread and cakes from a nearby bakery, the stink of marigolds crushed underfoot, the overlying exhaust of a vanished car in which the guy might have fled. "Maybe," Joe had said bitterly, "he can levitate like some would-be comic-book hero."

Whether the assaults exploded out of cruelty or were born of some unknown reason, or were a sick prank with no real purpose at all, no one yet knew. Nor had the attacker left a clue at any scene, no dropped possession, not even trace evidence of hairs or fabric particles, no lost button; the perp seemed as ghostly as if, indeed, he had materialized from some phantom life.

Nor was there ever a loiterer nearby to be questioned as a witness. With each incident, the cats' frustration grew apace with that of the detectives, the patience of both sets of sleuths wearing thin. The cats' usual pleasure at offering Molena Point PD a telling clue, the officers' stoic reception of mysteriously proffered information, all came to nothing. There was no information. Meanwhile lone senior citizens were being injured and frightened. Those older folks who had not been attacked, but who read the local paper, listened to the news, and gossiped among their friends, grew more wary and angry. One of the victims had been in a wheelchair, two walking with canes, folks out to take care of a few errands, get a little air. Each one was knocked down, wheelchair or cane cast aside. And the perp was gone, vanished, leaving the victim to the mercy of whoever might happen along and find them; but none of the marks was robbed.

When the assaults first began, MPPD had put on extra patrols: more squad cars cruising, officers on foot dressed in street clothes. Vacation leaves were postponed, overtime was increased. Of the seven who were accosted, one lady was a ninety-two-year-old music teacher living in a retirement home. A frail, retired banker, Ogden Welder, was fatally injured, the assailant gone before anyone heard his cries; Welder died in the hospital two days later.

No arrests and no witnesses. Only when someone heard shouts for help and arrived to find a frail person, frightened and angry, sprawled on the cement among spilled packages, was anyone aware of the crime. As more officers of MPPD worked the streets, their response to drug crimes, traffic accidents, shoplifting, and domestics demanded additional personnel that Max Harper didn't have. Like every police department in the state they were understaffed, their budget stretched too thin for adequate overtime. There was plenty of city money for beautification and tourism promotion, but never enough for law enforcement—money for the politicians, but not enough to protect those who voted them in. Max Harper's men and women grew ever more frustrated.

At the first assault, the cats' anger had flared. At the second one, on a lone, helpless citizen, their rage revved high. Slipping into Molena Point PD they had lounged in Chief Harper's bookcase, innocently reading field reports over his shoulder—though there hadn't been much that they didn't already know, that they hadn't read in the paper, heard on the news, or heard from Joe's housemate. Clyde Damen had grown up with Max Harper. Often over dinner or playing poker Max shared information that he knew—or thought he knew—would never go any farther than the Damens' kitchen table. There, as the cards were shuffled and poker chips tossed into the pot, no one paid attention to the gray tomcat and maybe Dulcie, too, curled up in the easy chair quietly napping. Who would notice the twitch of an ear, the flip of a tail at some interesting new detail of the street crimes? Joe Grey's own housemates were as secretive, regarding the tomcat's spying, as was Joe himself.

Now, at the edge of the roof, the cats alerted again at the sudden swish of tires approaching down the fog-wet street. They watched an unmarked white van slip into view, but it was maybe only the delivery truck of some small company bringing produce or bakery goods to one of the restaurants. Farther on, a lone runner trotted by heading for the beach; there were always runners, lean men or women, tanned and seemingly carefree. Soon, from the shore, a dog barked. A flock of gulls rose screaming, and then silence again; when they heard nothing more they lay down at the roof's edge and had a leisurely wash.

"I wish," Dulcie said, "Kit and Pan were home. Surveillance would be easier with four of us. Besides, I miss them," she said, giving Joe a green-eyed look.

"Just wish them home safe," Joe said crossly. He didn't

approve of the flighty tortoiseshell and the red tom-cat chasing off into a world that Joe himself could hardly believe in, a world Kit called magical. Except he had to believe there was such a place, when their human friend Kate Osborne had gone there. Kate told startling tales, and had brought back enough jewels and artifacts to convince even Joe himself—and to make him even more nervous thinking of Kit and Pan venturing down into those vast caverns beneath the earth. They had been gone only a few days, and still the thought of that journey made his fur crawl.

That land had fascinated tortoiseshell Kit even when she was very young, listening to a band of feral cats tell their stories. Only later when she was older had thoughts of those hidden caverns begun to frighten her. But Pan had no fear; he had traveled the length of California and Oregon on his own, a hobo cat, staying out of danger. Now, learning of the Netherworld, he had burned to see that farthest, most enticing realm of all.

Kit, half longing to go and half afraid, had given in, to please him. And, because her two human housemates had longed to be off on their own adventure. Lucinda and Pedric would never have followed their own dream, of an Alaska cruise, if it meant leaving their beloved companion alone at home. The little speaking cat was their treasure beyond all other joys. Kit knew that. She knew Alaska beckoned to her two housemates. But only if she herself journeyed away from Molina Point would her old couple feel free to take the leisurely, small-ship cruise they longed for. Lucinda and Pedric weren't getting any younger. "If you don't go now," she'd told them, perhaps with more honesty than finesse, "you may never go at all."

Kit had given Lucinda a soft purr. "Ryan's father and his new wife are keen to go with you—it will be an easier trip with another couple. Mike and Lindsey are quiet and steady, and—"

"And they are younger and stronger than we are," Lucinda said, laughing. "You needn't say it, they'll take good care of us. They'll be good companions to investigate the little ports and scattered villages."

Kit smiled, and nosed at Lucinda. "You will take your adventure, and Pan and I will take ours. That is what life is about. And then," she said, purring, "we'll be home together again. Oh, my! To tell each other all the wonders we saw!"

It was just a few days ago that they had said their teary good-byes. That Lucinda and Pedric, Mike and Lindsey boarded their plane for Vancouver—and Kit and Pan crossed the village up into the hills and joined the waiting group of feral, speaking cats who had lingered, waiting for them. Waiting to set out together down into the Netherworld; and none of the speaking cats, not even Pan himself, had any notion that Pan's father would soon lie ill.

Now, this foggy morning, Joe and Dulcie, left without enough cat power for efficient surveillance, were about to separate, each to watch the streets alone, when a siren's whoop and the wail of the medics' van brought them sharply alert. As the roar of the engines headed fast for Ocean Avenue, they glimpsed the van and two squad cars make a skidding turn onto the divided main street and vanish beyond the buildings. The cats marked where the sound of the engines died, heard vehicle doors flung open and men running, and they fled over the roofs toward the action.

2

OLD MERLE RODIN said later, it was his wristwatch that put him in the hospital. His wife wasn't home at the time. He was alone, dressed in old denim pants, a faded denim shirt and suspenders, working in his shop when he tore his watch-band on the corner of the vise. The soft leather was worn ragged anyway and had been ready to tear. And then, as he was cleaning up from painting the wooden chairs, he spilled turpentine on the band and he knew the wet leather would tear worse. He didn't want to lose the watch, it was the only kind he could read anymore, the new ones were all dots and squiggles. This was a good, reliable Swiss Army with big black numbers so a person could tell the *time*. Big dial, plain and no-nonsense. He left the watch loose on his wrist, finished cleaning up the workbench, got in his car and drove the few blocks into the village to get the band replaced.

He parked in a handicapped spot in front of the Village Inn. He eased out, pulled his crutches out, locked the car, and swung along the narrow walk that led behind the hotel to the little courtyard, to the row of small shops tucked in around a patch of garden, heading for the jeweler's door. There were miniature courts all over the village with their little, half-hidden vendors. Each retreat was, to a tourist, a new and exciting discovery; that's one of the reasons visitors came to Molena Point, for this kind of special charm.

He didn't like his reflection flicking along the fog-dim windows. His white beard and crutches, his hobbling walk made him look older than he was; some days he felt old, but he didn't like to see it.

The village was nearly deserted this early, the stores not open yet, and the streets so foggy. The few early tourists would still be holed up, and most of the locals, too. But the jeweler was always there early working on the books, cleaning up, puttering around; even if he kept the door locked, he'd let you in if he knew you.

The newspaper warned folks not to go into empty courtyards and alleys alone, since the attacks began. But this court was safe enough, being right by the hotel. The paper claimed the cops didn't have a lead yet to the source of the crimes—and the Molena Point cops were good at what they did. Too bad, nice little village like this, so much crime suddenly. Maybe he *was* getting old. He didn't like the changes he was seeing in the world, didn't like what the world had become.

Moving on into the courtyard, walking slowly, he placed his crutches carefully on the uneven bricks so not to stumble on the edge of a flower bed and tip over into the cyclamens. Their array of red and pink flowers had bloomed all winter among their intricately patterned leaves. They would die back soon now, once summer was on them. Sure enough, there were lights on in the jewelry store. He was heading across the court, for the glass door, when he was hit from behind. His crutches flew out from under him. He spun around, striking out at the attacker. He hit a glancing blow with his left fist and fell sprawling, his arm twisted under him. His legs twisted, too, tangled in the crutches. A violent pain dizzied him where his head was struck.

He didn't know how long he'd lain there, the wind knocked out of him, when he heard the siren, a blurred, faraway sound as if he were half asleep. One whoop, then silence. Then a tangle of voices, and people kneeling around him, putting machines on him to take his blood pressure, his pulse. A man wiping at his forehead with something cold and stinging. Uniformed medics lifting him onto a stretcher, covering him with a blanket, really careful of his arm, lifting it gently. He didn't try to move it, he knew it was broken. He didn't know, until later in the hospital, that he'd lost his watch.

He didn't know, and never would know, how the Swiss Army watch was found, that two cats found it lying in the flower bed deep beneath the cyclamens.

Joe Grey and Dulcie discovered the watch long after Merle Rodin had been lifted into the medics' van and driven away, after the cops had finished their search of the scene and the crowd had dispersed. Merle wasn't there to see the gray tomcat and his tabby lady slip down a vine from the hotel roof and trot across the courtyard to where he had lain; to see a discerning tabby nose and a gray and white nose sniffing among the cyclamens, twitching at the smell of turpentine that the cops, with their inferior sense of smell, had missed. Merle didn't see a soft tabby paw reach down among the leaves to investigate the wristwatch or see Dulcie sniff at it again. He didn't see the two cats slip out of the courtyard leaving the watch where it lay, the cats galloping fast up the street, noses to the faint breeze following the turp-scented air where the attacker had fled.

Fog held the stink of turpentine low against the sidewalk. But as Joe and Dulcie raced after the scent that had transferred to the mugger when Merle struck out at him, the smell vanished. It ended at the curb, replaced by the smell of exhaust as if the attacker had stepped into a car and sped away.

The street was empty. No car moved now in either direction. But then as the fog shifted, the heady smell of sandalwood drowned all other scents. The cats slid into the shadows as the proprietor of the oriental rug shop passed them, sandalwood aftershave drifting back to them as he paused to unlock his store. As he disappeared inside, Dulcie sniffed again at the curb.

"There's not only exhaust," she said, looking up at Joe. She watched as he, too, sniffed again at the concrete.

"Oil," he said, his yellow eyes brightening, "bicycle oil. Maybe he didn't get away in a car." He sniffed again, breathing deeply, his whiskers twitching. "But still a hint of the turpentine, too. Maybe we *can* catch him." Noses to the pavement like a pair of tracking hounds, they raced away, ran out along the street swerving past parked cars, glad there was hardly any traffic, that they needn't dodge moving wheels.

The smells they followed continued for three blocks but then suddenly the turp and oil were gone, vanished in the wake of a noisy street sweeper, its huge roller-brushes sucking away every leaf, every scrap of paper, and every errant smell. Its roar drove instinctive fear through the cats: every fiber of their beings trembled, fearful the hungry juggernaut would crush them if they drew close. They might be wiser than most cats, they might be brave when facing a human killer, but this monster reached down into their darkest, ancient instincts, terrifying them both.

Only when the sweeper had passed did they relax. They followed it, sniffing along its wake, but no scent remained. The giant spinning brushes had destroyed the trail. And the perp himself was long gone. A faint sea wind began to tease them, and to stir and thin the fog. Soon all they could smell was salty iodine, a hint of dead fish, and the pine and cypress trees that sheltered the narrow streets. Glancing at each other, the cats were of one thought.

Leaping up the nearest oak, they headed for Molena Point PD. By this time, Chief Harper would have information on the victim: driver's license, other identification from the man's billfold, maybe a hospital report on his condition. Maybe the responding officer's field notes were already on Max's desk. Off they raced over tiles and shingles, Joe's mind fully on the assaults. But as the gray tomcat tried to understand the perp's motive, Dulcie lagged behind, feeling tired again suddenly, feeling awkward and heavy.

She didn't like to think that as her pregnancy advanced, she would become truly clumsy, that she wouldn't be able to keep up with Joe. Who needed a fat, slow partner trying to do detective work? This frustration, plus having lost the trail of the attacker, plus her underlying distress over Misto, left the little tabby padding slowly and disconsolately across the tiled roof of the courthouse.

Ahead on the roof of the PD, Joe had stopped. He stood looking back at her, puzzled by her slow approach, his lady who usually ran circles around him. It was just as she joined him that a woman came out the door of the police station below, her high heels tapping. She didn't notice her scarf slip off her shoulder to fall among the bushes, a pink scarf hidden now beneath the bottlebrush blooms. Dulcie froze, watching.

The pale pink gauze excited her, brought her sharply alert, stirred in her a possessive greed she hadn't felt since she was a very young cat. Her longing for that soft, beautiful garment filled her suddenly with a keen, claw-snatching desire. She wanted that scarf. Her passion surged anew from her long-ago thieving days. The pink scarf was *hers*; the woman had carelessly lost it and now it was meant for her. Her passion returned for the silk stockings she had stolen, the satin teddies she had lifted from neighbors' bedrooms, slipping out through an open window, the lovely cashmere sweaters she had dragged home and hidden when she was very young—had hidden until Wilma found them, until her embarrassed and amused human housemate had called the neighbors and given them back their treasures. The disappearance of each item, which Dulcie had so cleverly stolen, had broken the little cat's heart.

Now, awash in her early passion for possession, she flashed past Joe and down the oak and into the bushes. Creeping under the dense and leafy shelter, she snatched the scarf, pawed it into a little bundle in her mouth, and ran, through the bushes and away. She paused only when the tap of high heels returned down the walk. Dropping the scarf, she reared up to look.

Peering over the bottlebrush blooms she watched the woman searching, watched her look all around and then turn back into the station as if to ask if she'd lost the scarf there. Gripping the soft scarf again, Dulcie hurried away beneath the leafy shelter. She stopped only when, glancing out toward the street, she saw a wheelchair coming down the sidewalk beyond the parking lot, a middle-aged woman gliding along turning the wheels with her hands; clearly she was being followed.

She was lean and tanned, her brown hair in a pony-tail threaded through the back of a golf cap. She wore cargo pants, the fabric folded neatly beneath a long steel brace on her left leg. Dulcie could see the corner of a blue shopping bag pushed, bulging, into the back pocket of the wheelchair. Four strides behind the woman, a boy in ragged jeans walked silently, the hood of his heavy black sweatshirt pulled up around his face. He moved slowly, keeping his distance and looking in the other direction, but certainly he was following her.

Could this be the mugger, this *kid*? Dulcie couldn't see enough of him to tell his age, but his walk was easy, like a boy. She sniffed, but at this distance she caught no turpentine scent, no smell of bicycle oil.

Was he waiting until the wheelchair had passed the PD and was in a more deserted part of the village before he attacked?

But again, why? What was his purpose? The attacker never stole anything; he shoved, pushed someone over, and ran. None of this made sense. A shout stopped the boy in his tracks, and stopped the woman. A shout from atop the roof, shocking Dulcie.

"Look out, you're being followed. You, boy . . . Get away from her!" *Joe's voice.* Oh, he wouldn't cry out in public, he wouldn't chance being seen!

She couldn't see above her, she was too near the building; but Joe would already be gone, safely hidden.

As the boy stood looking, the wheelchair-bound woman spun to face him. When she started after him, the boy ran. He was fast, disappearing in the traffic, dodging cars. She was fast, too, but she stopped at the curb. Two pedestrians had turned to stare, but their attention was on the woman. A bus went by; when it passed, the boy was gone. The two portly tourists, dressed in red sweatshirts, watched the woman for a long moment as she headed away down the street; they talked softly between themselves, then they, too, turned away—and Dulcie's thieving passion had cooled. Joe Grey's shout had sharply upset her. It took a lot for a speaking cat to expose himself like that, a lot of nerve even to whisper, in public. Leaving the scarf beneath the bushes, she slipped out into the parking lot where she could see the roof above.

From that distance, rearing up, she could see that the roof was empty. She thought Joe would be behind that tangle of heat vents, of weathered gray pipes and metal boxes that rose up against the clearing sky. She waited, crouching at the edge of the bottlebrush until Joe appeared, slipping out from the galvanized jungle, and came leaping down the oak tree. Dulcie joined him. She would return the scarf later, to the PD, would leave it for the clerk to find. Maybe the woman had left a phone number in case someone discovered it. Guilt touched her only a little; her surge of greed had been deeply therapeutic. She felt like herself again, her passion to steal, her wild dash dragging that soft and silken prize, had left her refreshed and wide awake and like her old, wild self once more—no longer just a pregnant cat growing heavy and lethargic. She was her bright, kitten-self again. Her joy burned young and rash, she was a whole cat once more: thief cat when the mood took her, mother cat, cop cat. She was all together now; she felt strong again, and complete.

Beside her, Joe Grey was frowning. If he was annoyed or amused at her thieving, he said nothing. "Should we report that guy? Head for your house, and call the chief?"

"What are we going to report? He didn't attack the woman. Maybe *she'll* report it, maybe she'll call in."

"But we saw him. A kid . . ."

"What did we see, Joe? Dark clothes, a black hoodie, and he was gone. We don't know if he would have attacked her. He was so bundled up, we don't know if that *was* a kid. Maybe a small adult."

Dulcie sat watching him, her tail twitching. "Let's wait, see if *she* makes the call. If we call in on something so vague . . . that doesn't help the department's confidence in us. They have enough questions about our phone calls, we don't need to make one that's so . . . uncertain." She looked at him steadily, her green eyes wide.

Joe Grey flicked an ear. He knew she was right. Every tip they offered the PD, like every bit of evidence, needed to be solid. Not just a quick glimpse of someone's back, when they couldn't identify him and didn't know *what* he meant to do.

They lingered in the bushes until two officers left the station through the heavy glass door. Slipping in past their heels, the two cats swerved to the right through prisonlike bars into the shadows of the holding cell.

This was not their usual mode of entry. Ordinarily they would stroll into MPPD as brazen as a pair of two-bit lawyers come to bail out a scuzzy client. But today, crouching beneath the bunk that hung from chains in the wall, wrinkling their noses at the stink of stale booze and stale sweat from generations of detainees, they peered warily toward the reception counter.

They would not be greeted today with joy and petting and a little snack from their favorite clerk. No homemade cookies or fried chicken, no hugs and sweet words from blond, pillow-soft Mabel Farthy. Mabel was in the hospital's rehab, recovering from back surgery. The cats missed her and they worried over her, as did all the department. And they knew, too, that if this sour-faced substitute clerk caught them in the station again she'd pitch a fit, would summon an officer to throw them out—though the officer would only smile, would listen to her complaint, but then would go about his own business, leaving the cats to do as they liked. And Evijean wouldn't snatch them up herself; she was too afraid of long claws and sharp teeth.

3

THE LOBBY OF Molena Point PD featured the one holding cell just to the right of the glass doors as you entered. Here a drunk could be temporarily confined or prisoners held for a short period while waiting to be booked. Beyond the holding cell was an austere seating area: seven folding metal chairs, no coffee table strewn with magazines, no potted plants to cheer the nervous visitor. Civilians waited here for their appointment with an officer or detective, perhaps to offer information, to identify stolen items, to pore through a gallery of mug shots, or to file a bad-tempered complaint against some unruly neighbor. To the left of the waiting area ran the long reception desk on which, over the years, Joe and Dulcie had enjoyed Mabel Farthy's gentle petting and ear rubs, her one-sided conversations and, most of all, her homemade treats. Mabel liked to cook; she often brought a freshly baked cake or cookies for the officers, and always the cats got their share. Mable could laugh and hold her own with the men she worked with; everyone loved her. Her replacement, Evijean Simpson, didn't know how to smile.

Evijean didn't bring treats for man or beast, she had no rapport with even the kindest officers, and certainly she had no fellow feeling for a cat. She didn't want stray animals, as she described Joe and Dulcie, to be slipping in contaminating the station with fleas and cat fur.

Evijean was so short that, from the cats' angle on the floor of the holding cell, she was barely visible behind the tall counter. They could see little more than the top of her head, her pale hair pulled back in a bun with ragged ends sticking out. She seemed hardly a presence at all as she moved about among the state-of-the-art radios and electronics. The cats watched until she turned away to stack papers into the copier; then they slid out through the cell bars, made a fast dash to the base of the counter below her line of sight. From there, a stealthy creep down the hall to the half-open door of the chief's office, where they crouched listening.

At first they heard only Max's voice, but then Charlie laughed. Comfortable husband-and-wife talk followed, implying no one else was present. Pushing inside, they saw the two were not alone.

Max Harper was in uniform this morning, not his usual lean western shirt and jeans. He sat at his desk alternately going through a stack of files and entering information on the computer. Charlie sat at one end of the leather couch texting on her phone, though such electronic preoccupation was not Charlie's habit. Her kinky red hair was freshly brushed, smoothed back in a ponytail. Her jeans and pink sweatshirt smelled of fresh hay and clean horses. She wore dangly gold earrings this morning, and had changed her work boots for a pair of handsome leather sandals, which meant that she and Max were probably headed out to lunch.

Detective Dallas Garza occupied one of the leather chairs, reading a report, his tweed sports coat thrown over the other chair, his polo shirt open at the collar. His smooth, tan face was clean-shaven, his short black hair neatly trimmed. He glanced up at Joe and Dulcie, his dark Latino eyes amused, as usual, at how the cats made themselves at home. Only occasionally did Dallas watch them with an uncertain frown.

Though no one in the department knew the cats could speak, they all knew, well, the phone voices of their phantom snitches. Max and the detectives had learned to trust implicitly those anonymous called-in tips; they took the information and ran with it, put that intelligence to good use. No one imagined the informants were their sleek, four-pawed visitors, the department's favorite freeloaders.

So far, the relationship between officers and cats was comfortable and efficient. During the cats' anonymous messages, no officer in the department cross-examined the caller or asked his name. They'd learned to trust the information they were given. If the cats dragged a stolen clue to the station and left it, with a phone call to alert that it was at the back door or inside a squad car, there were no questions. "Found" evidence, useful Visa bills, or a "lost" cell phone? The detectives used what they got and then generated their own follow-up investigation, digging out background facts that would stand in court.

If ever in the future the cats were careless and were caught in the act, discovered talking on the phone, Joe didn't want to think about the consequences. Their well-oiled and effective deception would be down the tubes, the work they loved destroyed in one careless moment. A cop was all about facts; his thinking was no-nonsense and meticulous. Clues, hints, anonymous tips, a good detective might put those together in new and creative combinations and come up with the missing piece. But no cop believed the impossible.

Hopping on the couch beside Charlie, Dulcie stretched out across her lap. Joe looked up into Charlie's lean, freckled face; Charlie always had a happy look even when life, for the moment, took an ugly turn. She petted them both, her green eyes amused at their private secret. She didn't glance up when Max's phone buzzed, but continued to stroke Dulcie and Joe. She did look when Max said sharply, "When? What time? Put Davis on."

He listened, scribbling notes on a printout that he'd inserted in a yellow pad. "You have his belongings? Davis, is his wife there? Stay with her, and see her home. See that she has someone with her." He listened again, then, "I'll talk with the coroner."

He hung up, looked over at Dallas. "Merle Rodin's dead. Cerebral contusion, from the blow he took. You want to go on over, finish up the paperwork while Davis takes care of the wife, gets her statement, makes sure she has friends or family around her?" This part of police work was never pleasant. They did what they could, to ease the pain that nothing could ease.

The Latino detective rose and pulled on his jacket. He gave Charlie a brief hug, and left the office, and Max looked across at Charlie, filling her in. "Lab has the brick that may have hit Rodin. A brick from the border of the flower bed, with what looks like bloodstains. Dr. Alder says there are particles embedded in the scalp that could be the same material." Now it was the coroner's and the lab's job. Charlie's hand was tense, poised on Joe Grey's shoulder.

She said, "He could have fallen on it? Or that street scum picked it up and hit him? That poor old man." Charlie was stoic about most village crime, or appeared to be. The cats knew she often concealed her distress from Max—he had problems enough without worrying about her, too. He didn't need a distraught wife. But these senseless attacks on frail citizens had left her enraged, feeling helpless—as frustrated as the department when the attacks continued and they had no viable clue yet, to give them a lead.

"The blood type on the brick," Max said, "matches Rodin's. But it will take a while for the DNA." The lab in Salinas was always backed up. Max turned off his computer and rose. The cats waited until he and Charlie left for a quick lunch, then they hit the chief's desk.

Pawing through the stack of files, Dulcie took the corner of Max's yellow pad in her teeth, pulled it out from under the folders, and opened it with her claws.

Beneath pages of notes was a printed list of the seven

attacks, with Max's penciled notes in the margins. The victims' individual files, with additional information, would be kept secure on the computer. This page needed no securing; most of this—until the attack on Rodin—had already been in the local paper, on local radio or TV. There had been seven previous victims including one death when banker Ogden Welder died in the hospital. Merle Rodin was the eighth mark, and the second to die. Max's new notation gave the hour, location, and date. Cause of death would wait for the coroner's report.

One interesting fact, new to the cats, was that three of the victims had only recently moved to the village from San Francisco; and that one had been vacationing there, taking a week off from his job at San Francisco General Hospital as a physician's assistant.

"So, San Francisco vectors in," Dulcie said. She cut a look at Joe, knowing what his take would be. Joe didn't believe in coincidence. If you dug long enough you could usually claw out a connection. The tabby gazed hungrily at Max's computer, thinking of the victims' files. With cool speculation, she reached a paw.

Joe stopped her with a quick swipe of claws. "If Evi-jean barges in here, finds us alone before the lit screen, you want to guess what would happen?"

Dulcie smiled a crooked smile, but she jumped down. They'd have to wait until Max or one of the detectives was into the program, some moment when they could lie on the desk idly washing their paws as they shared depart-mental information.

Or wait until one or two officers stopped by Joe's house after his shift, maybe for a few hands of poker with Max and Clyde. Max would talk freely in the Damen household, as would Ryan's Uncle Dallas. Dulcie looked at Joe. "How long do we wait for a poker game?"

Joe shrugged, he wasn't hopeful.

Dulcie said, "Talk to Ryan, she'll get something going." This wouldn't be the first time Ryan would conduct behind-the-scene assistance—she was deceptively casual when she eased Clyde into an unplanned poker night for Joe's benefit: Joe's dark-haired, blue-eyed housemate did love a conspiracy.

But now, "I don't know," Joe said. "As hard as she's working, and the cranky mood she's in, I'm not sure she's up for a poker night. Tekla Bleak, that woman with the remodel, she's driving Ryan crazy. New complaints every day, foolish and arbitrary changes. Ryan comes home at night as snarly as a possum in a trap."

They were quiet as two officers came down the hall. When they'd passed on by, Joe dropped from the desk and peered out toward the lobby. No sign of Evijean—maybe she was sitting at her desk, hidden by the counter. They made a dash for the front door as Officer Brennan came in herding a young man before him, unwashed and smelling of whiskey.

Slipping out the door behind them through the miasma of alcohol, they scrambled up the oak tree. They sat on the tile roof only a moment before they headed across the roofs again, moving south and east in the direction of John Firetti's veterinary clinic. Despite their preoccupation with the attacks, their strongest urge was to sit with Misto. *While we can still be with him*, Dulcie thought sadly.

Below them along the narrow streets the traffic was

heavier now. The fog was thinning, the shops were open, and a few tourists had left their motels, looking up at the sky hoping for sunshine. The smell of coffee and sweet confections rose from the little bakeries, the smell of late bacon and eggs from the small cafés, from clusters of tables in street-side patios. The cats were passing above a tree-shaded court when they stopped, looking down, watching two strangers below. A woman with a cane was limping through the patio toward one of the shops. Behind her a short, older man had turned into the courtyard, walking without sound following the woman, his eyes intently on her; she seemed unaware of him.

4

LOOKING DOWN FROM the roof, engulfed in the smells of café breakfasts, Joe and Dulcie watched the woman in tight black workout clothes limp along toward the back shops of the little courtyard, watched the man following her. Her cane was one of those folding aluminum models. Her face and arms were sun-wrinkled, her calves pale between her cutoffs and black socks. She wore sturdy black walking shoes and a black fanny pack strapped low at her side. She glanced uneasily now at the small, thin man behind her, a grizzle-haired fellow wearing a boy-sized leather jacket and jeans. He moved easily, like a boy. He slowed when the woman slowed and pretended to look in a store window. As she limped along she watched his moving reflections. Turning suddenly, she headed toward a small toy store that was just opening.

The cats could see the owner inside pulling up the shades, a tall, bald man in a pale blue sport shirt. As soon as he unlocked the door the woman stepped inside. The two spoke for a few moments, then she moved deep into the shop. The owner stepped out into the courtyard, stood facing the man with a forbidding look. Everyone in the village, it seemed, was on edge over the assaults. The ragged fellow stared back at him, turned away and headed for the street. Neither had spoken. The cats heard, from somewhere behind the shop, a door open and close as if perhaps the woman had slipped out the back, to the side street or an alley.

Within the store, the shopkeeper had picked up the phone. The cats, watching him, watching his gestures, felt certain he was calling the police, giving the man's description. He glanced out once to see which way the stalker had gone—as Joe and Dulcie turned to follow the little man from above. A few parking places down, he approached a white Toyota pickup. Slipping in, starting the engine, he pulled out into traffic between a UPS van and a pair of wandering pedestrians. The cats saw, behind him, the shopkeeper run from the patio and step into the street, stopping traffic, watching the pickup pull away with a hard, intent look as if he were committing the license to memory.

"He'll call that in, too," Dulcie said, smiling, flicking her whiskers.

But the cats had memorized the number as well. "If that was the same person as at the courthouse," Dulcie said doubtfully, "that we thought was a boy, then somewhere he changed jackets, maybe left the black hoodie in the Toyota."

"Why not?" Joe said. "Or maybe not the same guy. Maybe he thought to take advantage of the attacks. Snatch a few bucks and lay the crime on the real bully."

"So even if the real thug's never caught," she said, "the crime's laid on him, and this fellow goes free."

"He'll be caught," Joe said calmly. "A matter of time. Time and stealth." The tomcat never doubted that between cat-power and the cops, they'd catch the right man. "We'll call the department from Misto's house," he said, hurrying along.

"But the shopkeeper got the number, he'll be calling right now."

"Maybe. Or maybe he got it wrong, couldn't see it all." Joe didn't like to depend on chance when it came to humans. "We'll tell Harper about that kid, too, there in front of the PD following the woman in the wheelchair. If I hadn't shouted . . ."

Dulcie stopped, gave him a long, steady look. "This time, Joe, let's leave it. We don't know that either one was going to attack. We didn't *see* an assault."

His yellow eyes narrowed, his ears went flat. "We saw two stalkers . . . We—"

"Wait, Joe. Wait until we have something certain. We don't want—we can't afford to make niggling little tips that could turn out to be nothing."

His scowl deepened; his claws dug into the shingles.

"We can't shake their confidence in us, we don't want them wondering, every time we call, if *this* tip is worth pursuing." She nosed at him gently. "Leave the calls for the big stuff. The important information that we know they can run with. Don't throw it away on conjectures."

Joe turned and trotted away from her, over a low, shingled peak, toward Ocean Avenue. He badly wanted to get to a phone. He didn't like to admit that maybe, just maybe, Dulcie might be right.

She caught up with him quickly, nosing at him so he wouldn't be cross. But she stopped abruptly, peering over the edge of the roof at a plump couple in matching red sweatshirts: the couple from in front of the PD, the woman's unruly hair tangled around her jowly face. Joe had a sharp recall of the red-sweatered couple turning to stare at the would-be victim, then moving quickly away as if they didn't want to be seen.

When the portly couple turned into the low-walled patio of the Ocean Café, Dulcie followed them. Joe wanted to move on to a phone.

"Just for a minute," she said. "I want . . . there's something about those two." With Dulcie so keenly intent, suddenly so focused, Joe put aside the thought of the phone, his own curiosity tweaked, too, and he followed her.

The brick terrace was crowded with small round tables draped in red, blue, or green cloths. As soon as the couple in red was seated, the cats backed down a stone pine, dropped down inside the wall and behind a row of potted geraniums.

"From the looks of them," Dulcie whispered, "they could skip a few breakfasts," But glancing down at her own tummy bulge, she thought she shouldn't criticize.

No one was looking as the cats slipped under the table's blue cloth, avoiding the couple's canvas-clad feet; avoiding the woman's floppy carryall that she'd set on the floor, one of those flowered, quilted numbers that tourists couldn't resist. Crouched in the shadows, they listened to the rustle of their menus and to their discussion of what sounded good—blintzes, omelet, hash browns. The cats licked their whiskers. Dulcie's appetite lately had been way too demanding, another aspect of her secret that was hard to conceal from Joe Grey.

The click of footsteps and the deep voice of the waiter brought his black shoes gleaming just inches from their noses. The tinkle of ice as he poured water. He offered coffee and poured it, and the couple gave their matching orders: pancakes, eggs, ham, and apple pie. The sound of the server's shoes clicked away again. The restaurant and patio were crowded, so the staff didn't linger.

The woman's voice was grainy and low. "That was her, all right, Howard. She's colored her hair different, it was blond before, but the same big brown eyes with those little creases, same long face. Same tennis tan," she said with sarcasm. "She wasn't in a cast and wheelchair then, but that's the same woman. Bonnie something, don't you remember? Even the same gold hair clip and gold earrings, I remember those."

"So?" Howard said. "How would I remember? I wasn't there every day, like you. And she has as much right to come down here as we do. Half of San Francisco vacations in Molena Point—even if we do come down partly to see your sister. But that woman—Bonnie, you said?—and that Betty Porter, they have nothing to do with us."

"But we *are* connected, Howard. That's just the point. That Bonnie woman and that Betty Porter. We *are* connected, that's what's scary—scary, when Betty Porter was hurt so bad, Howard."

"Coincidence," Howard said gruffly. "An accident. What else could it be?"

They both had harsh, whiskey voices. Maybe the result of advancing age and thickening vocal cords, or maybe they liked their booze as well as a big breakfast.

But it was breakfast that quieted the two. The minute their orders came, all discussion ended; there was silence except for the clatter of knives and forks on plates. The sounds of greedy humans gulping their food made Dulcie feel queasy. Whoever said a cat didn't get morning sickness, even this late in the game, didn't know much about felines.

Ignoring her unsteadiness, too curious to be still, the tabby reached out a paw, and with careful claws she drew the floppy purse away from the woman's foot. With teeth and claws she loosened the drawstring, then gently pulled the bag open.

She peered in, then half crawled in, her head and shoulders down inside the bag. Joe watched the woman in case she reached down for the floppy purse, wondering what he'd do if she did reach. *Hurry up*, he thought, half annoyed at Dulcie, half amused.

Dulcie backed out from the depths of the carryall, her teeth clamped gently around a fat red billfold, trying not to leave tooth marks. Laying it on the brick paving, she worked the snap loose and pawed it open.

The two cats, ears and whiskers touching, studied the driver's license: Effie Hoop, clearly incised beside her wide-faced picture. Quickly they memorized the San Francisco address, both wishing they had Kit's keen, photographic memory.

Dropping the billfold back in the bag, and still with only the sounds of eating from above and no useful conversation, Dulcie and Joe slipped out from under the table, slid behind the geraniums again, and leaped up the patio wall. Landing lightly on the narrow edge, they were about to spring up the stone pine to the roof when they saw Ryan's truck coming down the street.

The big red king cab swerved in to the curb where a minivan was pulling away. With parking spots at a premium, Ryan was lucky. On the far side, the driver's door opened. The cats were about to drop off the wall, trot across the sidewalk, and join her when they saw that it wasn't Ryan. The driver was her new carpenter, Ben Stonewell, apparently running an errand. Yes, the bed of the long pickup was loaded with new kitchen cabinets, all carefully shrouded in plastic and cardboard, the logo of the cabinetmaker stamped on the wrappings. Ben entered the restaurant patio at the far end.

Ben Stonewell was a shy young man, quiet, reclusive, not much of a talker. He'd been in the village less than a year, working for Ryan. He had left a large construction company up the coast because they moved him around so often from job to job, from one city to another. He'd told Ryan he wanted to settle in one place, in a small, friendly town. He liked to hike and run on the beach. He was heading for the takeout counter at the back of the patio when he glanced across to where the red-shirted couple was seated. He paused, startled. He was still for only an instant and then, his face turned away, he moved on quickly.

Probably he was picking up lunch for himself and Ryan's red-bearded foreman, her uncle Scott Flannery. Usually the men brought their lunches, but once in a while they splurged on burgers and fries. At the counter he paid for a bulging paper bag, pulled his cap low, turned away again from the portly couple. Double-timing back through the patio to the street, he never showed his face to them. He slid into the truck fast, started the engine, and pulled away, heading back to the job.

From atop the wall, Dulcie looked after him, her tail twitching. "What was that about? Why would Ben hide from those two, they're tourists. How does he know them?" Leaping up the stone pine lashing her tail, she looked back at Joe, her ears flat in a puzzled frown. "This Hoop couple. The woman in the wheelchair. Betty Porter. And now . . . Is Ben Stonewell part of the puzzle? What are we seeing?"

"We're seeing bit and pieces. Too few pieces." The tomcat rankled at, but relished, this process of scattered hints slowly coming together, of clues falling one by one into place in ways he hadn't anticipated. Like cornering a mouse that darted in a hundred directions before it came to ground.

"It will all fit together," he said confidently. "All of a sudden. So simple we'll wonder that we didn't see it right at first."

He glanced down again at the couple in the patio, then leaped from the wall to the roof and they galloped away across the shingles toward Ocean Avenue, heading for Misto's cottage.

In order to cross that wide, divided street, they backed down a bougainvillea vine and entered the crosswalk close on the heels of three tourists, young Asian girls leading a fluffy brown dog. The little mutt looked around at the cats, put his nose in the air, and hurried along in disdain. The traffic halted obediently for human pedestrians, whereas drivers might not see a cat or a small dog. On the far curb Joe and Dulcie fled past the little group and up a honeysuckle vine to the roof of a furniture boutique. Only then did the dog start to bark, at the nervy cats.

But now Dulcie, trotting up and down the steep tiles, began to lag behind again. The last up-and-down climbs had been tiring. Joe Grey glanced back at her, his ears flattened in a frown.

She knew she needed to explain. She needed to tell him soon, before he started asking questions. But again unease kept her silent. How *would* he respond to the thought of kittens?

Joe was not an ordinary street cat to ignore, or even kill, his own young. To Joe Grey, with his wider human view of the world, new babies would be a responsibility. A burden that he might not welcome, this tough tomcat who was all about danger. Whose life bristled with spying on criminals and passing information to the cops. Would he *want* this tender miracle? Would he want his own affairs disrupted, his own stealthy contribution to police work shoved aside while he sat with helpless babies or taught them to hunt—instead of Joe himself off hunting human scum?

But she had to tell him. She prayed he would be glad. The kittens needed their father; they needed Joe's down-to-earth view of life, his level-headed and sensible teaching—just as they needed Dulcie's touch of whimsy, her bit of poetry, even her love of bright silks and cashmere. Their kittens needed both parents, they needed the contrast of two kinds of learning.

Well, she thought. *Whatever he says, here goes.*

She paused on the roof tiles, looking at Joe. The look in her eyes stopped him, made him turn back. "What?" he said. Suddenly worry shone in the tomcat's yellow eyes. "What's wrong?"

"Kittens," she said. "There will be kittens."

Joe looked at her blankly. "What kittens? Rescue kittens? The village has plenty of those, Ryan and Charlie have been trapping abandoned kittens—"

"*Our* kittens," she said. "*Your* kittens."

Joe stared at her. He looked uncertain, he began to feel shaky. His expression turned to panic. He hissed, his ears flat, his paw lifted . . .

But then his whiskers came up, his ears pricked up, his eyes widened. "*Kittens?*" he said. "*Our kittens?*" He let out a yowl.

"*Kittens!* Oh my God."

He backed away from her, amazed. He leaped away, raced away across the shingled peaks, twice around a brick chimney and back again, a gray dervish streaking . . . He spun twice around Dulcie, his ears and whiskers wild. Around her again and halted, skidding nose to nose with her.

"*Kittens?*"

He nuzzled her and washed her face. He stood back and looked her over. "You don't look like you're carrying kittens." He frowned. "Well, maybe you've put on an ounce or two but . . . Are you sure?"

"I'm sure," she said, flicking her whiskers, lashing her tabby tail. "Dr. Firetti *says* there are kittens."

Joe couldn't stop smiling. Strange that he hadn't noticed a different scent about her. But she always smelled of the garden flowers and the pines—maybe he hadn't paid attention to subtler smells.

She sat down on the tiles, licking her paw, watching him. He stood silently looking at her, speechless and grinning. When he could talk again he said, "Kittens! They'll learn to hunt as soon as they can toddle, I'll bring them mice to learn on. They'll learn everything they need to know, to hunt, and to defend themselves. And to be the best detectives ever."

Oh, my. Dulcie hadn't thought of that.

"They'll learn to read from police reports," Joe said, "right there on Max Harper's desk, learn so cleverly that Harper will never know . . ." On and on he went, happily planning. Dulcie watched him uncertainly, her tough, practical tomcat laying it all out . . . bragging over his clever babies, his rookie-cop babies . . . *Oh, my tender little babies*, she thought nervously.

But then she thought, *Okay. They'll grow bigger, they'll grow strong. Kittens grow up, you know. Cop cats*, she thought tremulously. *Well, I guess I can live with that. I'm pretty good at cop work myself.*

But they'll learn more than what Joe teaches them, she thought stubbornly. *They'll learn about poetry. About literature . . . and so much to know about the ancient past. They'll learn to dream*, Dulcie thought. *They'll learn to dream from me.*

45

5

Misto didn't spend his waning days in the veterinary clinic, but next door in the Firettis' cottage, tucked up in John and Mary's king-size bed among a tangle of soft pillows. Since John had discovered Misto's fast-growing cancer, which was already too widespread for surgery, he and Mary had kept their beloved companion as comfortable and well tended as any ailing human could ever be.

The Firettis' bungalow sat back from the side street, down a long stone walk through Mary's flower garden. The clinic was off to the right, its original two cottages joined now by a glass-domed solarium that had turned the structure into a tall and airy hospital. The rooms of one cottage offered the feline clinic, lobby and office; the other cottage held the surgery and examining rooms. The solarium itself housed the dog hospital and exercise yard.

Dr. John Firetti, tall and slim and quiet, had made the clinic a safe and welcoming sanctuary for his treasured patients.

But for John and Mary, their own Misto was the most beloved of all. He had come to them when he was an old cat, returning, after a long journey, to his kitten-hood home. The instant love between the three was solid and deep. The Firettis were heartbroken when John did not discover the old cat's disease early on. They were dis-traught that Misto had kept his secret as the illness fast progressed, that the old cat had hidden his early pains. Those first days, the yellow tom had shown no weight loss, no loss of appetite, no dullness of eyes or of coat. Certainly he showed no flatness of spirit; he was as lively as ever. Misto had no clue himself until, quite suddenly, he began to feel weak, deeply tired. Then the pain was fierce, and he knew.

For some time, he kept that malaise to himself. When at last he told John that something was wrong, the cancer had spread and was not operable. Indeed, Misto told them, he would not have wanted surgery. The big yellow tom seemed far more at peace with his illness, with the num-bering of his last days, than were his human and feline friends.

But now as the end of Misto's life drew near he had much to speak of. He remembered his earlier deaths more clearly, just as he remembered his earlier lives. He shared bright fragments with John and Mary from times long past and from distant places, the old cat lying before the hearth fire of an evening, telling his exotic tales.

Some days John would carry him over to the clinic, to

a comfortable bed on his desk. And when, at dawn, John drove the few blocks to the shore to feed the band of feral cats he cared for, Misto rode with him, tucked up in the front seat in a warm blanket. Misto loved the shore and the roiling sea. Those gleaming waters brought back times living among the fishing wharves on the coast of Oregon; the sight of the sea brought back earlier lives, too: a strange life at the edge of the Aegean Sea; the Welsh and Scottish coasts. But the best was here, on the shore of Molena Point where the yellow tom had been born, this very stretch of shore where John now fed the strays.

Here, as a kitten, Misto had been taken far away from the village by a caring couple. Now in old age after so many adventures he had traveled back again to his first home, to the long white beach and the little dock where the ferals still gathered. Now, even in illness, he was satisfied to be back where he was born. Sometimes John carried him up the rocky coast where the waves crashed wild and where, when the tide was out and the sea sucked away, little pools among the rocks reflected the changing sky; where with a careful paw he could tease small rock crabs and tiny, trapped fishes.

Venturing to the shore with John on his better days, he stayed in the cottage with Mary on bad days, tucked up before the fire, and at night he slept warm between them. The Firettis woke each time Misto woke; they doled out pain medication and brought him cool water, offered custards and warm fish broth; they tried not to show their grieving.

But just as the old, speaking cat had come back to the Firettis on his own, the arrival of Misto's son Pan, some months later, was a second wonder to John and Mary.

48

The Firettis had known about speaking cats for many years; John, since he was a boy. They had kept the secret well, but they had longed to share their home with just such a one. Now their family included both Pan and Misto—though the four had had only a short time together before Pan was off on his journey and before Misto began to fail. How deftly the old cat had kept his secret, to give Pan his freedom; and soon now Misto himself would face a new adventure. The yellow tom knew that when his pain grew too severe John would help him sleep, and sleep more deeply until his spirit rose up and he would fly free.

"We will be together again," he told John and Mary. "We will come round together again, in one life or another, as we are meant to do. This is the way of the universe," Misto told them. Mary had wiped a tear, cuddling him, and she couldn't answer.

Now Misto, alone for the moment in the Firettis' bedroom, was dozing when Joe Grey and Dulcie padded across the big rag rug, slipped up onto the bed, and settled among the pillows beside him. Only slowly did Misto's ragged ears lift, his whiskers twitch. Only when he was alert again did Dulcie touch a soft paw to Misto's paw.

"I told him," she said. "I told Joe about the kittens."

Misto grinned at Joe Grey. "About time you knew."

Speaking kittens were rare; speaking, mated couples seldom brought little ones into the world. Joe, still shaken, looked back at Misto and smiled foolishly.

"Now," Dulcie said, slipping closer to the ailing cat, "now, what else do you have to tell us? What about our girl kitten, that you didn't tell me earlier when you fell asleep? Now you can tell us both."

Beside her, Joe Grey went rigid with dismay. He didn't want to hear predictions. He was proud and happy about the kittens, but he didn't want Misto to lead Dulcie down some foolish path of what *could* be, what *might* be; he didn't want the old cat planting foolish dreams.

Misto's voice was weak but filled with pleasure. "Three kittens," he told Dulcie again. "Two boy kittens, and a calico girl. It is she I have seen in my dreams. A lovely little creature, a beautiful young cat with a charmed spirit. A kitten who is heir to past lives more amazing than you can imagine.

"Your own child, your bright calico baby. Her past lives are set into humankind's history, her portraits grace man's ancient art from centuries gone. You will find the antique paintings, the tapestries, the illuminated manuscripts, you will find her image if only you will look."

He glanced at Joe. "There is no other cat marked like her. She has moved through time with an elegance unique even to our own speaking race, this kitten who will be your child."

Dulcie's heart beat fast; she burned to search among the library's old volumes, to find their own calico child. Yet she was shaken with fear for the treasure she carried, fear at bringing such a one into the world, fearful of the challenge, the responsibility for that precious creature.

"Courtney," Misto said. "Courtney is her true name. She has carried it through much of time, she would welcome owning that name again." The old cat laughed. "A name bigger, right now, than the little mite herself. But she will grow big and strong, this kitten who is destined to a life of honor."

"What honor?" Dulcie whispered, even more stricken. *"Oh, my. What destiny?"*

But the old tom had dozed off again. As if, when he thought he had said enough, he escaped slyly into an invalid's sleep. Softly Dulcie moved to the foot of the bed beside Joe, where the gray tomcat sat rigid and uneasy; and strange imaginings filled them both.

It was now, with the two cats so nervous and unsettled, that Dulcie's housemate found them. Wilma slipped into the room beside John Firetti as the good doctor brought medications for Misto.

Wilma Getz was as tall as the younger doctor. She wore a tie-dyed sweatshirt today, a garment so old it was back in style, its soft reds setting off her gray hair, which was tied at the nape of her neck. John was in his white lab coat, having just come from the clinic. His light brown hair was short and neat, his sunburned forehead peeling, his light brown eyes kind as he greeted Joe and Dulcie. Moving to the dresser, he set down the tray with the syringe and medicine, to be administered when the yellow tom woke. He stood beside Wilma, looking down at the two cats sitting rigid and edgy. They looked deeply at Joe, then at Dulcie.

Dulcie flicked a whisker. "I told him."

Wilma smiled and stroked Joe Grey. "It will be all right," she said. "They'll be fine, strong kittens." She frowned at Joe. "What? They'll be healthy kittens, Joe. You'll be a fine father. What?" she repeated. "You don't *want* these sweet babies?"

Joe stared up at her, his conflicted look filled half with joy, half with distress. "Of course I want them! Our kittens!

Our little speaking kittens. It's a miracle. But Misto . . ." he hissed softly. "Does Misto have to make predictions? I don't need *predictions*!" Joe said. "I don't want to hear *predictions*."

Wilma and Dulcie exchanged a look and tried to keep from smiling. Dulcie rubbed her face against Wilma's hand. "Misto's prophecies were . . . they frightened us both," she said softly.

It was then that John interrupted—as if perhaps he didn't want to hear predictions, either? Or perhaps he wanted only to soothe Dulcie and Joe. "Let's have a look at you, Dulcie. Let's see how the kittens are getting on."

Moving his medical tray to a chair, he cleared the dresser and lifted Dulcie up. She stretched out, looking up at him trustingly, only the tip of her tail moving with a nervous twitch. She loved John Firetti, but even his gentle hands pressing her stomach filled her with unease, an automatic reaction to protect her babies.

But John's hands were warm and tender on her belly. "Feel here, Wilma. And here . . ." He watched as Wilma's familiar fingers softly stroked Dulcie's stomach. "It's a little late now to feel them properly," he said, "it was easy when they were smaller. There are three kittens. Come on, Joe. You'll feel better when you can see for yourself. Maybe you can wipe that scared look off your face."

Reluctantly Joe leaped to the dresser. He hesitated, then placed a careful paw on Dulcie's tummy.

"Feel along here," John told him.

Joe stroked Dulcie as soft as a whisper. As he found the faintest divide between each tiny shape his expression turned from surprise to wonder.

"Three little heartbeats," Dr. Firetti said, holding the stethoscope against Dulcie, then letting Joe listen. "I'd say about two more weeks, they'll be ready to face the world." Scooping Dulcie up again, he handed her to Wilma. "A ride home would be a good thing."

He looked sternly at the tabby. "You are to stop galloping all over the village. No more running the rooftops. No more racing up and down trees. No *climbing*. You'll soon be a mother, Dulcie. You have babies to think about. A little circumspection," he said. "You are to slow down, take care of the kittens. We don't want to lose these little treasures."

Dulcie laid her face against his hand. Of course he was right. No one said pregnancy would be easy; no one said she'd like being a stay-at-home cat, being quiet and calm and doing nothing. Sighing, Dulcie snuggled down in Wilma's arms. She guessed her theft of the pink scarf had been her last craziness before she accepted a dull and sensible boredom.

Wilma had once told her, *"To admit to boredom is to admit to intellectual poverty."*

That remark, at the time, had shamed Dulcie because she'd been bored and restless and didn't know what to do with herself. Now the thought nudged her again as they headed for the car.

We do have a snug and cozy home, she told herself. *I can curl up before a cheerful fire, we can read together, we have music, and we always have nice things to eat. And*, she thought, smiling, *there's Wilma's computer right there on the desk . . . Now, maybe . . . Now, if I must be idle, maybe more poems will come, maybe new poems. Why should my idleness be boring?*

As Dulcie and Wilma headed home, Joe raced away across the empty side street into a tangle of cottages, through a maze of gardens, and up a pepper tree to the roofs. Heading home himself, he was still getting used to the idea of kittens, to the fact that soon they would have their own family. His thoughts were all atangle, part of him annoyed at the interruption of his busy and sometimes dangerous life, part of him ashamed at such a thought. But what he felt most was an incredible tenderness for Dulcie and their babies, a fierce desire to protect them. What he wished was that the world was a safer place for their kittens—for all the innocent of the world.

These violent attacks on the frail and elderly seemed far darker, now, a cruel contradiction to what life *should* be. He didn't want to think about human evil just now, but he couldn't stop. Suddenly, passionately, with the amazement of kittens filling his thoughts, Joe Grey wanted no viciousness at all, anywhere in the world.

But that's the way the world is. This is the balance between innocence and cruelty that Misto talks about.

Still, Joe thought, *no one has to like it. No one has to accept the twisted humans who relish their brutal plots, no one has to accept the corruption of the world. I can hate it if I choose. And maybe,* he thought, *even a cat, once in a while, can do something to push back the dark tide.*

6

 THIS WASN'T A game, this was for keeps. It was that very fact that made it the best game of all. Dead is dead, losing *is* for keeps. Snuffed like a candle, and that was the end of it. Death for the real scum among the decoys and shills they'd set up, and most of those were elderly, they'd chosen those to help mislead the law. So far the actions they'd laid out had gone down just fine. One or two they'd had to back off, but they'd make up for that.

They hadn't liked moving to Molena Point, but this was where the marks had come. Prissy little place for retired rich people. Or for those who wished they were rich. That's what most of these people were, the want-to-be rich. Poking around the fancy shops, maxing out their credit cards, gaga over the big prices. Talking about the big-deal social events and wanting to be part of them, that's what these newcomers were about. Living beyond their means, trying to get a glimpse of the movie stars and big-time executives who lived on their high-toned estates back in the hills.

And in the town itself, little shops all too cute and pretty, sleazy tourists taking in the sights, dragging their fancy dogs on a pink leash. You couldn't move for tourists and foo-foo mutts with fluffy scarves around their necks, dogs even in the outdoor cafés. Well, but the crowds were part of the game, the crowds were cover, all these strangers from out of town worked right in to confuse the action.

Two people dead now, and before they moved down here two more taken care of in the city. According to the papers, both cases were accidents. Cops didn't have a clue. Too bad some on the list had moved away. New Hampshire, Georgia, Mexico.

As for these local cops, any town where the chief wore jeans and western shirts, and stray cats wandered in out of the station, had to have hick-town law enforcement despite their fancy money.

No, the game was playing out just fine. Every death, every name they crossed off the list evened the score one more notch. They'd keep on until they had them all, or as many as they could reach. Maybe in time they'd snuff every one of those killers, who themselves so badly deserved to die.

WHILE THE UNKNOWN bully entertained satisfying thoughts of success and while Joe Grey fumed uselessly at the evils of the world, across the village Dulcie sat in her window in the kitchen, purring and content at last.

Looking out at Wilma's bright spring flowers, at the rich alstroemerias and the last of the winter cyclamens, she licked her whiskers at the smell of broiling flounder. Tonight they would have their supper in the living room before the fire and then would tuck up together on the couch with a favorite book, maybe one of Loren Eiseley's that they reread every so often.

Maybe being pregnant wasn't so bad; maybe she'd better enjoy her leisure while she could. When the kittens came, tiny and helpless, she'd have her paws full. And later when their eyes and ears were open, when they had grown bold and wild, she wouldn't have a moment of her own.

Yes, now was a moment for herself, to rest, maybe think about the poems that insisted on waking her at night and wouldn't go away. Even as Wilma dished up their supper, a poem was nudging at Dulcie like a bright glow—though maybe this verse, she thought, amused, was born of a pregnant cat's ravenous hunger, and that did make her smile.

> *No thin beggar, never shy*
> *This lady dines quite royally*
> *Fine salami, leftover Brie*
> *Salmon freshly from the sea*
> *She is beautifully obese*
> *Who feasts on kippers and roast geese*

But as the poem slowly formed, and as she followed Wilma in by the hearth, she had a sudden flash of something else. Watching Wilma, she saw suddenly the darkly dressed boy, or small man, following Wilma on the street, alone on a foggy morning.

But how foolish. No one was going to attack Wilma, not without sprawling on the concrete themselves, seriously damaged. Wilma Getz might be up in years but she was strong, she was well trained, and she had a carry permit if she wanted to use it. Defensive tactics and firearm training put her in a different category from most of her fellow seniors. *Too bad*, Dulcie thought, *that more seniors have never availed themselves of such skills.*

Maybe, in the last few decades, life didn't seem so dangerous. Maybe, the way some people looked at their lives, only a very special need would lead one to consider such training.

But of course Wilma's training had come with her profession, in probation and parole. *Yet even now that she's retired*, Dulcie thought, *those skills are a plus. And any citizen can carry pepper spray or a cane, can learn how to use those simple weapons against a would-be mugger.*

She thought about earlier centuries, about the wild young years of the country, when *self*-protection was the only protection a person had, when there was no nearby law enforcement, when the skill to fight back was an essential way of life.

These trusting humans today, the tabby thought, *they need to rev up some anger, they need to substitute complacency for sharp teeth and claws. They need to find a little mean in themselves and learn how to use it.*

JOE GREY, HEADING for home over the rooftops thinking about the kittens and then about the street crimes, wondered again if it was time to call Max. He had nothing to tell the chief but a few vague observations: the smell of turpentine and bike oil after Merle Rodin's attack. The person following that woman in the wheelchair as if ready to attack her, racing away when Joe Grey himself shouted, then dove out of sight. That couple from San Francisco recognizing the woman, knowing her from the city and distressed to see her there in the village. What was that about? Ben Stonewell not wanting the couple to see him, and Ben, too, was from San Francisco. Wondering what these matters might add up to, well aware of their vagueness, he knew that Dulcie was right. They needed solid facts, needed leads that Harper couldn't brush off, that wouldn't make the chief lose faith in the phantom snitch.

Leave it for now, Joe thought. *Just leave it. This time, listen to Dulcie.*

Leaping from a pine branch to his own shingled roof, he trotted across to look down on the driveway. Ryan's parking spot was empty, she'd still be at work. No big surprise, she'd been late every night since she started on Tekla Bleak's renovation.

That Bleak woman was a pain in the tail. Ryan never should have taken on her remodel, particularly with so many sensible, likable clients waiting for Ryan to start on their own houses. Ryan's innovative design talents, her conscientious attention to construction details and fine materials had generated a long line of eager customers.

The Bleaks hadn't been in the village more than a few months when they bought the cottage just down the street from the Damens' house, and because Ryan felt sorry for Sam Bleak, in his wheelchair, she had agreed to work them in soon for the needed renovations, so they could live more comfortably. Meanwhile Sam and Tekla were renting a backyard guesthouse just a few blocks from the center of the village, a cottage so tiny there was hardly room at all for the couple and their teenage son, or so Tekla complained.

Now as Joe looked down at his own driveway, he could smell their supper, lasagna or maybe spaghetti sauce, and he thanked God Clyde could cook. Clyde's new green Jaguar stood in the open carport, a gleaming collector's item, the result of a three-way trade Clyde had managed, offering his fine mechanical workmanship on other vehicles, in trade for the Jag. Licking his whiskers at the smell of supper, Joe slipped into his glassed-in cat tower that rose atop the second-floor roof, padded across his tangled pillows, and pushed into the house through his cat door onto a rafter above the master suite. Below him, to his left, was the master bedroom: king-size bed, fireplace, TV, all the amenities. To his right lay Clyde's small study, and beyond it, Ryan's large, glass-walled studio. The tops of oaks and pines rose on three sides, forming a leaf-sheltered workplace which, like Joe's tower, blended with the woods and sky.

Dropping down from the rafter onto Clyde's desk, hitting a stack of paperwork, he barely managed to avoid a landslide. The entire suite felt empty. Even Clyde's leather love seat was bare, no little white cat and big silver Weimaraner curled up together. Snowball and Rock would be down in the kitchen licking their chops, waiting hopefully for spaghetti. The two would never admit they were geared for disappointment, that spicy sauces were not on their agenda.

Months ago Ryan had put both animals on a diet of lean cooked beef or chicken, a safe selection of fresh vegetables— and added taurine for Snowball. No treats from the table, none of the human-type food that Joe and Dulcie indulged in. Who could explain to them that speaking cats were different, that they thrived on food that would do inestimable damage to the organs of most animals?

Dr. Firetti was more than careful about regular check-ups for the speaking cats, but they always rated A-plus. Who could explain why? Except for John Firetti, the medical profession didn't know that talking cats existed.

Well, Joe thought, Rock and Snowball felt great on Ryan's diet; they were sleek, lively, and sassy. Ryan had tried only once to put Joe on the same regimen. He'd raised so much hell that she and Clyde gave him what he wanted—though he knew she was now slipping in a few vegetables. He admitted only to himself that they weren't bad, a little change of flavor that went down fine.

He wondered if Wilma was preparing similar special fare for Dulcie, to better nourish their babies? How would his lady take to that? Again a thrill of amazement shivered through him, another smile twitched his whiskers as he dropped from desk to floor, galloped down the stairs and into the big family kitchen.

Clyde stood at the stove stirring spicy tomato sauce, his short brown hair neatly trimmed, his tanned face showing only a hint of stubble after a long day at the automotive shop. He was still in his work clothes, pale chinos,

Italian loafers, a green polo shirt. He had substituted a navy blue apron for the pretentious white lab coat that he wore at the shop. Clyde catered to expensive foreign models, classic cars, and antiques; he liked to keep an upscale image: medical specialist to your ailing Maserati, the best in tender loving care for your frail old Judkins Brougham. As Joe leaped to the table, Clyde turned from the stove.

"What?" Clyde said, frowning at him. "What's the silly grin?"

Why was Clyde always so suspicious? "Bad day at the shop?" Joe asked coolly.

"What, Joe? Why are you smiling like that? What have you been up to?"

"Ryan still down at the Bleak job? Why does that woman show up every evening just at quitting time? Doesn't she know people have lives of their own? Doesn't she *understand* the term *quitting time?*"

"I said, 'What's the grin about?' What gives?"

"Tekla thinks Ryan has nothing better to do than hang around after work to hear her latest complaint." This remodel, which Ryan had sandwiched in among her larger construction projects, was just four blocks from their own house: a convenient location for Ryan to get to work, handy to run home for lunch. But hard to avoid Tekla Bleak. If Ryan wasn't right there on *that* job—among three projects she was currently working on—Tekla would come on down to their house to lay out her complaints.

"Arbitrary, useless complaints," Joe said angrily. "She makes them up to enrage Ryan."

"The smile," Clyde said patiently, stepping to the table, reaching for Joe. "What is the smile about?"

Joe raised extended claws and hissed in Clyde's face. A few things were none of Clyde's business; he didn't need to ask nosy questions.

Clyde looked like he was going to strangle Joe. "What . . . is . . . the . . . smile . . . about? You haven't stopped grinning since you got home."

"I am not *grinning*. The Cheshire cat grins. I do not grin."

"It's plastered all over your face. Even when you try to scowl." Clyde watched him intently. "What? Have you got a line on the mugger?"

"If I had a line on that dirtbag, would I be sitting here on the table listening to your rude hassling? I'd be upstairs on the phone to Max Harper." Hissing again, he dropped from the table. "I'm going down the street and hurry Ryan along. It's suppertime and I'm starved."

"What, hop on her shoulder and tell her dinner's ready? That should get Tekla's attention."

"I don't need to *say* anything. My studied glare speaks volumes." Turning his back he headed upstairs, leaped to the desk, up to the rafter, pushed out through his cat door into his tower. Out its open window onto the roofs and he headed south to the Bleaks' frame cottage, where, late as it was, he could still hear hammers pounding.

Galloping the four blocks, he leaped onto the roof of the small brown house. White window trim and white picket fence that still needed painting. New, thick roofing shingles under his paws, they smelled new. He crouched above the cracked driveway, looking down at Ryan's red king cab, parked directly below him.

The truck bed was no longer crowded with new

kitchen cabinets; they had been unloaded and would be neatly stored inside the empty rooms. Bellying down on the shingles peering over, he watched Tekla Bleak where she stood on the deep front porch telling Ryan off, her voice loud enough to bring two joggers to a halt, the young men staring as if Ryan might need help, but then moving on, fast.

Tekla was a small, skinny woman, her short brown hair awry, her long, baggy blouse draped over slim black tights. Her black running shoes were sleek and expensive.

"My husband," Tekla snapped, glancing down at Sam in his wheelchair where he waited patiently at the bottom of the steps, "can hardly maneuver his chair through that narrow gate. And you will have to do something about this ramp, you can *see* it's way too flimsy for a wheelchair. If it gives way, if Sam falls . . ." Tekla stepped closer to Ryan, her stance threatening. Ryan looked at her coolly.

Ryan's dark, short hair was spattered with sawdust, as were her neatly fitting jeans and her white T-shirt. She dangled a Skilsaw from one hand, where she'd been cutting a porch rail. "I have not yet torn out the gate," she said patiently. "You can see we have only begun on the new rail." She did not point out that Sam had no trouble at all with the gate, that his wheelchair slid right on through.

"And," she said, "the new wooden ramp is sturdy enough for an army. Concrete supports in five places. Sam has been up and down it every day and it's given him no trouble. You *wanted* wood, Tekla. Not concrete, as I suggested." Looking over Tekla's head, Ryan gave Sam a wink. The poor man never got in a word.

His eyes grew bright at Ryan's smile, though he listened meekly enough to his wife's haranguing. Joe thought it pointless for Tekla to make a fuss over Sam's comfort when, inside the house, adaptations for his wheelchair were minimal, at best. One bathroom and a small bedroom had been retrofitted for him, but most of the renovation was concentrated on fancy countertops, fancy basins and faucets. Ego appeal, not efficiency for a challenged resident. Even the bright new kitchen was not being adapted for a wheelchair; the counters were all standard height, not even a low, easy island where Sam might fix himself a snack, as Ryan had forcefully suggested.

How simple it would have been to design the job with prime attention to Sam's comfort. Whatever complaints Tekla had now were irrelevant to the main purpose of the project, and the woman's arguments were wearing Ryan thin. Demands that they tear out brand-new work, put in different light fixtures though these had just been installed, replace the new kitchen hardware because Tekla had changed her mind. The arbitrary reversals were at Tekla's expense, that was in the contract, but the extra time and labor had Ryan and her workmen increasingly frustrated. Even her foreman, big, red-bearded Scott Flannery, who was usually calm and reined in, was about at the end of his temper.

Ryan's nature was much the same as her uncle's; it didn't take much for their Scots-Irish blood to flare up. So far she and Scotty had been circumspect with Tekla, trying not to upset Sam; everyone felt sorry for Sam Bleak. Everyone but his wife.

It was Ryan's young carpenter, Ben Stonewell, who pointedly stayed away from Tekla, avoiding trouble. Joe could see how much the woman upset him. Now, after Ben's evasive behavior in the restaurant patio when he didn't want to be seen by the Hoop couple, Joe had to wonder if there was more about Ben than he was seeing. He hoped not, he liked the shy young man.

Only Billy Young seemed immune to Tekla's shrill complaints. Ryan's thirteen-year-old apprentice seemed more amused than angered. Joe had seen Billy, more than once, turn away, hiding a little smile at the storm of Tekla's raving. Joe watched Billy now as the boy put away the shovels and a pick from where he'd been digging a new water line. The tall boy looked older than thirteen, his brown hair trimmed short and neat, his thin face, high cheekbones, and black eyes hinting at his trace of Native American blood.

Finished cleaning up, Billy wheeled his bike from beside the garage and moved on up the drive to the street to wait for Charlie Harper. This evening, even Billy had had enough of Tekla.

The chief's wife often picked Billy up after work, when she came down from the ranch on an errand. Charlie and Max Harper had been Billy's guardians since his grandma died; they hadn't wanted to see him go into foster care. Max usually dropped Billy at work in the morning, throwing his bike in the back of his pickup. The bike got him to school for early afternoon classes; then he was back at work again, on the school's part-time apprenticeship arrangement. Now, as Tekla raised her voice louder, Billy wheeled his bike farther away, up the street. She was insisting on different flooring, when the new floor was already down in three of the six rooms.

"This is *not* what I ordered," Tekla shouted.

"This," Ryan said, "is exactly what you selected."

"It is not. You're lying! You're a liar!" Tekla snapped. "You got this cheap stuff at some discount sale!" Her accusation made every hair on Joe's body bristle. Crouched as he was on the roof, he found it hard not to leap straight down on Tekla's head.

"I don't lie," Ryan said softly, her green eyes steady. "You cosigned for the flooring yourself." She picked up a square of the sleek golden wood where a pile of scraps had been tossed on the porch; she showed Tekla where it was stamped on the back: "Same manufacturer, same style number, same color: *antique oak*."

"I don't believe you. Where is the order?"

Ryan pulled both the order and the delivery bill from her pocket. She held them so Tekla could look, but she didn't hand them over.

Tekla said no more. Joe dropped down onto the truck hood trying to keep his angry claws from scratching Ryan's red paint. He longed to dig them into Tekla. Ryan was beautiful and kind and Joe loved her; but Tekla's harangues sent her home every night with a headache, in a cranky mood that cut through both Joe and Clyde, that cowed Rock and sent the little white cat to a far corner— until Ryan got herself under control. Until she did her best to smile, and the household turned sunny once more. Now when Ryan glanced up at Joe, he laid his ears back and licked his whiskers, telling her, *Screw the woman. I'm hungry, it's suppertime! Dump Tekla and let's move it!* His tomcat scowl said it all.

Ryan tried hard not to laugh. Tekla looked at her

strangely, but at last she turned away and wheeled Sam to their van. Sliding open the side door, she pulled down the ramp and helped him in. Joe watched her fold the wheelchair and secure it beside him. Tekla might be small in stature, but she was strong; and she seemed to take adequate care of Sam—adequate physical care, anyway, if you could discount her spirit-bruising sarcasm. Their son, Arnold, was kinder to Sam than Tekla was. At least he acted kinder when he stopped by after school; he seemed far closer to his father than he was to Tekla.

Though somehow even Arnold gave Joe the twitches. As nice as the kid could be to Sam, there was something hard inside him. Something about Arnold Bleak that mirrored, exactly, the deep-down enmity of his mother.

Joe watched the van pull away, watched Ben head up the street for his small coupe, patting his coat pocket as he always did to make sure his phone was there and the little spiral-bound notebook that contained his building measurements and notes. Watching Ben, Joe edged from the hood of the king cab around through its open window and dropped to the front seat. At once Ryan joined him, slipping in through the driver's door, leaving Billy to wait for Charlie, leaving Scotty to lock up.

"How do you stand her?" Joe said as she started the engine. "You could break the contract."

She looked at Joe, frustrated. "With Sam in a wheelchair, they *need* this remodel. At least he'll have a convenient bath and bedroom. They have to be cramped in that little place they're renting." Her patience sounded kind and forgiving, but when again she glanced at Joe, angry tears filled her eyes. Ryan, who never cried. Who was usually high-spirited and in charge of a situation. "If she could just be civil," she said. "If she could just try . . ."

On the seat Joe snuggled closer and laid a soft paw on her arm. "You *know* she does it on purpose, you know she likes hurting people. Don't let that scum get to you with her power trip, you're better than to listen to her." Looking up, his eyes held Ryan's. "She won't take *you* down, you have more style, more everything. You can laugh at her."

Driving, Ryan smiled, and wiped at her tears. They were a block from home when she pulled over to the curb and gathered Joe up in her arms. Burying her face in his fur, she was silent for a long time, dampening his gray coat with her tears, needing a little time-out, needing Joe as she tried to get herself under control.

But suddenly she began to laugh. She laughed against Joe, she held him tighter, then held him away, laughing in his face, her teary green eyes bright with amusement. "You're right, tomcat. I can growl at her just as good as you can," and she hugged him harder. "If Sam can't silence Tekla, if he *won't* silence her, then maybe I will." She stroked and hugged him. "Why not? *I* can unsheathe my claws just as well as you can."

7

Tears still dampened Ryan's cheeks as she pulled into the drive—but she was still smiling, cuddling Joe close on her lap. Above them, bright reflections from the lowering sun flashed across her upstairs studio windows. She and Joe sat a moment enjoying the sight of their comfortably remodeled house, Ryan scratching Joe Grey's ears as she shook off the last of her anger. "Guess we have it pretty good, don't we, tomcat?"

Joe gave her a nudging purr. "Guess we do, now that you've added a little pizzazz to the old cottage. *And* to the family," he said, grinning. "Now that you've civilized Clyde," and that did make her laugh.

The Damen house had started out some fifty years earlier as a one-story weekend bungalow. It was now a spacious two stories with more air and light, and a touch of

Spanish flavor. It still amused Joe that the renovation was what had pushed the romance into high gear as Ryan and her crew worked on the remodel and Clyde often worked with them. What better way to get to know a person than working side by side, exhibiting your worst temper when you hit your thumb with a hammer, as Clyde was inclined to do, or when the wrong materials were delivered, nudging Ryan's temper. What better way to know someone than when a project turned out exactly right and they could share that glow of pleasure. As the couple learned each other's moods, as they began to see the truth of what each one was about, the romance bloomed.

Now, gathering Joe up in her arms and swinging out of the truck, Ryan hurried inside. Setting him down in the hall, she didn't go into the kitchen to kiss Clyde as she usually would, but headed upstairs to wash away the last of her tears. Joe heard the bathroom door slam as he followed the smell of spaghetti into the kitchen; then soon he heard the shower pounding.

"In a temper again," Clyde said, moving around the big table laying out napkins and silverware. "What does Tekla want now? Gold-plated doorstops?"

"Wants to rip out the new floors," Joe said, leaping up to the kitchen counter. "Said that floor wasn't the one she ordered."

Clyde snorted. "What did Ryan say?"

"Ryan showed her a floor scrap with the name and color number on it, showed her a copy of the order Tekla had signed. Why does Sam Bleak stay with that woman? Even in a wheelchair he'd be better off alone. You're setting four places."

71

"Just Scotty and Ben." Ryan's uncle Scott was a bachelor and was often there for dinner. Young Ben Stonewell was single, too. The thin, twenty-something carpenter, who was new to the village, was so quiet, so withdrawn and shy, that Ryan was inclined to mother him.

Clyde said, "It would be pretty hard for Sam to get along alone in a wheelchair. He needs someone."

"He has Arnold."

"Arnold's what? Maybe fourteen? And the kid's . . . he's kind enough to Sam, but there's something about him. The kid makes me uneasy."

Joe twitched a whisker. "With Tekla for a mother, no wonder. I don't get too friendly with him, I doubt he likes cats very much. He makes my fur twitch."

They heard Ryan descending the stairs. She came into the kitchen, her temper washed away, looking softer in a pink velvet jumpsuit and smelling of lavender soap—no longer smelling of anger. Her short, dark hair curled around her face, from the steamy shower. "Sam and Tekla have no one but Arnold," she said. "No other family that I know of. Both Sam and the kid need Tekla, and they sure need to have this house finished. If she'd just stop bugging us and let us get on with it."

Clyde moved away from the stove and took her in his arms. She melted against him, nuzzling into his shoulder. "Tekla's a lot less caustic," she said, "when Arnold's around. Is she ashamed to pitch such a fit in front of their son?"

"I'd be ashamed," Clyde said. He stroked her hair, then turned back to the stove, where the water for pasta had begun to boil. He eased in the dry spaghetti, then opened two cans of beer, handing one to Ryan. He stood watching the pot, ready to turn it down when it boiled. At the sink Ryan washed tomatoes and began cutting up salad greens. Joe moved down the counter away from her splashes and then sailed across to the table. He hoped he wouldn't have to move again when their guests arrived. After all, it was only Scotty and Ben. At the other end of the long kitchen, the big silver Weimaraner and little white Snowball watched the proceedings with nose-twitching interest, though their own bowls of supper had already been licked clean. As Joe settled down between the place mats, Clyde turned from the stove to fix him with a piercing look.

"Okay. Now Ryan's home. Now we're all together. Let's hear it."

Joe looked up at him blankly. Ryan turned, watching them.

Clyde sipped his beer, his gaze never leaving Joe. "You were grinning when you got home this afternoon, grinning until you left again. You're scowling now, after a half hour with Tekla. But that smug look is still there, underneath. Come on, Joe. Spill it."

Ryan looked closely at Joe. She reached out one slender finger and tipped up his chin, studying his wide yellow eyes. "I didn't notice, down at the Bleaks' or in the truck, I was too caught up in . . . too damn mad. You do look a bit smug," she said. "What, Joe? What *is* that look?"

Joe Grey sighed.

He told himself he was blessed to have Ryan and Clyde, to have a loving family. That he was blessed he hadn't remained a homeless stray in the San Francisco alleys. That he was more than fortunate that Clyde had rescued him, back when he was a starving kitten. Told himself he was lucky beyond dreams that Clyde had married Ryan Flannery.

But there *were* times when they didn't have to be so damned nosy. He lay between the place mats staring back at his housemates' stern and unblinking assessment, the two of them waiting for him to explain that inner joyousness that he couldn't seem to hide or quell: two stern humans banded together in silent interrogation, as hard-nosed stubborn as a pair of old-time detectives. If Clyde *thought* he had a secret, Ryan *knew* he did. Her green eyes saw too deeply into his wily cat soul.

He *wanted* to share his and Dulcie's news. He was eager to tell them about the kittens and see their excitement. But he felt embarrassed that he *was* so excited. And he dreaded the fuss they'd make. They'd start worrying over Dulcie; they'd caution him to take care of her when he and she were out running the roofs and streets. They'd tell him not to let her climb trees, just as John Firetti had told Dulcie herself. They'd go on and on, he could only half imagine their concern.

But he had to say something. The two were still staring. There was no getting out of this. Besides, Dulcie was already starting to show, if you looked carefully. Pretty quick now, her condition would be too obvious to hide. Then everyone would start asking questions. If he or Dulcie didn't break the news, Clyde and Ryan, or Charlie, would start to interrogate Wilma, whom Dulcie had so far sworn to secrecy.

Well, hell, he thought, fighting his prideful embarrassment, and he laid it out for them using Dulcie's own words. "Kittens," he said, "there'll be kittens."

Clyde stared.

"We're going to have kittens," Joe said slowly.

Ryan's eyes widened and she began to smile. Clyde's expression was numb. Dulcie and Joe had been together a long time, with no sign of ever expecting babies. Kittens born to speaking cats were a rare occurrence. The idea still amazed Joe himself, still left him only half believing. "Dulcie is with kittens," he repeated, watching Clyde.

But Ryan flew around the table and grabbed Joe up in her arms. *"Kittens! Oh, Joe.* How *many* kittens? Do you *know* how many? Has she seen Dr. Firetti? When are they due? How soon? Has she told Wilma? Wilma hasn't said a word . . . *Oh!"* She kissed the top of Joe's head, then kissed his nose. Beneath his fur, Joe had to be blushing. *"Oh, kittens,"* she said. *"Little speaking kittens . . ."*

Snug in her arms, Joe didn't point out that there was no guarantee their babies would speak. Ryan and Clyde knew that, if they'd thought about it. John Firetti had told them, long ago, that the gift of speech didn't always happen, that sometimes the talent was not passed on, that it did not appear at all. Just as, once in a great while, a little speaking kitten would be born to an ordinary, nonverbal litter.

A recessive gene? An anomaly surfacing out of nowhere? Joe found the tangle of genetic paths daunting; he didn't comprehend the math of it at all, or the implications. He wondered if anyone understood this particular scientific puzzle. How could geneticists study and understand a creature they didn't know existed? No more than a handful of people in the world could know there even *were* literate, verbal cats.

Most people, Joe thought, *wouldn't believe in talking cats if one shouted obscenities at them.*

Those few who *knew* the speaking cats and loved them kept their secret well, to protect the cats themselves; to shield them from human exploitation in a world where any creature rare and different was open to human greed.

Settling deeper into Ryan's arms, Joe worried that the babies might *not* be able to speak. Dismayed, he looked solemnly at Clyde and then up into Ryan's green eyes, so tender now as she fussed over him. But Clyde was saying, "Kittens! My God, Joe. If they're half as stubborn and hardheaded as you . . ."

"Or if they're half as smart and decisive as Joe," Ryan said, "and as clever and sweet as Dulcie . . . oh, a baby shower, Joe! We'll have a shower for Dulcie—little kitten toys, a soft new cat bed. Baby books, little kitty primers to—"

Joe drew back in her arms and pressed a paw to her lips. "You're not having a *baby shower*!" Ryan never gushed, he was shocked at her gushing. "Dulcie's not having a *foo-foo baby party* like some . . . some giddy . . . *human* mother."

"Why not?" she said, hugging him. "Little toy mice, some pretty little blankets . . ." She was never like this, his steady, sensible housemate, the woman he counted on for a calm and balanced view of the world when Clyde might be off the wall. The tomcat's voice was sharper than he intended.

"We don't want a baby shower!" he hissed at her. *"Don't you think you should ask Dulcie if—"*

A loud explosion stopped him, then a deafening metallic clatter as the top blew off the cook pot. Clyde and

Ryan spun around, Ryan hugging Joe tighter, backing away from the stove, where a geyser of steam blasted toward the ceiling. Pasta was boiling over in a white cascade of froth, bubbling over the sides of the pot and across the stovetop and burbling down into the burners. The metal lid spun rattling across the floor. Clyde dove for the pot and pulled it off the burner. At the same moment a series of loud thuds rattled the front door and a deep voice echoed through the intercom. "Supper ready?"

8

Ryan held Joe forcefully over her shoulder, having grabbed him away from the geyser of steaming water as she hurried to the living room to let Scotty in—leaving Clyde to deal with the erupting pot. Reaching for the door, she tossed Joe on the mantel among the tangle of photographs. He hissed at her and settled down to collect himself, to ease his jangled nerves. Washing his paws, he listened to Clyde in the kitchen swearing and banging pots.

Chaos was nothing new in the Damen household. Joe should be used to calamities. But deep in his feline nature burned that ancient instinct for self-preservation, that fight-or-flight inborn shock at loud noises, every fiber geared to slash or race away until he'd sorted out the cause of the trouble.

Reflex response, he thought, *and where would a cat be*

without that instant reaction? As he sat on the mantel calming himself, in the open doorway Scotty gave Ryan a big bear hug, happy to see her though they'd worked together all day. Her uncle's voice was so deep and comforting that soon Joe's fear reflexes had eased. He began to purr, and then to smile as he saw again the lid of the spaghetti pot blow off, and Rock and Snowball streak out through the dog door to the safety of the backyard.

Stretching out among the small, framed photos, he was washing his shoulder when the phone rang. He heard Clyde answer, but not until he realized the call was from Kit's traveling housemates did he drop to the rug, beat it to the kitchen, and land on the table, to listen.

Clyde had pushed the boiling pot off the burner and opened the windows to clear out the steam. The trash can was filled with sopping paper towels sticky with starchy water. Was this the end of their supper? Was the spaghetti ruined? Joe eyed the mess with dismay. He wasn't about to choke down a serving of cat kibble.

But no, there on the stove the spaghetti itself was piled in a colander glistening with olive oil, balanced atop a deep bowl. And the covered pot of tomato sauce looked tame enough, nothing bubbling out, nothing running over the side. As Clyde talked on the phone he wiped the last of the sticky gray liquid off the stove. *"Lucinda,"* he mouthed at Joe, silent because Scotty was headed through to the kitchen. *"It's Lucinda."*

Clyde's words didn't cheer Joe. If the Greenlaws had arrived home before Kit and Pan returned from their own journey, if the older couple found them still absent they'd be beside themselves. But then, listening to Clyde,

Joe realized that Lucinda and Pedric were in Anchorage. They were talking about the shops and a native arts museum, Clyde asking questions to avoid the subject of Kit as Scotty and Ryan entered. " . . . yes, they are, Lucinda. Kate says the new garden plants are fine, she checked the watering system yesterday."

Lucinda, aware that someone had come in, talked for only a few minutes more, then ended the call. Did Clyde's *"Yes, they are, Lucinda . . ."* answer her most urgent question, tell her that Kit and Pan were still away? Had she hung up burdened by that news?

"Lucinda," Clyde said to Ryan and Scotty. "They're in Anchorage." He looked at Ryan. "Your dad and Lindsey have gone on to the Kenai River for a day or two of early salmon fishing. Lucinda wasn't sure whether they'd be coming home together or separately, she wasn't sure which flight they'd take." The travelers hadn't been gone long, but it seemed to Joe like forever. He hoped Kit and Pan *would* be home before the Greenlaws; even this short parting had been hard for the older couple, and surely was hard for Kit, too. The three had never been parted since the amazement of their finding one another just a few years ago up on Hellhag Hill. The frightened tortoiseshell kitten, a lonely stray, hadn't ever imagined she would discover humans she could speak with, humans she could trust to keep her secret, humans she could love and who would love her as she had never dreamed.

As for Lucinda and Pedric, long immersed in the Celtic myths that told of speaking cats, to imagine encountering such an astounding creature in real life was beyond their dreams. Such a longing was only whimsy, fanciful thinking; they hadn't dared suppose that a speaking cat would appear before them there on those green hills, wanting to share their picnic—to share their lives. A chance meeting born perhaps of a deep and inherent need within the two humans and within Kit herself. Their close bond now had made it hard indeed for the three of them to part. *They'll be together soon*, Joe told himself hopefully, *nothing bad will happen*.

At the kitchen table Scotty took his usual place, absently petting Joe where the tomcat lay sprawled across the place mat, his paw on Scotty's spoon. Scotty was never annoyed at Joe's boldness but only amused; he nodded thanks as Ryan handed him a can of beer and a frosty mug.

"Ben will be along," Scotty said. "He stopped by his place to feed his rescues." They had all been pleased when young Ben Stonewell, even in his tiny rented room, had taken in three rescue cats, giving them safe temporary quarters until real homes could be found. Scotty laid a sheaf of drawings on the table. "I swung by Kate's to pick these up—the changes she'd like for the outdoor shelter rooms."

Joe watched Scotty with interest. His mention of Kate brought a vulnerable look to the Scotsman: he glanced down shyly, seemed suddenly off center, making Joe Grey smile.

Blond, beautiful Kate Osborne, their good friend who understood the speaking cats so well, had at last succeeded in buying the old Pamillon estate. The acreage and crumbling mansion had languished for generations in the hills above Molena Point, caught up in a tangle of legal disputes. Kate's attorney had finally wound a legal path through the mire of too many heirs, too many overlapping trusts and wills. Now the property was through escrow, Kate and Ryan had all the building permits, the plans had been approved by a hard-nosed county inspector, and they had begun construction of a fine new cat shelter. It rose just south of the fallen mansion with a low hill in between. Ryan's larger crew of carpenters was working up there, Ryan dividing her time between several jobs, but always happy to get away from the Bleak renovation.

The shelter project was part of CatFriends, their volunteer rescue group. The refuge was a special dream of Kate's, to care for abandoned cats. Kate had lived in the village before she left her philandering husband. It was here in Molena Point that she discovered her own strange relationship to the speaking cats. She had, while investigating that connection, found her way down the hidden tunnels beneath San Francisco's streets into the Netherworld, where Kit and Pan now traveled. Though Kit and Pan's route had taken them, not from the city's tunnels, but from here in the village beneath the estate itself, down a cavern discovered by the band of speaking, feral cats who made their home among the Pamillon ruins.

Kate, at the moment, was living in Lucinda and Pedric's downstairs apartment looking after their house and garden while they were away—watching for Kit and Pan's return, just as she waited eagerly for Lucinda and Pedric to arrive home again, safe.

"She was working on two more drawings," Scotty offered. "She said she'd drop them by later." Again Scotty had that off-center look that made Joe and Ryan glance at each other.

"She wants to add two more outdoor group rooms," Scotty said, opening up the folded plans. "For the ferals that want to see outdoors, cats who get upset being shut inside." The plan was, the ferals would be neutered, given their shots, and turned loose again into the colonies where they had been trapped. That way, the whole colony was healthier, the cats wouldn't reproduce but could live happy, productive lives hunting the rats and mice and destructive ground squirrels that bedeviled the village cottages. CatFriends' volunteers were currently feeding three such colonies, supplementing their rodent diet and seeing to it that they had plenty of fresh water.

The rescue group's plan for the shelter had begun at the time the economy faltered so badly that many homes and cottages were foreclosed and families moved hastily away, searching for new jobs, cruelly abandoning their pets to fend for themselves or find new owners. Members of CatFriends had patiently trapped the lost, frightened animals and found temporary foster homes for them until the shelter could be built. There would be roomy cages and two big group rooms for the cats who got along well together. Rescued dogs went to the SPCA, which had larger facilities for them.

A lot of thought had gone into CatFriends' shelter. Their group meetings included Charlie Harper, Ryan's glamorous sister Hanni Coon, Ryan and Kate, and five other members. Joe and Dulcie had sat in on a few gatherings at the Damens'—had sat in, finding it hard not to offer their own opinions. How could humans design a cat shelter without consulting an expert? Sometimes they even wanted to argue with Kate.

Joe had been amused when Scotty started attending the meetings. Scott Flannery was not a cat person and was not inclined to women's groups. But then Ryan's shy, quiet carpenter Ben Stonewell had joined. Ben *was* interested in the rescue operation. Scotty was more interested in Kate; he would come to the meetings with Ben but leave with her, "for a walk on the beach," he would say, or, "a nightcap in the village."

Scotty was Ryan's father's brother. Detective Dallas Garza was her mother's brother. The two men had moved in with Mike Flannery after the children's mother died, when the three girls were very young. Together the men had raised them, adjusting work schedules to be sure someone was at home for them, teaching them not only to cook but to do household repairs, to carpenter, to carefully handle and care for a firearm, and to help train Dallas's bird dogs. Dallas and Ryan's beautiful sister Hanni were good hunting partners.

But it was Scotty who stirred Ryan's interest in construction, teaching her the more intricate use of carpentry tools and the basics of strong construction, years before she went on to art school to study design.

Now, at the sink tossing salad, Ryan turned at a knock on the front door, and went to let Ben in. The young carpenter hadn't used the intercom; he was wary of that simple device, though he was comfortable enough with the high-powered carpentry equipment.

The thin, pale young man entered the kitchen shyly. He looked freshly scrubbed; he wore his brown hair shoulder length, but it was clean and neat. He always seemed pleased by the big family kitchen, the homey room with its flowered overstuffed chair and bookshelf at the far end, by the resident animals looking up smiling at him, by the warm sense of family. He was more outgoing with the two cats and the big Weimaraner than with humans. At the sight of Ben, Rock left the braided throw rug and came to lean against the young carpenter's knee. Ben had changed from his work clothes to tan slacks, a brown polo shirt open at the collar, and loafers. Ryan pulled out a chair for him and fetched him a beer. He looked up at Clyde. "Smells good," he said. "Real good," and he grinned more openly. "Can I help?"

Clyde shook his head. "All under control." The rescued pasta draining in the colander seemed none the worse for boiling over—there was enough spaghetti for a small army. The Damens always made extra. Leftovers went in the freezer for a handy future meal. That is, what leftovers Joe Grey didn't get into during a midnight foray. Joe had learned, when he was very young, to open the refrigerator, though he was not as agile as Dulcie. The Damens' refrigerator, as well as Wilma's and the Greenlaws', had emergency interior handles; these were Clyde's invention, built at the automotive shop by one of his mechanics.

Scotty set the salad on the table, and Clyde dished up the spaghetti. Joe leaped off the table to the end of the kitchen counter where Clyde had set Joe's own plate. He could never understand why Clyde thought he deserved a smaller plate than everyone else. Though he *was* amused by its pattern of fat cats. Ryan said it might encourage Joe to watch his waistline. In fact, looking at those prancing, greedy kitties only made him eat faster.

They were all seated, Ryan serving the salad, when

Scotty said, "Kate told me . . . she saw another assault this evening."

Everyone paused, Clyde's beer mug half raised.

"When I got to the apartment she was just home from the PD, from filing the report. She was still mad, upset that she hadn't caught the guy. She said he ran like hell, and Kate's pretty fast herself."

Clyde said, "She got a look at him?"

"Not much, just his back. He slid into an alley. She wasn't that far behind, but when she got there he was gone, not a trace."

Scotty sprinkled cheese on his spaghetti. "Slim guy, Kate said. Thin and small. Dressed in black, black cap with earflaps. Could have been a kid, or not. She was coming out of the drugstore when she saw him half a block away, saw him knock a woman down. When he saw Kate he spun away and ran. She grabbed her phone, got a blurred picture of his back, just a smear of the dark figure careening around the corner. She called 911, then chased him. When she lost him she turned back to help the woman. Officer Brennan was already there, and the medics.

"Kate said the woman didn't seem hurt too bad. While they were taking care of her, Kate went on into the station, gave her statement to Detective Davis, and they copied the photo from her cell phone.

"They'll enhance the picture," Scotty continued, "but I doubt they'll get much. The woman told Brennan she was all right, she didn't want to go to the hospital. She went into the station with him, gave her own statement, and he took her home." Scotty laid a copy of the photograph on the table.

Joe, leaping to the table pretending to sniff at Ryan's spaghetti, got a good look at the picture, but it didn't offer much, just a dark, blurred figure running, very like the hooded figure who ran when Joe shouted from the roof of the PD.

"What does this guy want?" Scotty said. "These attacks seemed no more than cruel pranks—until the murder. And then the second death, that could be either murder or unintentional manslaughter. None of it makes sense. Everyone in the department's edgy."

Joe knew that. He was more than uneasy himself.

At Scotty's first mention of the attack Ben looked uncomfortable. "If people were half as decent as animals," he said, "were as kind as animals, the whole world would be at peace."

No it wouldn't, Joe thought. Watching Ben, the tomcat found it hard to keep his mouth shut. He wanted to point out that predatory animals weren't so decent, that wolves, coyotes, jungle cats, were all cruel killers, that was the way God made them. Wolves, for instance, began eating their prey before the poor animals were dead; a wolf would pull half-born calves from their mothers, or would mortally wound valuable young heifers and not even bother to eat them. They would leave their prey slowly dying and move on to kill the next little calf, as they taught their cubs how to hunt. He wanted to say that it was only the *victims* of the wolves and coyotes that were without cruelty.

And, Joe thought, only half ashamed, *even a mouse might not die quickly in the jaws of a hunting cat.* The tomcat's own dual nature sometimes left him conflicted; he really didn't like to analyze such matters—and now he could make no reply to set Ben straight. His opinion was locked in silence.

He realized he was scowling only when Ryan gave him a faint shake of the head, a look that said, *Back off, cool it, Joe. You're too interested. Suck up whatever you want to say. Get out of Ben's face with that angry and superior stare.*

Embarrassed, Joe turned from Ryan, leaped from the table to the kitchen counter once more, and licked clean the last of his spaghetti.

Only when Ben talked about his rescue cats did his eyes brighten. He launched into an amused and loving description of his three charges, of how well they got along together and how all three slept with him at night. *Maybe,* Joe thought, *if Ben finds a larger apartment he might keep the three homeless cats.* Ryan said his apartment was so small there was hardly room for the bed, a tiny refrigerator, and a hot plate. The little basement room and bath huddled beneath a tall old house that overlooked a shallow canyon east of the village. Ryan had described, to Clyde and Joe, the rough concrete walls, the decrepit metal windows on the two daylight sides of the corner room. She said Ben had lined up the two spacious cat cages before the windows, further darkening the little apartment but giving the cats light and morning sun. Ben's landlord rented out rooms in the house above, but people were seldom home. No one seemed to care that Ben kept cats. Joe expected he'd find a better place soon. He'd only moved down from San Francisco less than a year ago.

Well, Joe thought, *the Bleak job will finish soon and Ben will be working full-time to finish the shelter; he'll like that better.* Though Joe did wonder why Ben was so uncomfortable around Tekla, more upset at her harassment than seemed warranted.

Well, who could blame him? Joe avoided the woman, too. Now, watching Ben, the tomcat had no idea that by the next morning his idyllic picture of the young man would have changed radically—and that Joe himself would be thrown into the middle of the tangle.

9

THAT BLONDE THAT spotted the attack had nearly messed them up, she ran faster than you'd expect, almost got a good look and ruined it all. A hasty retreat and no harm done, but way too close—left a person shaking with nervous sweat.

But that was the only time there was trouble. All in all, every new assault was a blast. Shadowing the victims, learning their habits, learning the paths they took among the village stores, knowing where they lived and where they shopped. Watching the places they worked, where they ate if they ate out. Pausing in a doorway, waiting, silent in the shadows, that was the best part. The sudden hit—slip up with no sound, one good shove and it was done. See them fall scared and struggling and you were gone before they got a glimpse. A fast attack, then gone. How easy was that?

Well, it should have been the same this time except the damned blonde got in the way. She had a cell phone—*did* she get a picture? If so, it couldn't be much. A running smear from the back. Hell, she didn't see anything. What could she tell the cops? Anyway, that mark had been just a shill. Tomorrow would be a real one again. Tomorrow's target knew something, knew too much and needed taking out. Tomorrow when they'd be alone, just the two of them.

IT WAS NEAR dawn when the setting moon angled into Joe Grey's tower so bright that, even deep in sleep, he tucked his face under the pillows. But the afterglow stayed in his head, brought him half awake. Wriggling around, he scowled out at the offending yellow orb. Damn moon brighter than a streetlight slanting in through the oak and pine branches.

The moon had been high when he galloped home from hunting late last night, his belly full of mice atop his earlier spaghetti supper—a good hunt even if Dulcie *had* wanted to stay to the grassy hill that rose behind her own cottage. He was chagrined that he hadn't been concerned, days earlier, when she preferred to stay within the village instead of out on the far hills. *Why wasn't I puzzled that my lady was slowing down?*

Tomcat inattention, he thought. *All wrapped up in my own interests. Expecting her to be as irate at these new crimes as she always is at village violence. I never wondered at all why she was so preoccupied.*

But even though he hadn't noticed Dulcie's motherly

condition, he *had* seen a different look in her eyes. That alone should have clued him in. He'd wondered only briefly what that calm look was, that deep contentment in her easy glance. He'd put it down to some passing mood, thinking, *Who can understand females?* He should have paid more attention, should have figured it out without having to be *told*. But no, not for one minute had he taken time to wonder.

Ryan had said, late last night as she climbed into bed and Joe leaped to the rafters, ready to head out to hunt, "Be careful with her, Joe. Hunt close to home, and hunt easy." She'd pulled the covers up over her silk nightie. "Please be careful, you don't want to stress her. Not with those precious kittens."

Well, hell, he knew that.

"Listen to Dr. Firetti," she'd scolded. "We're all eager for those little kittens to be healthy and strong."

Joe had flicked his ears in annoyance, bolted across his rafter and out his cat door.

But he'd made sure Dulcie had an easy hunt among the tall grass where the field mice thrived. He had watched her gobble mice as if she couldn't get enough.

"Taurine," she'd told him when at last she'd stretched out in the grass to rest. "Cats need taurine, and maybe I need more now for the kittens. We don't make our own, like people do." Where did she get this stuff? From Wilma? Did she and Wilma find these things online? Or had Dr. Firetti told them? *Taurine*, he thought. No wonder a cat craved mice.

It had been around two A.M. when he'd escorted Dulcie through her cat door and headed home himself. He found it hard to get used to his tame, sedate lady, hard to forget her wild days when, too often, he'd had trouble keeping up with her. He guessed those times would return. He hoped so. He felt tender and frightened for her, but he missed her devil-may-care fearlessness. Now, rolling over among the pillows again to block out the setting moon, he burrowed under and slept once more, deeply.

It was a reflection from the low rising sun that pulled him from the depths this time, that stirred him just enough to smell coffee brewing. Then an urgent banging, which woke him fully. He leaped from the pillows to stare around at the dawn-bright roofs and treetops. The pounding came again, from below, from the front door, and Billy Young's voice, "Ryan? Clyde?" A quavering, shaky voice not like Billy. Joe pushed out through the tower's open window, leaped across the shingles, and peered over.

The slim, brown-haired boy stood with his back to the front door, pressed against it watching the street fearfully in both directions, his thin face white, even his high, ruddy cheekbones white, his fists clenched. The door opened so suddenly behind him that he nearly fell inside.

Swinging around, he pushed in beside Ryan and slammed the door closed.

Startled, Joe Grey fled in through his tower onto the rafter, hit Clyde's desk, and was downstairs before Ryan and Billy reached the kitchen. Clyde, startled, turned from the stove where he was frying eggs. Joe leaped to the table as Ryan urged Billy to sit down. He was trembling and out of breath, his dark eyes huge. She reached for the freshly brewed coffee, added milk for him. "You ran here from the job?"

Mutely, Billy nodded.

Putting the cup on the table and fetching her own coffee, she sat down next to him. At the stove Clyde dished up the eggs and set them aside. Refilling his coffee cup, he joined them. Both were quiet, waiting for Billy to collect himself. When Joe heard the familiar sound of Max Harper's truck go by, Billy heard it, too, and glanced nervously in that direction. When Ryan took Billy's hand, gently undoing his fist, he gripped her fingers hard, needing that strong human touch.

Only Joe heard the softer sound of the medics' van slip by the house, following Max. No one else looked up. The medics were not using their siren, as if they didn't want to be heard heading for the building site. What had happened? Surely there'd been an accident—but who was hurt, to call out the rescue team?

Oh, not Scotty, Joe thought. Ryan's big redheaded uncle was often at work early—but the tall Scots-Irishman seemed as indestructible as stone. *Is it young Ben Stonewell?* He thought, shivering. *But maybe only some local, poking around the building, fell over a stack of lumber?* It was hard as hell to sit still, not to race out and follow the action.

"Max dropped me off at the job," Billy was saying, "and went on to work. I was early, Scotty wasn't there yet. No one . . . I used my key, went on in. Opened the garage from inside, then went out again and around to get some tools . . ." He cupped his hands around the warm mug, sat silently staring into it. Seeing what ugly replay, that he could hardly talk about?

At last, quietly, he looked up at Ryan and Clyde.

"Ben Stonewell," the boy whispered. "Ben is . . . Ben

is dead. Lying there, the ladder fallen over him . . . blood everywhere. I . . . I called Max on my cell. Dead," he repeated, looking at them, lost and pale. "Lying there in the side yard, so much blood . . . the ladder down on top of him." He wiped his eyes. "I guess he'd been working on the roof gutters. I thought at first he fell, then I saw the blood . . . then the bullet wound. A terrible hole, had to be a gunshot." He wiped at his eyes. "He couldn't have lived . . . A hole in the back of his jacket and up through his throat. Blood underneath where he fell . . ."

Ryan put her arms around the boy. She held him tight, her cheek against his forehead, her hands gripping his shoulders to steady him.

"I shouldn't have left him there alone," Billy said. "Dead, and alone. I was afraid the killer . . . that they might still be there. That they'd think I saw them and would come after me, too."

"*Did* you see anyone?" Clyde said.

"No one." Billy looked up at Clyde. "Ben never hurt anyone, never wanted to hurt anyone. How could someone . . . Why would somebody . . . ?"

Joe stretched out across the table close to the boy, put his paw on Billy's arm. Billy had already been through the trauma of his gram's death. The shock of seeing Gram's frail, charred body on the medics' stretcher, covered with a sheet outside their burned cabin, a memory that could never go away. That had been about a year ago, when Billy was twelve. Now Joe hurt for the boy in a different way than he hurt for poor Ben. Ben was dead, was at peace now from whatever horror had happened to him; he was hopefully in a kinder place. But Billy was feeling it all, the shock, the pain, the terror. Why would someone hurt Ben Stonewell? What had he done that someone wanted him dead?

IT WAS A while before Billy quieted, before he grew steadier and some color returned to his face. When he seemed stronger, he and Ryan and Clyde piled into the king cab and headed for the remodel. Joe Grey, slipping out behind them, leaped into the truck bed among the tools and folded tarps and old jackets. A stack of oak boards was strapped to one side. Clyde's glance back at him, as Clyde stepped up into the passenger seat, told Joe he'd better make himself scarce at the scene.

Clyde knew that no one could keep him away. Clyde's *Get lost* look was only an empty threat. Riding in the bumpy truck the four blocks to the brown cottage, Joe, despite his pain for Ben, was thankful it wasn't Ryan or Scotty or Billy lying dead. Had some drug-crazy vagrant, seeing the property vacant and under construction, maybe camped there overnight? And when Ben came to work early they'd panicked. Maybe the killer had a record, maybe there was a warrant out for him. He didn't want Ben calling the cops, and in a panic he'd shot Ben? Maybe someone on drugs with his brain all scrambled?

According to Billy, Ben must have been up on the ladder when he was shot, working on the roof minding his own business, not confronting some trespasser. *But they shot him anyway*, Joe thought. *And what if Billy had gotten to work first? Would they have killed Billy instead? A murder as coldly senseless as the random street attacks.*

Senseless? Joe thought. *Random? We don't know that. No one thinks those attacks were without reason.*

Ryan slowed the truck a block from the remodel and drew to the curb. Officer Jimmie McFarland stood in the center of the intersection rerouting traffic, sending rubberneckers down the side streets. McFarland with his boyish smile, his brown hair fallen over his forehead, looked like he should still be in college, not in a police uniform. Seeing it was Ryan and Clyde, he waved them on through to the next intersection, which was blocked off with sawhorses. There, when Ryan parked next to the coroner's van, Joe leaped out of the truck bed and into the bushes. The Bleaks' cottage was three doors down. He hightailed it through overgrown back gardens and beneath the yellow crime tape that now marked off the Bleaks' weedy property. At the far side of the cottage he slipped into the neighbors' hedge and peered out.

Max Harper and Detectives Garza and Kathleen Ray were working the scene. Kathleen stood against the house a few feet from Ben's twisted body, photographing the scuffed earth with its tangle of footprints from the building crew, angling for shots of the fresh prints on top. Dallas and Max were working on grids and a rough map, and making notes. Outside the crime tape the coroner waited to seal up and remove the body. Dr. John Bern was a thin, pale man, his dark-framed glasses placed firmly on his small button nose; his hair was graying, but he still looked strong and fit.

Joe watched Dallas kneel beside Ben, photographing the body from different close-up angles, then taking blood and debris samples with as little disturbance as possible. Ben lay twisted from the way he had fallen, his jacket skewed around him, the ladder still lying across him. The blood on his face and jacket bristled with dirt and debris. Dallas reached to remove the items from Ben's pockets, but he paused, looking at the blood and dirt smeared down across Ben's lumpy pockets and down into the folds of his clothes. He looked up at Max. "The removal of his possessions will be better done at the morgue. This mess—we could contaminate a lot, here."

Max nodded and glanced at Kathleen. She would, Joe assumed, be accompanying the coroner and the corpse. "You'll want a second witness," Max said. "Get Jane Cameron over here."

This meant Detectives Ray and Cameron would have custody of the evidence, would examine and photograph it, log it in, seal it in the appropriate individual bags, and transport it to the station to the evidence room. Joe watched Max and Dallas remove the ladder. Dallas shot another round of pictures and then, with John Bern, carefully lifted and wrapped the body in clean sheets—as clean as they could be kept. Joe watched them seal Ben into a body bag. Feeling sick and cold, he started suddenly thinking about Ben's construction notebook.

He had seen Ben, alone at odd hours, as during a coffee break, writing in the last pages of the little spiral-bound tablet. Not making his usual brief measurement and product memos on the front pages, but writing away in longer passages at the back, frowning, deeply occupied; he had watched Ben drop the notebook in his pocket if anyone came to join him. What was on those pages?

Could Ben have known the killer? If this wasn't a random shooting, if someone had killed Ben on purpose, would the notebook shed some light on the murder?

He'd like to have a look, but there was no way. He watched Max and John Bern carry the body to Bern's van. When they had him strapped in place, Dallas turned back to the house, picked up the ladder that he had already fingerprinted and photographed, set it in place and climbed up to examine and photograph the roof where Ben had been working. Watching him, Joe crouched in reflex when Tekla's angry voice echoed sharply from down the street. He reared up above the bushes to look.

Down at the corner, Ryan and Clyde stood facing Tekla Bleak, her angry harangue exploding in their faces. She was alone, Joe didn't see Sam. Maybe she'd left him in the van, parked beyond Ryan's truck nosed into the sawhorse barrier. Tekla's voice was shrill enough to take a cat's ears off. Joe had to grin at Officer McFarland's annoyed scowl.

"Of course it's your fault! Whose fault would it be! One of *your* people murdered right here in my house. How could you let such a thing happen! Why would you allow this? I can't live where someone's been *murdered*, where there's been a dead body! How could you . . ."

Joe threaded through the hedge, raced through the backyards to the corner and slipped under a lavender bush. The murder was Ryan's fault? Right. This woman was certifiably nuts. He wanted to leap in her face, show her what claws felt like.

"It's a good thing Sam isn't here, I can't have Sam upset and distraught—"

"Where is Sam?" Ryan said, to distract her. "He's always with you."

"Why is that *your* business? Sam's home with Arnold, the boy has a cold. Don't change the subject, *Ms.* Flannery. I cannot have this mess in my yard. I cannot have police all over my property. This is intolerable. I won't—"

She looked shocked when Clyde forcibly took her arm and turned her toward her van. "I suggest you wait in your vehicle, Tekla. Captain Harper will want to talk with you. You don't want to tramp around mingling your footprints with those of the killer?" Clyde asked, smiling. "You don't want to add *your* footprints to the possible evidence? This is a crime scene now. This is police territory."

Tekla jerked her arm away from Clyde and turned her back. She was standing stiffly by the barrier glaring at Mc-Farland when a second squad car drew up, nosing into the shade beneath a cypress tree. Detective Juana Davis got out, square, dark uniformed, and severe. The no-nonsense officer was still limping, her knee replacement giving her trouble. Ignoring Tekla, she put her arm around Billy and took Ryan's hand, her dark Latina eyes warm and caring. She talked softly with them for a few minutes, then turned to Tekla, her black eyes unreadable, a cop's closed look. Silently Tekla looked at her. Joe settled more comfortably among the bushes hoping Davis would question Tekla right there, where he wouldn't miss anything—Davis would question Billy and Ryan, too, for whatever information they might have, whatever they had observed.

These first interviews were best done at the scene,

when the crime was fresh. Where had the ladder been stored? Did Ben have a key to the house or garage? Did Billy? Had any of them given someone else a key? Did Ben always come to work so early? Was Billy sure no one else had been there when he arrived? But it was Tekla's answers that Joe burned to hear. Davis would ask where Tekla had been this morning, would ask for all kinds of details while, later at the station, Dallas would repeat those questions and more, the detectives alert for incongruities, for conflicting answers.

Now, at the far side of the house, Dallas was searching for trace evidence where the body had been removed. Soon he would photograph the ground there, would process for fingerprints on the window frames, would examine and take samples from all the surround. Before they finished up this morning, the officers would search Ben's car and his apartment; both were now a part of the crime scene. Meanwhile Joe waited impatiently for Tekla's interview, for Davis to sit her down right there, on the porch steps, to conduct the inquiry

But instead, Davis walked Tekla to her squad car, got her settled, and began the preliminary questions. Joe was poised to slip over under the car or ease up on top beneath the cypress branches when Max came out of the house and down the steps. He put his arm around Ryan and drew Billy to him. Curious, Joe waited.

"Juana can do your interviews later," he told them. "As soon as Davis is through with Tekla, she's headed for Ben's apartment. I'd like you two to follow her, get the rescue cats and their cages out of there so she can work that part of the scene. I have an officer up there, he got a key from the landlord. I don't want the place unguarded until we're done with it." The rescue cages were unlikely receptacles for any item of interest, but in a search, they needed to be cleared.

Ryan and Billy waited through Juana's interview, sitting on the steps close together out of Dallas's way. Joe did slip under the squad car but he couldn't hear much; Tekla's voice was sullen and low. When at last Tekla stepped out scowling and got into her van, and Ryan and Billy headed for Ryan's king cab, Joe Grey slipped into the truck bed. He was startled nearly out of his paws when Dulcie landed beside him in a flying leap from beneath the hedge.

"What the hell!" he hissed. "How long have you been here? Can't you be more careful! Those are *our kittens* you're carrying! My God," he snapped. "Are you all right? Are *they* all right?"

Dulcie smiled sweetly. "I'm fine, the kittens are fine. It was just a little leap." She rubbed her whiskers against him. "Wilma heard the call on the police scanner." She yawned in his face. "Scanner woke me up. Guess I slept in this morning, I was so full of mice. She . . . Wilma called the station to find out what had happened. I left her crying," Dulcie said sadly. She settled quietly on the folded tarp beside him, and there were tears in her own eyes. "I still can't believe it. Ben. Such a dear, gentle fellow."

Joe clawed at the jackets that lay tossed in the bottom of the truck, pulled them up onto the folded tarp to make a softer bed for her. She gave him a whisker kiss and curled up there. She looked so sad. The engine started and they were on their way, following Juana's patrol car up to Ben's place. Joe supposed that until Ryan found new foster homes for Ben's rescue cats they would reside in the Damens' downstairs guest room.

Riding in the truck bed close to Dulcie, he wondered if Ben's notebook *had* been in his jacket pocket when he died, along with the cell phone he always carried. Why did the notebook keep nudging at him, why did he think it important? And now the phone, too—the phone he'd seen more than once aimed casually at Tekla's feet as Ben stood near her ordering supplies or checking on a delivery.

Was his curiosity one of those moments Dulcie called cop sense? *"Cop thought,"* Dulcie would say. *"Detective intuition? Feline intuition? Who knows?"* Now, curling closer to her, Joe was glad she was beside him.

But then, heading for Ben's place, the truck slowed too soon, in only a few blocks. Joe tried not to be seen in the side mirror as he reared up to peer out—at his own house. Why were they stopping? Did Ryan not want him and Dulcie in on the search, did she mean to haul them out and leave them? That would be tacky, she wouldn't hear the last of that.

Or maybe she didn't want Billy to know they were riding along. Billy was too perceptive, he was sure to wonder why the cats had hung around the crime scene and why now they wanted to ride up to Ben's place. The cats trusted Billy, but enough people knew their secret: Ryan and Clyde, Wilma, Lucinda and Pedric, Kate Osborne, the Firettis. Every new confidant became, unwittingly, a new danger to them. One careless word, one innocent remark that might imply too much, and their cover could be destroyed.

Pulling into their drive, Ryan got out but didn't turn

back to the truck bed; she didn't snatch the cats out and dump them on the lawn. She and Billy headed for the garage. Joe and Dulcie, slipping behind the tied-down lumber, watched the two return with three cat carriers and extra blankets, safe transport for Ben's rescues. Ryan loaded these in the truck bed, hastily tying them in place as Billy stepped back in the cab. Ryan's scowl into the shadows of the lumber said clearly, *Stay out of sight! Stay out of the way and out of trouble or* I'll *make trouble.* Swinging into the truck, she headed up into the hills where crowding cottages overlooked a wild canyon, where Ben Stonewell had rented his small basement apartment.

10

In Anchorage, as Lucinda and Pedric Greenlaw prepared for their trip into Denali Park, worry still rode with them. They couldn't get their minds off Kit. Shopping, adding a few things to their light backpacks for the trip, adding heavier boots and canvas jackets, they toured Anchorage for another half day—but all the while their minds were on Kit. As they walked the town's rough streets, with the great, snowcapped peaks towering over them above the steep rooftops, unease nagged the gray-haired couple. Worry followed them as it had for the whole excursion, even as they thrilled at the sight of calving glaciers, at polar bears swimming in the icy waters and roaming the shores, at hundreds of bald eagles descending together toward an icy fjord. All the while, their thoughts didn't leave Kit and Pan for long.

When Lucinda had asked Clyde on the phone if Kit

and Pan were still gone, when he really couldn't talk much, all he said was, "Yes, they are, Lucinda . . ." Someone came into the room, and then shortly they had hung up. Not a satisfactory discussion. She knew he'd call when they did return. Meanwhile, she and Pedric fretted. Lucinda pictured the two cats back in the village curled before a warming hearth fire, maybe with Kate in the downstairs apartment or with Wilma and Dulcie. If she thought hard enough, maybe she could make it happen.

B UT KIT AND Pan were not curled before any fire. They were shivering cold, their paws nearly frozen as they clawed up through the dark earthen tunnels, up and up the wet, slick boulders, climbed in blackness, leaving the Netherworld behind them.

They had taken their leave with tears and with longing from that land of green light, of rolling fields and jagged cliffs, that realm of gentle unicorns and dwarves and elven folk; from the short-tempered Harpy who had carried them aloft winging through the green glow of the Netherworld's granite sky.

They had left their own kind, too. Had left behind the small clowder of speaking feral cats with whom they had traveled down from their own land, who had chosen to stay longer in the one Netherworld realm that welcomed and understood their singular feline race.

The green light followed them into the tunnel for only a little way, staining the ragged walls but quickly growing dim, eaten up by shadows. Kit grieved at leaving but she yearned for home, for her own loved ones. They trot-ted close together, Kit's mottled black and gray coat dark against the heavy stone walls, Pan's red-gold coat glowing for a little while and then darkness swallowed them.

In the Netherworld they had stayed clear of the blighted kingdoms to the west that had long ago grown corrupt and lost their own magic. They had cleaved to the one small country where life still throbbed with the bright hopes and endeavors of its peoples, the one unspoiled cor-ner of that lost and phantasmic world.

Now, ahead they could see only the faintest shadow-shapes in the blackness, their own eyes wide and black with their night vision. Echoes led them, echoes of a mewl to see what might bounce back to them, echoes of their own claws scraping stone. Vibrations against their whis-kers led them, too, as they padded up and up in the velvet dark; up and up through the dense and incomprehensible earth, Kit's yearning fierce for home, for space and light, for Lucinda and Pedric, for Joe and Dulcie and Misto, for all their human and cat family.

Is this always the way? Kit thought. *You long so hard for something, as we longed to see the Netherworld. You reach that place, you dive headfirst into the wonders there, you embrace those who greet you, who take you to their hearts—but then you start to grieve for home and all you left behind, to grieve for those you loved first?*

Oh, she thought, *will Lucinda and Pedric be home, will they be there to hug and welcome us? Or are they still in Alaska? Will the house be empty and dark, no cheerful blaze on the hearth, no one to hug and snuggle us, no good smells of supper cooking? Are they still there at the top of the world even as we leave the world's very depths?* She imagined Alaska's mountains of glacial ice breaking and falling, its huge and hungry beasts; she saw the two tiny figures in that vast land which, to Kit, seemed far more threatening than the enchanted realms that they had left behind. Now the last breath of the Netherworld had long ago vanished. The higher they scrambled up through darkness, the deeper up into the vast and heavy earth, the more they longed for the open sky. For their own stars, billions of light-years above them, for the night winds blowing down from heaven, for their own bright moon. Crowded against stone shoulders too close to the edge of dropping chasms, they knew fear: fear of falling, panic sometimes at the tunnel's confinement, terror that they were lost, but they mustn't let fear take them. On they climbed, drawn by their terrible longing, up and up, it seemed forever in the overwhelming dark.

JOE AND DULCIE bounced along in the back of Ryan's pickup, slyly peering out. She pulled up before a tall old dark-shingled house that hugged the side of the canyon. Two stories plus a peaked attic and, down at the day-light basement level facing the canyon, a small apartment tucked into the concrete foundation. Even the sight of Ben's small home brought tears to Dulcie's eyes and left Joe grim and silent.

Beside the house, the driveway from the street had been widened so one could pull on back next to the lit-tle rental. Ryan turned the truck around, backed down against a heavy wooden barrier, and set the brake. Beside

Ben's plain front door, a wide window faced the drive. Through it the cats could see two big cages facing larger windows that looked down the falling canyon. There could be no other windows, the way the apartment was tucked beneath the big house, up against the hill. The inner space looked cramped and dim. Both cats shivered, both cats felt for an instant that in that shadowed room the spirit of Ben might linger, that Ben wasn't ready yet to leave this earth, to leave his new home, his friends, his little cats. Joe and Dulcie ducked out of sight when Juana's patrol car pulled down the drive and parked beside them.

Ryan stepped out of the truck, untied and retrieved the three small carriers—and gave Joe and Dulcie another warning look. *Stay put. Do not make trouble in front of Davis. Do not slip in and try to toss the apartment—until Davis leaves.* Joe scowled at her but obediently the cats crept deeper behind the lumber. Ryan was getting as bossy as Clyde. When everyone's backs were turned, Juana unlocking the apartment door, Ryan and Billy hauling the carriers inside, Joe and Dulcie scrambled out of the truck bed, up over its roof, in through the driver's open window, and to the backseat. With its dark-tinted glass, they could see out but remain nearly invisible. Only the white strip down Joe's nose was a problem, but maybe it would look like a simple reflection of light.

It was one thing to lounge on Max Harper's desk snooping and listening; the department was used to free-loading cats making themselves at home. But their presence at a crime scene was never smart, particularly one as out-of-the-way as this. Why would cats hitch a ride way up here? Why would they hitch a ride anywhere? Most cats, unlike dogs, didn't enjoy going along to savor new smells or new views; most cats didn't like the noise and jolt of a car or truck.

Though sometimes a cat would crawl into a warm vehicle unseen, maybe a mover's van, go to sleep, and end up half a continent away. That cat might make the national news if he was discovered, identified, and found his way home again via human intervention. Or not. He might spend the rest of his life as a homeless stray, or might luck out and adopt a new family but never see his own people and his own neighborhood again. All because he had foolishly chosen to nap in the wrong hideaway.

Inside the dim apartment Juana flicked on the dull overhead bulb; she left the door open for additional light as she examined the small, shadowed room.

Knowing that Ben would never again sleep in that narrow bed, eat a meal at the little table, or pet his three rescue cats made Joe swallow hard and look away.

As Juana examined the big wire cages, the three rescue cats eyed her warily: a half-grown black female, a big white tom, and a black-and-white tuxedo male. Juana photographed the cages, the walls, the concrete floor, then began to lift fingerprints from the cage handles and from their flat metal latches. Why would the killer, if he *had* been in there, have any interest in cat cages? Why *would* the killer have come there?

Had he planned to kill Ben here in the apartment this morning, but Ben had already left? Or did Ben have something he wanted, something so valuable that before following Ben to work he had slipped in here to search?

This whole case seemed so senseless. Innocent victims, four of them dead. Banker Ogden Welder; Merle Rodin; James Allen, who had been attacked while wiping the windshield of his car, and died shortly afterward, in ER. And now Ben Stonewell. While the other assault victims had been left alive as if their attacker had no desire to finish them. *None of this*, Joe thought, *none of it adds up*.

He watched Juana bag a cluster of short black hairs from the bed, and that gave him a start. Anything involving cat hairs unsettled him. But those weren't his hairs, they'd belong to one of the rescues. When Juana finished with the main room, Ryan and Billy lifted out the three rescue cats and put them in the carriers. Setting these outside the front door, they got to work breaking down the big cages into flats. Davis watched them carefully; civilians were never left alone at a crime scene, even the most trusted friends. That was, in part, for their own protection, if questions should arise later about the possibility of contaminated evidence.

Fighting the bolts on the old cages, Ryan and Billy slowly removed the sides and tops. Before loading the big wire flats in the truck, Ryan stepped outside with her cell phone. The cats, slipping into the front seat beneath the open window, crouched listening. She made two calls, the first to Wilma, to tell her that Dulcie and Joe were safe, and to talk a moment about Ben. But then when Wilma asked if Dulcie was all right, the tabby hissed and lashed her tail. *Do they* have *to fuss over me? Just because I'm with kitten, do they have to treat me like I'm helpless?*

Ryan's next call, to Celeste Reece, was a long and tearful conversation. The cats could tell from Ryan's gentle words that Celeste was shocked and upset. After a long while, Ryan said she'd bring the rescues on over if Celeste had room. Ryan listened, nodded, and hung up. As she and Billy loaded the flats into the truck bed, Joe peered out, torn between staying with them or remaining behind. He glanced at Dulcie. "We could just slip inside, search in the shadows behind Juana."

"*Oh, right.* Just how do you propose, in that tiny space, to keep out of Juana's sight? You know her better than that."

Waiting wasn't Joe's style, but they stayed sensibly in the truck. Peering from the cab window into the apartment, they watched Juana meticulously photographing the little table beside Ben's cot, paying close attention to some kind of marks on its surface. Juana stepped outside once, as Ryan headed for the backseat with the first carrier. "Did Ben have a laptop? And a printer?"

"He may have," Ryan said. "He submitted a printed résumé. But he could have done that anywhere. Library, UPS, Kinko's." Ryan looked at Juana questioningly.

"Table's a bit dusty," Juana said. "Two items have been recently removed. Clean underneath and with slide marks. Did Ben have a smartphone? Did he take and print any pictures?"

"He had a smartphone. I never saw any prints he'd made. I think he took some shots of work in progress. Probably just for the record and didn't bother to print them. I keep the same kind of record. Unless . . ."

Ryan paused, frowning. "Unless Tekla criticized something more than I knew. Unless she was on *his* back, too, when I wasn't around, and he wanted proof of the work he'd done? If he did take pictures for that reason, I'd like to know what it was about. I guess his phone would be at the coroner's, he usually kept it in his jacket pocket."

But Juana had already keyed in a call to Kathleen Ray.

"You're still at the coroner's. Did you find a phone, was there one on the body?" She waited, then, "And Dallas didn't find it at the scene?"

Joe wanted to shout, *Ask about a notebook, too! Did she find a spiral-bound notebook?* Beside him Dulcie was strung tight, they both wanted to slip into the apartment to scent the marks on the table, see if they could detect what a human sleuth might miss. But one look at Ryan, as she opened the back door of the king cab, and he knew they'd better stay put. They were already in trouble for not staying in the truck bed.

They watched, peering back between the bucket seats as she strapped the cat carriers onto the backseat. When she'd finished, they leaped to the floor back there, in the shadows where Billy might not notice them. Glancing up at Ryan, they tried to look small and defenseless, but Ryan only scowled.

Billy got in the front next to Ryan, she started the engine, and they headed down the hills to deliver the rescues to Celeste Reece. Maybe by the time Juana got back to the station, she'd have found something of interest, have pulled more pieces together. Maybe by the time *they* slipped into the station again, Davis's written report would be on the chief's desk? And, with luck, Kathleen's list of Ben's possessions? Maybe she would find the notebook. Maybe then the odd bits of intelligence might start to make sense. Then, it would be time to slip away and call Harper.

K IT AND PAN pressed on up the tunnels in blackness, their whiskers brushing outcroppings, their keen ears catching the echo of empty spaces that halted them in their tracks. They found their way sometimes by the luminescence of scuttling crabs, the iridescence of blind fishes flashing through dark rivulets. Scrambling up through the blackness toward their own world across underground springs that soaked their paws, they didn't know day from night. They crossed stone bridges trusting their whiskers, trusting the tiniest movement of air. They wondered if they *were* following the same path that they had descended. Or would they keep climbing and circling forever?

"I don't think. . . ." Kit began. But Pan eased closer to her and purred and licked her ear to steady her and on they went, Pan's bold attack on the darkness soothing and calming to the tortoiseshell. And then at last as they rounded a bend the tunnel grew wider—and they saw ahead the faintest glow, the thinnest shaft of light. "*Sunlight!*" Kit whispered. "*Oh, sunshine!*" Soon golden light blazed in at them, the portal shone wide open, and they bolted out into the brilliance. "*Our* sky, *our* world," Kit cried, reaching tall, whirling around on her hind paws, staring up into Earth's infinite spaces that swept away forever; beside her Pan, too, leaped for the sky. They were home, reveling in the vastness of their own bright and endless domain, their own universe.

11

CELESTE REECE WORKED hard for CatFriends' rescued strays, finding homes for lost and abandoned cats. She lived south of Ben's place, down along the canyon nearer the village, a square, sturdy woman, her iron-gray hair layered short and neat, her voice low. Her way with a cat was understanding and always gentle. She attended CatFriends meetings at the Damens' house where Joe liked to lounge among the group and slyly enjoy the variety of snacks laid out on Ryan's tea cart.

Now, from the floor of the backseat, Joe and Dulcie could see nothing as Ryan pulled up into Celeste's drive and parked. Only when she and Billy had lifted the three small carriers out, and their footsteps moved away, did the two cats leap up onto the seat and press their noses once more to the dark window.

Celeste's one-story stucco cottage stood on a narrow lot flanked by older houses crowded close together above the canyon among olive and pepper trees. Behind Celeste's yard a lone pine loomed tall, a dark exclamation mark against the pale spring sky. The stucco walls of the cottage smelled of fresh paint, the color pale ivory beneath a black shingle roof. The front windows were narrow and tall, reaching nearly to the ground, three at either side of the carved front door.

An old, discarded basketball hoop lay at the side of the yard atop a stack of folded painters' tarps. Part of the driveway was wet. A bed of flowers and bushes along the drive gleamed where they had just been watered. The rest of the yard, an expanse of pine bark and bushes, was dry. The marks of wet bike tires crossed the drive, swerving in and then back to the street. Beside the house a wheelchair stood tucked against the porch rail and the two shallow steps. In the back pocket of the wheelchair a blue shopping bag peeked out: it was the wheelchair from in front of the station—but that hadn't been Celeste Reece in the wheelchair, spinning around to face a possible assault.

Ryan and Billy set the carriers on the porch. The door opened at once, Celeste stepped out, gave Ryan a big hug and put her arm around Billy. Her jeans and T-shirt were old and faded, her short hair shone fresh and clean. Leaving the door ajar, she knelt to look in the carriers.

Two of the rescues pushed forward, greeting her with interest. The black-and-white tuxedo kept his distance. She spoke gently to the small black cat and to the white tom but ignored the wild tuxedo as she could see he preferred. She looked up at Ryan. "My sister's down from the city, she'll help me with the cats. These three make twelve, about all the room I have. I hope we can find homes for them."

"We usually do," Ryan said, "*you* usually do. And soon we'll have the shelter. Didn't your sister . . . ?"

Celeste nodded. "Bonnie. You remember, she married Gresham Rivers. Yes, she recently lost Gresham in a shocking accident. She was hurt, too. Now that she's out of the hospital and through the memorial, now that she's beginning to heal, she needed to get away, get out of the city. Away from every painful reminder, at least for a little while."

"I'm so sorry," Ryan said. "How can Clyde and I help?"

"Thanks, but there's nothing at the moment. She's doing fairly well. It was a terrible accident. It's been hard for her, alone suddenly, the shock of Gresham's death, so cruel and senseless. Come, let's set up the cages."

Leaving the rescues in their carriers on the porch, Billy and Ryan followed Celeste as she opened the garage from outside. Inside, five tall cages stood against the far wall, each with several tiers.

Joe and Dulcie could see pale shapes within, interested eyes looking out. They dropped down quickly as Ryan passed the truck, Celeste and Billy behind her, ready to unload the wire kennels.

Watching the three friends haul out the big flats, thinking about Ben taking care of his rescues in that small apartment, Joe's voice was hardly a whisper. "We need to tell Misto about Ben. Misto was fond of him." He thought about how, before Misto got sick, Ben would come to the shore to help John feed the ferals and would always carry

Misto around with him in his arms. About how, that first day when they knew Misto had a malignancy, Ben had gone to the clinic and spent a long, quiet time with the frail old cat. Golden Misto, even for those humans who didn't know he could speak, had woven himself, with his indomitable spirit, into the lives of them all.

"Misto needs to know about Ben," Joe repeated, "but I don't like to hurt him. He . . ."

"Maybe he does know," Dulcie said softly. "Maybe, in that mysterious way he has, maybe he already knows, maybe he knows where Ben is. Where . . ."

"Where Misto soon will be?" Joe finished sadly.

A soft step by the truck window, and Ryan looked in. "I came back for my gloves. I heard you whispering," she said quietly. "I'll see that Misto knows. I'll call Mary. The Firettis will gather him to them and hold him; they'll tell him gently that Ben is gone. Two strong humans, to tell him and hold him."

Joe looked up at Ryan and swallowed and didn't answer. He looked toward the garage where Celeste and Billy were at work setting up the cages. Ryan reached into the truck seat for her gloves, gave the cats a pet, then returned to the garage. Joe and Dulcie were watching the cage sides being bolted in place when, at the house, the front door swung open again and the woman in the leg brace hobbled out, the woman from in front of the courthouse, Bonnie Rivers, lean and tanned, wearing her metal brace.

Leaving the door ajar behind her, she didn't approach the wheelchair. She came down the two steps using only her cane and headed for the garage. And the cats heard again in memory the woman in the red sweatshirt, *That was her, all right, Howard . . . same long face, same tennis tan. She wasn't in a cast and wheelchair then . . . Bonnie something . . .*

How was Bonnie Rivers connected to the couple in the red sweatshirts? Somehow, through San Francisco. And was she connected, as well, to the Molena Point street attacks?

As Bonnie limped toward the garage, Joe Grey and Dulcie waited until the little group had their backs turned working on the cages, then slid out the open window, Dulcie breaking her fall among the bushes. Quickly they crossed the dry part of the garden to the open front door—but the smell of the wheelchair stopped them.

They stood sniffing, wrinkling their noses at the unexpected scent. A faint hint of Vicks VapoRub. But a strong, fresh scent of Hoppe's, said Joe. There was no mistaking the smell of gun-cleaning solvent. Its aroma drifted all through the offices of MPPD, as well as at home on occasion when their housemates cleaned their own firearms. But Hoppe's on the wheelchair? The smell brought them up sharply.

The Hoppe's was on the handlebars. The hint of Vicks clung to the edge of the seat where Bonnie's legs would have touched. Sore muscles in the injured leg they could understand. But Hoppe's? That was more interesting. Glancing toward the garage where the four were at work, they fled through the partially open front door into the house, shaking pine bark from their paws.

The large living room had also been freshly painted, white and airy. Big bay windows at the back, white canvas slipcovers on the upholstered furniture. A pale wood floor, no throw rugs for a cane or wheelchair to get caught on, the room uncluttered and welcoming. They had no trouble following Bonnie's scent to the guest room, which appeared to share a wall with the garage. Slipping in, they could hear the mumble of voices where the four were working, heard small metallic clicks as the cages were bolted together. Following the smell of Hoppe's to the dresser, they leaped up.

They landed nose to barrel with a businesslike revolver.

Dulcie backed away before she saw that its action was open and empty, the weapon bright from a recent cleaning. It lay on folded newspapers beside gun-cleaning equipment, a bottle of Hoppe's, gauze patches, a long rod, and a little brush. Beside these lay a box of .38 cartridges.

They wanted to paw the box open to see if any rounds were missing, but they didn't want to smear fingerprints. They still didn't know if pawprints would be picked up. But why not? They had never yet gotten in trouble over pawprints, but the thought haunted them.

The sounds from the garage changed suddenly. They heard water running as if bowls were being filled, hands being washed, the chores were done. Dropping to the floor they fled the room, fled the house. They were through the truck window, in the backseat of the king cab, when Ryan and Billy headed their way. Dropping to the floor, Dulcie was panting with tension and exertion. Joe nosed worriedly at her.

He'd been so interested in Bonnie Rivers and the gun

that he'd nearly forgotten his lady's condition. *I nearly forgot the kittens, nearly forgot how stressed Dulcie must feel, ramping around the village trying to sort out this tangle while she worries about the kittens.* Gently he licked her ear. Maybe all Dulcie really wanted was to loll around the house enjoying little treats and listening to music. Maybe she didn't want to be out chasing a killer, just wanted to be calm and cosseted, for herself and for the kittens.

How much strife can the kittens sense, he wondered, *when they're still inside the womb? We don't want frightened babies. Will the tension that Dulcie feels, will that weaken them or strengthen them? Make them more fearful or make them bold and strong? Maybe*, he thought, *no one knows the answer to that.* But for his lady and the babies, he'd prefer restful and tender care.

KIT AND PAN had emerged from the tunnels among the Pamillon ruins just where they had entered to go down seeking the Netherworld. Emerged from beneath a stone porch between tumbled pillars and vine-covered buildings. "*Home.*" Kit mewled again softly. "*Oh, we're home.*"

They stared up at the endless sky above them; they drank in the scents of pine and cypress, the smell of the grassy fields and of the distant sea. This world's breeze caressed them, rippling through their fur, made them race in circles. They were fiercely hungry. In the tall grass among the broken carvings Pan lifted his nose scenting for mice, for rats or squirrels, for anything edible, and Kit did the same. The tunnel had provided water and an occasional blind lizard or sightless fish snatched from the black waters, but never enough, nothing substantial enough to truly sustain them. Now they dodged through the ruin on the trail of a wood rat, doubled through overgrown bushes working together hazing the little beast until they took him down. Quickly they shared their kill, but left the tail. They spied and cornered a big wharf rat, attacked it with businesslike urgency. Soon, killing and gorging and feeling stronger, they finished off their meal with a pair of small and succulent field mice.

They drank from a little spring within the overgrown garden, and at last, sated, they lay washing blood from their paws. They wanted a nap after their long and stressful climb, but Kit hungered too passionately to be home. Had Lucinda and Pedric returned? Would they snatch her up and hug her and cry over her and comfort her? Would they hold her warm and safe and hug Pan, make a loving fuss over both of them? *Were* her humans home to welcome and comfort them?

Eagerly she headed down the hills, Pan following close beside her, down and down where the hills dropped away, dotted by cottage rooftops. Down they fled, racing belly-deep in grass, paws flying, crushing dandelions and wild nasturtiums, leaping through tangles of honeysuckle. Down and down the familiar hills where, far below, the sea reflected late afternoon sun; down through cottage gardens that smelled of onions and rotted leaves, down until at last they could see Kit's own roof among the distant oaks. She could see her tree house. Racing steeply down they bolted at last into Kit's own garden.

The house towered two stories above them. Kit's tree

house thrust higher still. Up the oaken trunk they scrambled, up into her aerie into scattered leaves and cushions. Kit rolled among her pillows, lay on her back looking up into the tree's sheltering crown, up into the sky beyond. *Her* sky, *her* tree, *her* house, *her* gardens all around. *Their* world, *their* village, *their* rooftops stretching away where they could travel the shingled byways as familiar as other cats' firesides. Among the leaves and pillows Pan sprawled beside her, his amber eyes laughing. "*Our* world," and it was theirs, their own sky rising high and away without any stone barrier, high and away forever.

But even now, even so content, Kit couldn't be still. Restlessly she rose again from among the cushions, peering toward the big house. Were they home? Could she hear them? Could she catch their scent?

She heard no sound. She saw no movement at the kitchen windows, the shades were still half drawn. There was no smell of cooking, no lingering scent of recent and comforting meals. The big house smelled distant and empty.

But maybe . . . Maybe they'd just gotten home, maybe they had just now come in. Maybe . . . Leaping from her aerie, Kit raced along the thick and twisted branch that led to the dining room window. In through her cat door that was set into the lower pane. One leap from the windowsill and buffet to the dining table, Pan close beside her, the cat door swinging behind them.

No one cried out at hearing the flapping door, no one came running. All was still. The house was empty. But even so they went racing through the hollow rooms, one room to the next, and in each room scenting out and listening and rearing up, looking for an open suitcase, sniffing for some hint of new smell.

All was still. All was as Lucinda and Pedric had left it. Nothing in the house was changed, no book or magazine moved from where Kit had last seen it. Wastebaskets empty, clothes hamper empty, clean towels hanging on the racks neatly folded, double bed carefully made, bedroom shades at half-mast. Nothing out of place in the kitchen, trash basket empty when Kit stood on the foot lever and Pan reared up to peer in.

The only change was the stack of mail piled on Pedric's desk in the living room, where Kate must have brought it in. Yes, Kate Osborne's faint scent where she had been through the house making sure no tap was leaking, no intruder had entered.

"Maybe Kate's home," Kit said, "the downstairs apartment," and she was out the cat door again, along the wandering branch and down the oak tree, Pan close behind her.

"Her car isn't in the drive," Pan said behind her, but Kit paid no attention; down the hill she fled and around the lower wall of the house to Kate's sliding glass door.

They could smell her scent stronger there, beneath the edge of the door. They pawed at it, Kit yowled, they tried the knob, swinging and kicking, but that did no good, the dead bolt was in place. They pawed and scratched and meowed together in a fine chorus, but there was no answer. They scrambled up bushes to peer in through the windows. At last, discouraged, they gave it up and headed for Wilma and Dulcie's. They needed welcoming. Kit needed hugging. And, in spite of being full of rodents, they longed for a bite of home-cooked supper. No wood rat or even field mouse was ever as succulent as a meal prepared lovingly by human hands.

They had left Kate's door, were crossing the neighbors' roofs when a brown car came along below them and stopped at the curb. A Dumpster stood across the street before a vacant lot where a dozen dead trees had been felled. Two men sat resting from cutting the logs with chain saws. The big metal bin was nearly full of smaller branches.

As the brown sedan slowed, a passenger stepped out, emptied a bag of old shoes in under the twigs and leaves, swung quickly into the car again, and it moved away. The workmen glanced up but paid little attention—they were only dumping old shoes. The cats didn't recognize the make of the car; they didn't see either the driver's or the passenger's faces. They moved on toward Wilma's hoping for a hot supper.

ALONE IN THE stone cottage, Wilma had put on a CD of Pete Fountain, a favorite among her collection of early jazz. These days when Dulcie was gone and Wilma worried, the lilting clarinet eased her. But now even as she paced the cottage worrying over the pregnant tabby, she knew she was being foolish. She knew very well where Dulcie was, from the police scanner that sat on the cherry desk and, later, from Ryan's phone call. She felt ashamed keeping such a close watch on Dulcie, but just now, considering the tabby's condition, she and Ryan might both be forgiven.

She'd known, early this morning when Dulcie bolted out her cat door, where she'd gone, had known when she turned on the scanner, and then from calling Ryan. Young Ben Stonewell had been shot. The murder sickened her, she was . . . had been fond of Ben; he was kind and caring and nothing cruel about him. Why *this* death? Was there something about Ben that they hadn't known? *Could* his murder be connected to these other crimes?

She had been tempted to drive over to the Bleak renovation this morning, but with the department working the scene she didn't like to get in the way. Pacing the cottage, across the Persian rug, brushing by the flowered couch, thinking about Ben's murder, and worrying about Dulcie, she hardly saw the room at all. She jumped when the phone rang, and snatched it from the cradle.

"The cats are fine," Ryan said, knowing how she worried. "They're with me, we're moving the rescues from Ben's place. Celeste is taking all three. We'll swing by the department so Billy and I can give our statements— Dulcie and Joe will be right there in our faces, you know that. Dulcie will be just fine. Joe Grey," Ryan added, "Joe has grown very attentive."

Wilma laughed. "He'd better be, he's responsible for this miracle—half responsible."

There was a smile in Ryan's voice. "I'll bring Dulcie home when we're finished. Please don't worry about her."

Hanging up, Wilma put on another CD and stretched out in the easy chair. Listening to the haunting clarinet helped to push away her worry, helped to ease life's dark side. She dozed off listening to Pete Fountain. The CD was nearly to the end when a different sound stirred her from sleep. The soft flap of the cat door, then a demanding mewl that startled her wide awake.

HAVING RACED OVER the roofs heading down toward the village, Kit and Pan paused several blocks above where the shops began. Scrambling down a pine they fled through Wilma's bright garden and in through Dulcie's cat door—but at the sound of music, they paused. Music filled the house, the clear notes of a clarinet, the dulcet riffs of the one musician in all the world who could speak to a cat's very soul.

Listening and smiling, but then curious, they padded into the kitchen. Wilma seldom put on a CD unless she or Dulcie were celebrating some special joy, or unless they were very blue and needed that soul-healing music.

Kit and Pan, lonely and hungry and needing loving, did not want to face some sadness. Which was this they were hearing? The lilting clarinet to ease an unwanted sadness, to assuage unexpected bad news? Or was the bright music a celebration of some wonderful event, of which they knew nothing? What were they to find?

Hesitantly they crossed the dining room beneath the big table. Softly they padded toward the living room prepared for either extreme, ready to offer comforting if that was needed, or to add their own joy to some bright and mysterious celebration. The cozy room was so welcoming, the soft oriental rug under their paws, the smell of recent baking, the flowered couch and overflowing book-shelves, sunlight streaming in on the cherry desk. In her easy chair, Wilma had stirred from sleep, an open book in her lap. Kit, watching her, gave a loud and startling mewl. Wilma jerked up, fully alert. She leaped up and knelt before them, grabbing them both in a hug, laughing, nearly smothering them in her joy, in her delight at their return.

12

 In the lobby of MPPD two men and a young woman waited in the folding chairs, a chair between each as if they had come in separately. The thin woman, in pale blue workout clothes, had focused on the younger man, grousing to him about the unfairness of the police, how that cop had pulled her over just because she was talking on her cell phone. Both men glanced away, their minds on their own problems. Ryan and Billy stood near the desk, waiting for a detective to come out for them, to escort them back to one of the offices to take their statements.

Joe Grey and Dulcie, having slipped into the holding cell, crouched under the bunk, trying not to breathe the mixed fumes of sweat and Lysol that so sharply stung their noses. They watched Detective Davis come out to get Ryan, watched the two disappear down the hall, leaving Billy at the mercy of Evijean Simpson; but Evijean had all she could do to deal with an enraged wife who had come to bail out her husband. "Of *course* he drinks," she snapped at Evijean. "What do you think *I* can do about it? Why should *I* be hassled and embarrassed because of the trouble *he* gets into!"

"You don't have to bail him out," Evijean told her as Dallas came up the hall, motioning Billy back to his office. At the same moment the front door flew open and Tekla Bleak stormed in demanding to see Captain Harper. Evijean, already overwhelmed, took one look at Tekla's scowl, backed away, and buzzed through to Harper.

The minute Max appeared, Tekla lit into him. "I want that woman off my property at once. I'm surprised you haven't already done that. I *told* you, with this murder . . ."

Max listened in silence, with only the hint of a smile.

"That Flannery woman has no business there after what happened. Why didn't your people make her leave? *She's* responsible for this and she's made no effort to evacuate the premises, to move her equipment, get her workers out of there. I want her out now. She refuses to honor the contract and of course it's *in* the contract, about damages caused. What worse damage *could* there be than this disgraceful murder, and I told her as much."

Max waited, letting her vent. In the holding cell, beneath the bunk, Joe Grey and Dulcie looked at each other with the same amused disbelief as the chief.

"This is police business, *Captain* Harper. It's *your* business to get her out of there *now*."

Max looked at Tekla for a long moment. "The property is a crime scene. Nothing can be moved or removed.

And how is your contract with Flannery Construction any of our affair?"

"*She's* turned our house into a crime scene! *That* is your affair. *She's* the one responsible for hiring that Ben person—he was obviously involved in something shady or he wouldn't have been murdered, but she refused to admit *that*. It's up to you to make her leave, or I will see my lawyer."

"Right now," Max said, "we'll want your statement, what you actually witnessed at the scene. Come back to my office, we can take care of that at once. Then you can call your lawyer."

Across the room, the two men and the young woman seemed to have forgotten their own troubles as they enjoyed the entertainment. Under the bunk, Joe and Dulcie were more frustrated than entertained. They wanted to follow Max and Tekla and listen, and they didn't dare cross the room. They watched them vanish down the hall. They heard Harper's door close, hard and decisively. Then silence. Their line of communication had gone as dead as an unplugged phone.

Cut off from eavesdropping, they curled up beneath the bunk into that drowsy seminap that serves a cat in times of annoyance, when things don't go as planned.

Maybe Max would record Tekla's statement at the same time that he made written notes; maybe they could listen later. But to what end? What would they learn? The woman was all vitriol and hot air. They were dozing and waking, listening for Max's door to open, when Ryan came up the hall with Davis, and Dallas and Billy behind them. Ryan stopped at the desk.

"Evijean, we're going to do some errands. Will you tell Captain Harper we'll be back, so Billy can ride home with him?"

Evijean scowled and nodded. Ryan, turning away, was just beside the holding cell when she dropped her car keys.

Leaning down to retrieve them, she glanced in at Joe and Dulcie—she knew just where they'd be, with the lobby full of strangers. Her look said, *Are you coming?*

Both cats looked back at her blankly, their ears down in a *no, we're not, get out of our faces* stare that made Ryan hide a laugh. Rising again, she went on out, following Billy. Joe knew she'd meant to drive Dulcie home to Wilma, not leave her running the roofs; but Dulcie backed away stubbornly.

There were only two civilians waiting now, the young woman having been seen and sent on her way. Joe was wishing they could make a dash for Max's office when they heard his door open, heard Tekla whine, " . . . but you're the police. It's your—"

"As I explained, Mrs. Bleak, this is not police business. This is between you and Ms. Flannery. If you want to file charges of misconduct, which I think would be hard to substantiate . . ." He was walking behind Tekla; she halted when she saw Ryan and Billy disappear out the glass door to the parking lot.

"What are *they* doing here?"

Max just looked at her.

"You *will* file charges against her!" she said shrilly.

As Evijean called the remaining two civilians to the counter, and Max walked Tekla to the door, behind their backs Joe and Dulcie made a dash past the counter and down the hall to the chief's office.

When Max returned, Dulcie was curled up on the leather couch. She looked up purring at Max's indulgent glance. From the bookcase, Joe got a gentle scratch on the head as Max sat down, picked up the form where he'd recorded Tekla's statement. He scanned it into the computer, then slipped the sheets into a file in his desk drawer. Turning back to the computer, he pulled up the first section of Kathleen's report, which she had sent from the coroner's office. It included details of the condition of the clothing and of the body as clothing was removed. Joe skipped down to her list of Ben's personal belongings: pocketknife, small grouting spatula, car and house keys, oversize bandanna, wallet, and a neatly folded packet of receipts from various building supply houses. No cell phone, no notebook.

Had these two items disappeared after the shooting, lifted from Ben's pocket by the killer? Or had Ben somehow been able to hide them before he died? Standing on the ladder working on the roof, had he heard an uneasy noise behind him? Had he glimpsed someone standing below in the shadows of the surrounding trees? Had he seen the gun? In that split second, had he, in desperation, quickly stashed the items he didn't want someone to find? But hidden them where?

Dallas had searched that whole area, had taken Ben's toolbox as evidence, had climbed the ladder and searched the roof for debris and trace elements.

Did Ben have those items when he fell, and the killer snatched them? *Or,* Joe thought, *am I chasing shadows?* Is the notebook of no interest? Was there nothing in the back but a few personal thoughts, like a diary? Nothing among the phone's pictures but building details? Am I fretting over nothing more than a collection of building specifications and material lists?

Juana had searched Ben's apartment and searched Ben's car for evidence, and Dallas had worked the rooms of the remodel. The detectives knew Ben had a phone and a notebook, so they should be as interested as Joe to know what they might contain—but they had found neither. Now he watched Max remove another file from the drawer and pull out a yellow pad, the kind on which he made random notes. Hanging half off the bookshelf, Joe scanned the chief's brief notations about those who had been attacked. The full reports would be on the computer. Max made no move to bring that up on the screen—even for Joe's convenience. The yellow pad was a place to contemplate, to perhaps jot down random thoughts about the victims.

Betty Porter, leaving work, M.P. Drugstore, streets stormy, nearly dark, hit from behind as she approached her car. Nothing stolen. Still had her purse, her billfold with credit cards and cash. Sent to ER, her spleen removed, recuperating at home, twenty-four-hour nurse.

Hazel Curt, walking home carrying groceries, again nearly dark. Hit from behind, knocked down, not badly hurt. Again, no robbery. She walked on home, called the department. No sign of attempted break-in. No further occurrence reported.

Luella Simms. Late afternoon. Attacked in parking lot of Village Grocery, loading shopping bags into backseat, knocked down but saw no one, nothing stolen. She was helped by a passerby, refused transportation to ER. Reported bruises, no injuries.

Elsie Rice, walking from her cottage at Pineview seniors' residence to the dining room for breakfast, 9 A.M. Hit from behind, fell into bushes. Saw no one, heard no running. Davis took the call, photographed footprints in the damp lawn. Victim was cared for at the facility. No enemies in the facility that she knew of.

A notation in the margin: "Have received so far two dozen frightened phone calls, citizens sure they were being followed. Conducted interviews. No useful information."

The last four names were the murder victims, Max had marked three with a penciled note: "San Francisco connection?"

Ogden Welder. 84-year-old retired banker. Walking home from the beach, 6:40 P.M., attacked from behind, critically injured, died, MP Hospital. Lived alone, Jasper Senior Apartments. Listed by the facility as having no family.

James Allen. Attacked 6:30 A.M. in driveway of his house, in his walker as he wiped windshield of his car. Had an order in his pocket for routine blood work, was headed for the lab. Heard nothing. Knocked to the ground, heard someone running, light footsteps like rubber soles. Saw no one. Statement was short, in severe pain. Died in ER 1:03 A.M. of a ruptured aorta. Attending doctor: Robert Ingleton. Officers Brennan and McFarland canvassed neighborhood. No witnesses, no newspaper delivery yet. Allen moved to MP from San Francisco with wife two years ago, bought small cottage on First Street.

Merle Rodin. Hit from behind, patio garden outside McKee Jewelry approx. 9 A.M. Found by passerby, transported to ER. Cause of death: blow to head with brick, severe contusion, blood but no prints on brick. See coroner's report: Kathleen Ray.

Ben Stonewell. Shot in back of head while standing on ladder at construction job. Approx. 7:15 A.M. Dead when he hit the ground. See coroner's report: Kathleen Ray. Moved from San Francisco eleven months ago. Unmarried. Went to work the same week for Flannery Construction. Basement apartment on Hayes.

Joe burned to see the full reports, but even Max's notes jolted him. It was time to add his own information about *San Francisco*, it was time to call the chief. Tell him about the couple in the coffee shop patio, and about Celeste Reece.

He wished that right now he could lean out from the bookshelf and whisper his message in the chief's ear. He hid a smile at the thought—but when he glanced across at Dulcie she was staring hard at him, her green eyes wide with alarm. Hastily he backed deeper into the shelf, put his chin down on his paws and closed his eyes. How did she know what he was thinking? How did she do that?

When he looked again, her green gaze was languid, only gently scolding.

But then when he looked deeper he saw something

else, something strange and unfamiliar in his lady's eyes. He saw a need, deep and urgent, a fear he didn't know what to make of—he saw a look of entrapment. And Joe felt, in his own being, Dulcie's shaky uncertainty.

This was her first litter. She was thrilled but she was scared. Scared of the birthing? Joe guessed he would be, too. Scared of taking care of those tiny mites? And was she fearful because life was so upside down—the two of them entangling themselves in these ugly attacks when she should be at home thinking only about the kittens? Joe saw, suddenly and clearly, Dulcie's need for quiet and repose, for a new kind of tenderness. His lady, he realized, was far more vulnerable than he had ever guessed. Vulnerable and frustrated, right down to her soft tabby paws.

He didn't know how to handle this. He was observing a kind of confusion that perhaps only another female would know how to deal with. He wanted to leap off the bookshelf and cuddle her. He wanted to lick her face and comfort her. But in truth, he felt clumsy and inept. He had helped make these kittens. Now he didn't know what to do about it.

Dulcie needed another female, another lady cat who understood the frightened, excited, lonely confusion that must be a part of motherhood. She needed Kit. Kit had never been a mother, but she was female. She would know how to ease Dulcie, Kit could lay on that special tenderness that even the most loving tomcat didn't quite know how to handle. But Kit wasn't there. And across the room Dulcie, seeing Joe's own confusion, turned her face away, curled up in the corner of the couch and pretended to sleep, pretended that she was just fine.

Yet even now, as he tenderly watched her, the tomcat's mind was of two opposing passions. He was struck with worry over his lady, but yet he burned to claw deeper into the case at hand. To see the full reports, to anonymously call Max and add his own information to the mix.

Max knew the key to the attacks lay somewhere in San Francisco, but neither of them knew what that key was, what element drew the varied victims together. Joe was kneading his claws on the shelf, wired to race home and call the chief, when Ryan knocked at the open door, Billy behind her.

"Interviews done?" Max said, motioning them on in.

They stepped inside. "Done," Ryan said, "and we've run our errands. Evijean *did* tell you we'd be back?"

Max scowled and shook his head. "Not a word." He reached for the phone as if to speak to Evijean, then seemed to change his mind. He looked up at Billy. "I won't be long," he said, "a little paperwork to finish. Charlie's up at the rescue building. We'll be home in time to feed the horses and we can start dinner."

A smile lit Billy's brown eyes. He liked cooking bachelor style with Max. He sat down on the couch beside Dulcie, gently stroking her.

Max glanced down at Kathleen's notes, then looked at Ryan. "Ben always carried his cell phone?"

"Yes," she said, sitting down beside Billy. "Juana went over that, in my statement. He always had it, either in his shirt pocket or his jacket. He never set it down on the job or left it in his car, he never mislaid it. Juana *searched* his apartment, his car, searched the jobsite and my truck that he uses to pick up supplies. No phone. She's concerned about what pictures he might have taken before . . . right before he was shot," she said softly.

Max nodded; they talked for a few minutes about Ben, his habits, his interests, his deep caring for the rescue cats. Joe guessed that Juana would have covered most of that, too. But another take was always good. Max said, "Did Ben ever tell you why he moved down from the city? Did he have family there?"

"He had no family at all. None. I was wondering . . . about a service when the body is released?"

"We'll put something together," Max said. "Talk with Charlie about it. Maybe that little cemetery out by the water. You're sure he was all alone in the city? No girl-friend?"

"He said, in the city he was hardly ever home. The construction firm he worked for put him out on jobs in Sacramento, Redding, up the coast—all too far to com-mute. He said he was tired of that, he wanted to live near his work. He said once, 'How did I have time to date, to even meet anyone?' He liked the smaller town atmosphere of the village, he wanted to settle in one place, he loved the small community. He was lonely, Max. He was just so young, he was just getting started making a life for him-self."

"And you're sure he had no other problems? Bad trip with a girlfriend that he didn't want to mention? Any other reason to leave the city, besides his dissatisfaction with work?"

"Not that he ever said. Surely you're not thinking drugs, not that clean-cut boy."

Max was quiet, looking absently at his notes, his

thoughts to himself. Ryan, seeing that he had no more questions, rose and scooped Dulcie up from the couch. "Come on, my dear, I'm taking you home, you need some supper."

Watching them, Joe dropped down to the desk and came to the edge—thinking of a phone, a fast ride to the nearest phone. Ryan gave him a startled, then amused look. She came around the desk carrying Dulcie and gave Max a hug. She scooped Joe up over her shoulder and they left the office.

And Ryan, like Dulcie, seemed to know exactly what was on Joe's mind. She hurried out, thinking, *Phone, he wants a phone. That wild, intense look in his eyes—like he wants to shout right out at Max. He's been scanning Max's desk, reading everything in sight. Something he found really grabbed him; he's burning for a phone, burning to share it with the chief.*

13

WITH THE TOMCAT twitching to get to a phone, Ryan took him home first. She meant to pick up Rock, drop Dulcie off to be coddled by Wilma, then head for the beach. No matter how heavy her workload or Clyde's might be, the big dog needed his twice-a-day gallop. The minute she stopped in their own drive Joe scrambled over her shoulder, out the driver's window, and up to the top of the king cab. She watched him leap to the roof and vanish across the shingles. He'd be through his tower and onto Clyde's desk before she'd backed out again. She could hear Rock pounding down the stairs barking, ready for his run. As she let him out the front door and loaded him up, she envisioned Joe on the phone talking with Max—the gray tomcat sitting straight and tense at one end of the line, Max Harper swinging his feet off the desk, sitting up, alert, when he heard the snitch's voice—and that too-familiar craziness hit her: that *Alice in Wonderland* giddiness. None of this was happening, none of this was possible. But all of it was happening, right now, right in her face.

JOE DROPPED TO Clyde's desk, listening to Rock thunder down the stairs, to the front door slam and the king cab pull away. Then listening to the silent house, the upstairs rooms empty and still, a few golden dust motes floating. He looked across at little Snowball curled up on the love seat all alone now, one white paw over her pink nose. When he leaped to the couch to nuzzle her, the cushions were still warm where Rock had lain napping beside her. Joe snuggled close for a few moments, gave her a warm lick on her ears, but then he returned to the desk.

He didn't use the house phone, he pawed the hidden cell phone from among a stack of papers, the phone that Clyde had bought him and registered in a false name: Joe's insurance against some moment of failed caller ID blocking on the Damens' landline. He sat for only a moment washing his paws, going over the items he needed to tell the chief, hoping Max and Billy hadn't left yet. Turning on the phone, he punched in the single digit for the desk at MPPD. Half the time, Max didn't turn on his own cell, knowing he could be reached by radio. Joe was sorry to hear Evijean answer.

Any of the younger officers who might be standing in for a moment would have put him directly through to Max. Speaking patiently, he asked for Captain Harper. He knew what was coming. Evijean's voice was cold and authoritative. "What is your name? You will need to give me your name."

"This is a personal call, Evijean. Everyone in the department knows my voice. I need to speak with Max now."

"I can't connect an unidentified caller, that's against departmental rules. You will have to identify yourself."

"Rules? What *rules*?" The woman was nuts. "What? *Security* rules? What damage do you think I can do over the phone? If you don't connect me, Max will know it pretty quick and you, my dear, will be pounding the street for a new job."

He could feel Evijean's rage through the phone line, could almost smell the smoke.

"I cannot connect you without identification."

He thought of calling Max's cell, but it would probably go to voice mail. He didn't want to leave a message, he wanted to talk with Max. He could try for Juana or Dallas, but he'd get the same routine. The silence stretched out unbroken and then there was a click. Evijean had hung up.

Immediately he called her back. "I have information for him regarding the current murder investigation. Put me through to him *now*."

"If you want to see Captain Harper you'll have to make an appointment."

"What do you think the chief will say when he finds out you are blocking confidential information in the murder of Ben Stonewell? And that you are getting in the way of the investigation of the other three murders? No one, *no one* else in the department treats a valued informant so rudely." Ears back, claws bared wanting to slash her face, he listened to another long silence, expecting her to hang up again.

A very long silence. But then he heard a click and Max came on the line.

The chief sounded short and impatient, as if he might be headed out the door for home. When he heard Joe's voice, he calmed. Joe imagined him settling back in his desk chair, picking up a pen and notepad.

The tomcat laid it all out for him: the San Francisco connections he had found, people other than the dead victims but involved with them. Bonnie Rivers in her wheelchair, not a victim but she *could* have been when she was followed there in front of the station. Bonnie's husband recently killed in a San Francisco street accident, and Bonnie herself injured. And then, in the home of her sister, the .38 revolver on Bonnie's dresser, a weapon that had been newly cleaned.

Joe didn't like blowing the whistle about the gun— maybe the .38 had nothing to do with Ben's murder. Maybe Bonnie was one of those rare Californians who had a carry permit? He wondered how she'd managed that. If she had a permit, maybe she'd been target practicing at some gun club on her way down from the city? Or she carried the gun without a permit, sufficiently frightened after her husband was killed that she balanced her own life against California's restrictive gun laws. Whatever the case, he felt shabby, implicating the woman when he didn't even know what caliber weapon had killed Ben.

Still, Bonnie was connected to this tangle somehow. What *was* that incident in front of the department, when the boy followed her and then ran? What was her relationship to the portly couple in the red sweatshirts, the woman so uncomfortable at seeing her? He gave Max the couple's names and their San Francisco address. But besides passing along his uncertain tips, there were questions Joe himself would like to ask.

Oh, right. Harper had never yet answered the snitches' questions. Nor did his detectives. It was all take and no give. Maybe if he were a human snitch, a drinking buddy, someone they talked with in the shops or on the street, it would be a different matter.

Yet the questions ate at him, and what harm to try? "*Is* there," Joe said boldly, "a connection here, to San Francisco?"

"What's your take?" Max said, shocking Joe clear to his paws. Max never asked his opinion.

"Maybe some soured workplace relationship?" Joe said. "A fired, disgruntled ex-employee out for revenge? Or . . . Illicit investments? Some kind of Ponzi game? The victims were on to the scam, someone trying to scare them off, stop them from reporting it?" But Joe shook his head. To torment the victims, yes. But to kill them? Still, the way crooks killed today, for no reason, anything could happen.

But what he really wanted to know was about the gun. "What weapon," he asked Max, "*did* kill Ben? *Could* it have been Bonnie's .38?"

He expected no response. Max was still for a long moment, then, "Not that gun," the chief said. "It was a .32-caliber automatic." He paused, then added quietly, "I've never given you information before. I expect the same courtesy of confidence that the department proffers to you."

"You have that," Joe said, his voice shaky. "Now, can you tell me whether in fact you found Ben's phone? And the small spiral notebook he carried?"

"We've found neither," Max said, rather tightly. "There's the possibility they contain useful information, maybe photographs in the phone. We'd be indebted for a lead."

Joe could hardly breathe. A whole new world had opened up, an enhanced one-on-one cooperation that made his head spin. Suddenly the chief was working *with* him, not just using the information that Joe or Dulcie provided.

Why the change? Why Max's abrupt, increased confidence in the snitches he'd known and worked with—*at paw's length,* Joe thought—through so many long and satisfying cases? What was happening here?

"I'll do what I can to find them," Joe said softly.

"Thank you," Max said. And before Joe could say more he heard the soft click as Max broke the connection.

Switching off his cell phone Joe Grey sat on the desk absently batting at Clyde's scattered invoices, mulling over the change in the chief's response. Almost, he thought with interest, almost as if the chief were proud to be working the case right alongside his two snitches.

And didn't that set a cat up!

Or, he thought with alarm, *almost as if Max knows something?*

As if Max had guessed the identity of his informers? His furry, four-pawed informants? And a deep, icy chill held Joe.

But no, not Max Harper. Not that hardheaded cop. If

Max ever for a moment imagined that his snitches might be cats he'd . . . Joe couldn't guess what the chief would do, he didn't want to think how Max would respond. *Sign up for psychiatric counseling? Check himself into rehab?* The very thought gave Joe shivers.

No, Max doesn't know. Maybe he's just mellowing, growing more comfortable with his longtime snitches, easing into a more direct relationship. That's it, Joe thought, and the idea pleased him. If Max really believed his snitches were cats he would have challenged them straight-out, would have *made* them speak to him in person.

Whatever the case, I'm not solving anything prowling the desk messing up Clyde's tax receipts. Leaping up to the rafter, he pushed out into his tower. He'd just gallop across the rooftops to Ben's apartment, for a little break and enter. The notebook and phone had to be in there, and somehow Juana had missed them.

But Juana seldom missed anything. Like all Harper's detectives, Juana Davis was nosy and thorough, prodding and snooping until she had found every last thread and torn fingernail. No, Joe thought at last, to search Ben's apartment after Davis was finished was an exercise in futility. He sat down in his tower among the pillows, stared out through windows at the streaks of sunset trailing above the Pacific. He thought about Ben, who never forgot or misplaced those two items. Why, this morning, would he have left them at home? He thought about Ben at work, the phone and notebook safe in his pocket. The sun just pushing above the eastern hills. Ben, alone, up on the ladder nailing down the new roof gutter . . .

He glimpses a shadow move in the yard below? Maybe hears

the click of the automatic as a shell slides into the chamber? He turns, sees the gun, sees the killer? He knows in that split second that he will die there, so his gut reaction is to hide whatever evidence he carries, leave it for the cops to find. He turns, shoves the notebook and phone—not in the gutter but hides them under the roof tiles, slips them under those pliable composite shingles.

Now certain where the phone and notebook had to be, Joe fled out his window, racing across the rooftops heading for the remodel. He could almost see the two items tucked down under the black shingles. As thoroughly as Dallas Garza would have searched the scene, Joe thought this time the detective had missed that small hiding place. Had missed Ben's message that lay waiting. With stubborn certainty he *knew* Ben had seen his killer and had left a trail for the law to find.

14

RYAN AND ROCK arrived home fresh and sassy from their walk, both smelling of the sea and the tide pools, and covered with wet sand. She took the big Weimaraner around into the backyard and gently hosed him off. She dried him with a towel, dried his feet. She removed her own shoes and socks, and in the privacy of the walled patio she pulled off her jeans, shook everything out in the flower bed. Leaving Rock sunning on a lawn chair, she rolled up the wet items, carried them in through the kitchen to the laundry and dumped them in the washer. Her face burned from wind and sun; her short, dark hair was sandy and windblown. Rock had chased half a dozen seagulls, threatened a big Rhodesian Ridgeback until she called him off, and had run her some three miles up the hard, wet shore. She wished she had more time with her dog. She envied Clyde the mornings that he took Rock running, pulling on his sweats, returning an hour later feeling just as high as she felt now, and of course just as hungry.

But in the kitchen, meaning to fix herself a snack, she stopped, shocked at the sight of Joe Grey: the tomcat lay on the table on his belly, his head down between his paws, his ears down, his eyes closed in misery. She hurried to him, but she touched him only gently. "Are you hurt? Oh, Joe! What is it, what's wrong?"

He stared up at her, forlorn.

"*Where do you hurt? What* happened? *Was there an accident?*" She slid soft fingers down his side and his legs, feeling for an injury. "Talk to me! I'll call Dr. Firetti." Leaving him she stepped to the phone.

"No." Joe shook his head and closed his eyes again.

"What's the *matter*?" she repeated. Then, alarmed, "*Is it Dulcie?*" She turned back to the phone, but Joe grumbled and sat up.

"Dulcie's fine." He stared grimly at Ryan. "Prescience, hell," he said. "Cop insight is all rubbish, I don't *buy* that stuff!"

Ryan sighed and sat down. "What? You act like you're dying, and all that's wrong is . . . some investigative glitch? You made a wrong guess?"

He scowled at her, ears and whiskers flat. She was getting as cranky as Clyde.

"Joe, every *cop* has bad days! Just because you're a cat, why should you be any different?"

Silence.

"Tell me!" she snapped, losing patience.

"I thought . . . Dulcie says sometimes I have the same

precognition as a cop. A subconscious thing . . . putting together vague hints . . . coming up with a solid fact." Joe looked up at her balefully. "Sometimes she has me believing it."

"So what happened? You had an idea, you put things together and . . . it didn't fly?" Ryan willed herself to speak softly.

"I was so sure. Ben's phone and his notebook *are* missing. When neither Juana nor Dallas found them, I thought—I had a clear picture of the phone and notebook tucked down under the roof tiles, I could almost see Ben shoving them there." Joe sighed. "I bought into Dulcie's theory and thought it was second sight, a cop's intuition."

"And you found nothing."

"Only the smell of Dallas's aftershave, where he'd already looked."

"Then maybe he found them," she said logically.

"He didn't," Joe said with certainty.

"Maybe the department is holding back."

"They're not," he said with equal conviction. From the look on Joe's face she didn't ask how he knew that.

"Max would have told me," he said. "Max . . . Max talked to me this evening. When I called. He answered *my* questions. A real two-way conversation," Joe said, looking at her with amazement.

She was as surprised as Joe, then as uneasy. "He gave you information when he never has before?" She looked at him, frowning. "Why would he do that?"

"Trust?" Joe said hopefully. "He's decided after all these years that I'm an informant he can trust?"

They looked at each other, questioning.

"It's no more than that," Joe said, feigning a conviction he didn't feel.

"Yes," she said uneasily. "But *I'd* call what you were thinking no more than common sense. Ben was on the ladder. He saw or heard something, maybe heard the gun click. If the phone and notebook do contain something of value, he hid them in the only place handy. But what could be so important about the notebook? Ben used it for measurements and lists."

"And maybe other things," Joe said. "I saw him more than once watching and listening to Tekla, frowning, moving away when she noticed him."

"Maybe Tekla has some suspicion about who this assailant is, about why he's doing this? Maybe she said something to Sam, and Ben overheard? Ben made notes, trying to figure it out, to make sense of it?

"But," she said, "if Tekla had a suspicion, why wouldn't she talk to the department? Why didn't she speak up this morning, the minute she knew Ben was dead? Why didn't she tell Dallas or Juana?"

"Tekla wouldn't talk to a cop. All she could think of was how inconvenient and embarrassing the murder was for *her*. She doesn't care who killed Ben. She doesn't trust cops any more than she'd trust the killer."

Ryan rose, took a glass from the cupboard, opened the refrigerator, and poured herself a beer. From a big covered bowl she dished up Rock's supper, a concoction she cooked up every week for Rock and Snowball, and kept frozen in manageable portions. Setting the bowl in the microwave for a moment, she put it on the floor. She stood back as Rock rushed to his meal, scarfing up a mix of meat and a variety of steamed vegetables. She smiled when Snowball came trotting down the stairs, yawning, and tucked into her own bowl, close beside Rock's gulping muzzle. Gently the big dog made way for her, not touching her food.

"Snowball might be getting on," Ryan said, "but with this new diet you'd never know it." She looked down at Joe, sprawled across the table patiently waiting for his own supper, for Clyde to get home and start cooking. Joe wasn't having even the most artfully prepared dog food. Ryan was saying, "If you'd just try a few bites . . ." when the intercom buzzed. She turned on the speaker.

"It's Charlie, we're just headed home."

Ryan buzzed Charlie and Billy in. Charlie's red hair was tucked back into an intricate twist. She was wearing black tights and a long, many-colored, hand-knit shawl. "Kate and I were at the gallery," she said. "A little private preview. The group show looks great, Kate loved it. And five of my large horse etchings have already sold. I'd hardly gotten there when Max called, wanted me to pick Billy up at the station. Something about a phone call just as they were starting home. He was headed up to talk with Celeste Reece and her sister," Charlie said, puzzled.

At the mention of Celeste Reece, Joe Grey came to attention. So his phone call *had* been important, had sent Max up there double time to talk with Bonnie, and surely to have a look at the gun.

"Kate left the gallery and headed back to the shelter," Charlie said, smiling. "She can't leave it alone, has to make sure every detail is the way she wants it, has to pet and play with the few shelter cats that are already settled in, the few we've made room for. She's up there more than the carpenters are. And . . ."

But Joe Grey hardly heard her as he dropped off the table and melted away through the living room. With his thoughts on Max Harper, on Celeste Reece and her sister, he bolted out his cat door, scrambled up a pine tree, over his own roof and the neighbors' roofs, heading for Ocean Avenue and the roofs rising up the hills beyond. The scents from the surrounding restaurants followed him, the smell of steak and lobster reminding him that he'd left home without his own supper. On the other side of the divided main street he hit the peaks and shingles, streaking up over the little shops and crowded cottages; hoping he'd beat Max to Celeste's house, and knowing he wouldn't.

He just hoped he could get inside where he could hear what they talked about; he had a lot of questions about Bonnie Rivers. Above him the orange-streaked sky was darkening, the sun gone, the streets below him growing shadowed. Approaching Celeste's freshly painted, bright ivory cottage, he saw above its dark roof the first stars begin to gleam. Max's truck was parked in the drive.

15

 **W**ILMA, HAVING HUGGED and cried over Kit and Pan home from their long journey, had made supper for them, then saw that they were tucked up on the couch in the folds of her quilt. She had served them leftover shrimp Alfredo heated in the microwave, warm milk, and a nice bowl of custard, all of which vanished swiftly. The poor cats were starving, and exhausted, too, from their long climb.

Now, full of their warm meal and happily back in their own world, they tried to tell her of their travels but all they could do was yawn—neither one could stay awake. Even as she stroked them, sitting on the couch beside them, the cats yawned and yawned and dropped into sleep. She sat looking down at them, so beautiful, Pan's red-striped fur tangled against Kit's mottled black-and-brown coat; the two cats so lovely but so small and vulnerable—and yet so bold and courageous in the adventure they had undertaken, in the dangers they must have faced. She wanted to grab them up again and keep holding them or to snuggle down warm between them. She left them at last, let them sleep and restore their strength, restore all that they had spent. She wanted to call Ryan and Clyde, call Charlie, call Kate, call the Firettis to tell them all that the cats were home, but she put that urge aside. Let them sleep, don't encourage anyone to come racing over to love and hug them, to see for themselves that they were well and safe, to welcome and celebrate them. Let them sleep around the clock if they chose.

But she did call Lucinda and Pedric, they would be so relieved. She called from the bedroom, shutting the door, speaking softly. When she couldn't get them on their cell phone she called the lodge in Anchorage.

The Greenlaws were in Denali, their cell phone out of range. The lodge called them on the radio, then put her through to them. Lucinda's yelp of joy and her flood of questions wavered with static. When Pedric came on the line, his voice was shaking. Wilma couldn't stop smiling. Now, their worries put at rest, Kit's beloved housemates could get on with their own adventure.

"Don't wake them," Lucinda said. "We'll talk later. We'll call as soon as we're back from Denali."

Wilma, wishing them a happy journey, had hung up and headed for the kitchen when she heard the cat door flap open and Dulcie came bolting in. Glancing out the kitchen window, she saw Charlie's red Blazer pulling away. Charlie waved, tooted the horn, and was gone. Wilma spun around at Dulcie's excited mewl. In the center of the kitchen, Dulcie stood up on her hind legs, her ears up, her tail twitching, one paw lifted. She had caught Kit's and Pan's scent; she was poised to bolt for the living room when Wilma grabbed her up.

"Don't wake them," Wilma whispered, cuddling Dulcie. "They're worn out. They had such a long, hard journey up those endless tunnels, let them sleep."

"Oh, my," Dulcie said softly. She slipped down from Wilma's arms, padded silently into the living room and reared up, looking at the two cats so deeply asleep on the couch. She longed to reach out a paw and gently touch Kit, but she only looked, every line of her tabby body curved into pleasure, to see the two home again. Kit was safe, they both were home and safe. *And won't they be surprised when we tell them about the kittens? Oh, my*, Dulcie thought, *won't Kit make over them and spoil them.*

But maybe she would spoil them more than they needed, this tattercoat Kit who was still, in spirit, a wild and unruly kitten herself. *What kind of influence*, Dulcie wondered warily, *will Kit be on our innocent babies?*

FROM THE SHADOWS beside Celeste Reece's front door Joe Grey could hear Max's voice clearly. He wouldn't need to find a way inside as long as Celeste didn't close the windows. The front door was shut tight, but the tall glass panes flanking it stood wide to the evening breeze. Joe could smell coffee from within, and some kind of peanut butter confection that reminded him again he'd had no supper. The bright white room, clean and uncluttered, smelled not only of coffee and dessert, but a lingering scent of roast beef that didn't help his emptiness, either. Max must have arrived just as they finished their meal.

The windowsills were so low he had to crouch down in the petunias so as not to be seen. Celeste and her sister, Bonnie, sat on the white couch, Max in a matching chair, his dessert and coffee beside him on a small table. He had just finished asking a question that Joe missed; he looked at Bonnie expectantly for an answer.

Bonnie, tanned and slim, was dressed in pale jeans and a light blue T-shirt, her metal brace snug to her left leg. "It was me they were after," she said shakily. "Not my husband. They didn't . . . they didn't care who else they killed."

Celeste said, "The trial itself was stressful enough for Bonnie. And then, all those weeks later, the accident—what we thought was an accident. I headed for the city, stayed in the hospital with her. It was terrible. Gresham gone so suddenly, that long surgery on Bonnie's shattered leg . . ." Celeste looked across at her sister and went quiet.

Bonnie's direct, steady voice was more in control now than her sister's. "After all those days sequestered, sitting in the cold, stuffy courtroom, finally it was all over, the ugliness, the stress. I was just beginning to feel normal again. Gresham and I needing to be with each other, staying close, going out to dinner at our favorite little restaurants, going to movies, long walks through the park. And then . . . the accident."

Max was quiet, giving her time. Then, "The jurors," he said at last, "could you identify them all, do you remember their names?"

"I'd know them to see them. I'd know their pictures, of course. But I'm not sure I can remember all their names—in most cases, just a first name.

"But I'll try," she told Max. "I'll start a list, write down descriptions and the names that I can remember. Maybe the full names will come to me. After the accident, it took me a while to realize what . . . what had really happened—that it wasn't an accident. When I read about that waiter, Jimmie Delgado, going home from work after midnight, his bicycle hit, Delgado killed . . . he was on the jury. It was then I began to put it together and got scared."

"I'd like you to come down to the station," Max said gently. "Tomorrow morning if you can. See if you can identify the murder victims? I can have someone pick you up, if you like. If I'm not there, one of the detectives will work with you, show you the pictures."

Bonnie nodded. "I read something in the paper about James Allen, saw the paper some time after he was killed. I remembered him, maybe because it's such a simple name, and because he was in a walker. An older man, nearly bald, gray fringe of hair around his ears. He complained, said he was too old to be on jury duty. But I guess the attorneys didn't think so."

Max said, "We may need to get a release of the names of the jurors, that may still be sequestered. A list would help you put names and faces together." He was quiet, then, "You're sure you didn't know the boy who followed you?"

Bonnie shook her head. "All bundled up. A boy? A small man? I'd say a boy, though. A good runner. But the couple you mentioned, in red sweatshirts? A rather portly pair. I recognized them, but they weren't on the jury, I never knew their names. I saw them in the visitors' gallery several times. And during the verdict and sentencing? She was crying, both days. He had his arm around her, hugging her. I couldn't tell whether she was crying from grief or was happy. It was that kind of crying," she said, looking across at Max.

Max nodded. He picked up some newspaper clippings from the arm of his chair. "May I make copies of these, return them when you come in?"

"Yes, of course."

Joe glimpsed the headlines for only an instant as Max folded the articles into his notebook and slipped it in his briefcase.

. . . dies when car goes over cliff north OF . . .

. . . ON A RAINY STREET SOUTH OF . . .

Bonnie said, "Would first thing in the morning suit you? Say, eight o'clock?"

"That's change of watch," Max said. "I'm tied up until, say, nine?"

She smiled. "Nine's fine. That will give Celeste and me a chance to have breakfast out, splurge a little."

When Max rose, the tomcat backed deeper into the petunias. Though the evening was growing dark, his white paws and white nose were always a problem, too bright in the gathering dusk, even among the tangled leaves. Watching Max head for his pickup, Joe wanted to leap in the truck, ride home with him unseen, slip into the Harper house, paw through Max's briefcase and read the clippings. What trial *was* this? What was the offense? Who was the plaintiff? If someone was out to kill the jurors . . . a friend or relative of the plaintiff . . . then he must have received the ultimate sentence . . . life in prison or the death penalty. Joe wished he had run faster over the rooftops, that he hadn't missed half the conversation, missed the telling facts.

But now, as much as he wanted to know the rest of Bonnie's story, he decided not to hitch a ride, not chance getting caught snooping up at the Harper ranch. He'd see the clippings in the morning, once he hit the station. Though even that wait annoyed him, he was wired with curiosity. He watched the chief cross the yard, step into his pickup and back out—and Joe Grey hit the rooftops, his paw-beats thudding across the shingles of the neighborhood cottages as he headed not for the Harper ranch, that long haul up the hills, but for Ben's place.

Maybe Juana had missed nothing at all—and maybe not. Either way, she was sure to have cleared the scene by now.

Maybe, in the process of removing crime tape, she had aired the apartment of cat-box smell, had opened the windows and, if luck were with him, she had not relocked them all. Not likely, knowing Detective Davis, but he meant to find some way inside.

Up across the roofs and oak branches, racing above the dropping canyon until he saw the tall old house ahead, Ben's small basement apartment at the back. The outdoor security lights were on, but no interior lights at all, even in the big house. He came down two gardens away.

There was no sound from within as he crossed the darkening yards onto the brightly lit lawn. Juana had removed the crime tape, and luck was with him. She, or maybe the landlord, had left the apartment wide open, to air. *Strange*, he thought, *to leave it unlocked at night*. Maybe that's why the security lights were on, shining brightly into the tiny room, brighter than Joe wanted. His nose twitched at the lingering stink as he leaped to the sill of an open window.

The screen was old-fashioned with just the kind of latch he liked. With careful claws he ripped a small hole in the bottom. Reaching through, he flipped the hook, pulled the screen open, ducked under, and dropped down inside.

The room was just as it had been except for the empty space before the windows where the two big cages had stood. Dent marks from their stands marked the carpet. He scanned the room looking for a hiding place that Juana could somehow have missed. Though still he found it strange that Ben would have left notebook and phone at home that morning. There was a better chance the killer already had them. Joe couldn't get it out of his head that Ben had secretly taken pictures that he felt might lead to perpetrator of the street crimes—pictures that Ben didn't know might lead to his own killer?

In this little square room, *could* there be some hiding place so small and out of the way that even Juana had overlooked it? She had surely gone over the carpet feeling for lumps underneath. Beside the narrow bed was a little writing desk that served as a night table, cluttered with cough drops, a battery-operated travel clock, a couple of paperback mysteries. Marks in the thin coating of dust described the shape of a laptop and what could be the feet of a small printer. Maybe one of those giveaway color jobs where the company made most of its profit selling cartridge replacements. In the far corner of the room a tiny refrigerator stood beneath a small counter with a bar-sized sink. On the counter were a dozen cans of cat food, a few clean mugs and plates, and a microwave. And now, even with the windows open to air out the lingering stink of cat kennels, another scent touched Joe. He could smell, when he took a good whiff, the whisker-licking aroma of young mice.

Having missed supper, he spared a few moments to stalk the trail, hoping to assuage the hollowness in his belly. Slipping across the room following the mousy enticement, he had doubled back where it was stronger—when a swift small shadow fled past his nose. Damned mouse exploded right past him! Enraged to have missed it, he leaped where the shadow paused for an instant. He missed again, the tip of its tail vanishing beneath the bed. Well, hell!

Bellying under the bed among inert dust mice, he found where the little beast had disappeared. Where the molding was warped, concealing a sizable hole behind the wooden trim.

Crouching to peer in he saw a tangle of chewed-up paper, and the smell of mouse was strong. He was staring at the edge of a mouse nest: torn papers deep and cozy. He tensed when something small stirred within. Hungrily he flashed his paw in, fast as lightning he grabbed—and drew back faster, hissing, pain shooting through his paw.

A half-grown mouse clung to his paw, its sharp teeth sunk deep in his tender pad. The tiny animal glared at him with rage. Joe shook his paw and backed away, the angry mouse clinging.

In all his days, in all his battles with enemies twice his size, from fighting raccoons to enraged dogs, he had never been attacked by a mouse. He stared at it, shocked; he was about to pull the cheeky youngster off his paw and crunch and swallow it. But it was so small and so damned *nervy*. The stupid mouse had way more courage than sense. Joe bared his teeth over it. One chomp and it would be gone, warming his hungry belly.

In the second that he hesitated, the mouse bit him harder. Angrily Joe swatted the little bastard off with his other paw. It was so bold he couldn't eat it. It stared up at him, squeaking angrily, then fled back into the hole.

Peering in, Joe prayed the little varmint wouldn't charge out and grab his whiskered nose. He couldn't believe the nerve of the creature.

But now the nest was empty, the mouse had vanished. There were no others. Had they run away at his disturbance? Nothing there now but the soft paper bed itself. Joe studied the tangle of chewed-up paper, each piece colored as bright as Christmas wrappings. Tiny scraps gleaming red, green, blue: a nest of scraps as brilliant and shiny as . . .

As brightly colored photographs.

Photographs, diligently chewed into hundreds of pieces, torn to line a rodent's nest.

Gingerly he reached a paw in, hoping the coast was still clear. Carefully he examined the edges where the mother mouse's mastication had not been so thorough. She had created a soft bed in the center, but had left the outer portion in larger scraps only lightly torn apart. Joe clawed out a few pieces, some nearly an inch across.

Yes, torn photographs. A shot of green grass with a streak of muddy path. The toe of a jogging shoe, mud-stained. The cuff of black jogging pants. All common items, but views that had, for some reason, stirred Ben to record them.

Once he'd printed them, had Ben hidden them in the hole not thinking about mice? And the mouse, typical opportunist, had begun at once to line her nest. Or had Ben hidden them somewhere else in the room, and the mouse dragged them here to make her nest?

He imagined Juana, in her straight black uniform skirt, having to crouch low, her face to the floor to peer into the opening beneath the warped baseboard. Crouching so low might have put more stress on her mechanical knee than she wanted, and she'd made short work of the search.

How, Joe wondered, *do I report the torn photographs without making Juana look bad for missing them? And how, in fact, do I report this at all without hinting at my identity? How many snitches crawl around under beds looking in mouse holes?* Why had this supposedly human snitch thought to peer inside a mouse nest; why would he ever imagine a mouse might be hoarding useful evidence?

Maybe he should just forget this one, abandon this particular tip. Were the torn photos *worth* reporting and thus stirring anew whatever suspicions Harper already had about the snitch? Maybe the department would gather enough information without this very dicey report.

But as he leaped to the windowsill and slipped out of the apartment, latching the screen behind him, he knew he would make the call. This one was too good not to pass on to the chief. *Time to head home and call Max again*, he thought, smiling. And, listening to his rumbling stomach, *Time to hit the refrigerator—leave the mouse, go for the cold spaghetti. Then call Max.* Licking his whiskers, he took off across the rooftops.

16

JOE'S SECOND CALL to Max was disappointing.

After the intelligence that Max had shared with him earlier in the day, he'd thought their relationship had geared up to a new and more intimate confidence.

Not so.

As Joe sat on Clyde's desk using the cell phone, trying to maintain the heightened relationship, telling Max about the mouse nest, the chief dropped back to his close-mouthed demeanor of earlier calls, the one-way snitch-to-cop dialogue that Joe was used to. Well, what could you expect? Listening to Joe's wild tale of a mouse and torn photos, of course he'd clam up. "What were you doing poking around in mouse holes, what were you doing in Ben's apartment? That's a crime scene."

"The crime tape was gone," Joe said. "The windows

were open. I was standing at the window looking in, wondering if your detectives missed anything, when this mouse ran across the floor. I guess mice take over right away when a place is empty. It had a piece of shiny red paper stuck to its fur.

"I remembered what you said about photographs. That paper was bright and shiny enough to have been chewed off a photo, and it made me wonder. I climbed in the window, had a look under the bed where the mouse had gone, and found the nest."

Max's heavy silence made him want to hang up and pretend he'd never made the call. Sitting among the clutter of Clyde's bills and catalogs, he knew he'd talked himself into a corner.

But then Max said, sounding only slightly reluctant, that someone would investigate the mouse hole, and he thanked Joe and hung up.

Now Joe lay in his tower speculating on what would come from that phone call. Hoping the photos would be worth the effort—his bitten paw still hurt. And then thinking about the one missing fact that Max and Bonnie Rivers knew and that he didn't. About the real heart of the puzzle: the rest of the information on the San Francisco trial, the facts that he'd missed when he arrived late at Bonnie's to eavesdrop through the front window.

A murder trial, but whose trial? What kind of murder? And when? He had left Celeste Reece's house knowing more than when he arrived, but not knowing enough, not knowing what the department knew.

First thing in the morning he'd find out, when he hit Harper's office. Now, curling among his pillows, looking out his tower windows at the night, he tried to be satisfied with that. At least now his belly was full of supper: cold spaghetti and smoked salmon that he'd scarfed down before he called Max. Yawning, he was dropping into sleep when below in the house, the phone rang. Two rings, then Ryan or Clyde picked up on one of the downstairs phones; he could hear no voice from Clyde's study. All was silent again and he drifted off, he was down into heavy sleep, into a deep dream, when the doorbell rang and Ryan's excited squeal jerked him wide awake.

Ryan never *squealed*. It was not a scream but a high, delighted exclamation. He heard several voices all at once, excited male and female voices jangling together and then Ryan pounding up the stairs, Rock thumping and barking beside her. Her voice rose among the rafters and through his cat door as if the house were afire.

"Joe! Joe, are you there? Wake up! They're home! They're here!"

Joe yawned. Lucinda and Pedric? Well, good, it was about time. To go running off to Alaska just when—

"Kit and Pan are home. Kit and Pan are here! Wake up!"

He shot out from among the pillows, belted in through his cat door, and crouched on the rafter staring down. Ryan stood looking up at him, her velvet jogging suit wrinkled, her dark hair tousled. "Kit's home! Pan's home! Oh, come down! They're here! Wilma brought them."

Clyde appeared behind her, Rock crowding between them. Wilma hurried up the stairs, too, Dulcie tucked up in a fold of her red cloak. Kit and Pan raced up past them, flew up the stairs, and reared up, staring at Joe. He wanted to leap down yowling, wanted to pummel Pan and caress

Kit as he'd done when she was a youngster—but even as delight rushed through him, Joe felt sick.

He looked down at the two cats crowding between Ryan and Rock, the red tomcat serious and silent, Kit's black-and-brown fur all atangle, her yellow eyes huge. For a moment their looks were steady with satisfaction at being home. But then they let their pain show, their deep and terrible pain.

They knew. They knew that Misto was dying.

"Dulcie told us," Kit said in a small voice. Pan's amber eyes were filled now only with rising dread, his distress terrible to see. Joe dropped to the desk and to the floor and pressed against Pan. He put his chin over Pan's shoulder, in a tomcat kind of hug. Pan pressed his face hard against Joe; they stood so for a long time before Pan turned away, hanging his head, and Joe moved to comfort Kit. But Ryan picked Pan up, holding him close, pressing her face against him, her dark hair tangled over his red coat. He snuggled his face into her throat, shivering.

And as Joe licked and nuzzled Kit, her yellow eyes were filled with such conflicting emotions. Her tears, her pain for Misto were terrible, her devastation at the old cat's illness. When Misto had first arrived in Molena Point, Kit had followed and followed him over the rooftops, begging for his stories, listening to his ancient tales. He was the closest to a father she'd ever had.

But now Joe could see, even through Kit's pain for Misto, a spark of wonder, too. Despite her hurt and grieving, he could see in her eyes a rising joy at the thought of Dulcie's kittens. Sadness and wonder burned together, now, within Kit's small tortoiseshell being.

Joe was hardly aware when Clyde picked him and Kit up and they moved down the stairs. Wilma carrying Dulcie, Ryan hugging Pan over her shoulder, they made a strange procession through the house and out to the drive. They all tucked up in Wilma's car, Clyde beside Wilma, Ryan in the backseat, the cats cuddled among them. They headed for the Firettis' cottage, dreading the moments ahead. Kit, in the front seat beside Wilma, pressed against Pan. Pan licked her face but then turned away, grim and withdrawn.

Dulcie had told them about Misto's illness only a long time after she burst in the house catching their scent and letting out a mewl of joy. Going quiet, letting them sleep, she had waited in silence for a long while, tucked up in Wilma's lap. But then when Kit and Pan did wake, and Kit jumped down to nuzzle Dulcie, she backed away with a yowl of surprise. Dulcie smelled different. "Oh, my!" Kit stared at Dulcie, her yellow eyes wide. "Kittens! You're carrying kittens!"

Dulcie laughed and lashed her tail and looked very proud of herself. Pan came close and sniffed, and backed away again with a typical tomcat shyness.

It was only after Kit had sniffed Dulcie all over and asked too many questions, and Pan asked questions, only later that Dulcie put out a paw at last to silence them, and sat quietly looking at them both.

Kit and Pan grew immediately very still, shivering at Dulcie's solemn look. When, gently and softly, Dulcie told them about Misto, Pan had slunk away into the hall by himself, where he curled up against the wall, nose to tail, rigid and grieving.

It was a long time more, after Pan finally joined them again, stoic and resigned, that Wilma had called the

Damens. That she and the three cats got in the car and headed for Ryan and Clyde's house.

Now, driving the few blocks from the Damens' to the Firettis', Wilma stroked Pan softly. "Don't grieve, please don't, Pan. Don't let Misto *see* you grieve, he doesn't want that." And, to Kit, "Please don't cry, my dear, he doesn't want sadness. Misto himself is not sad—except to be parting from you. He is certain he is parting for only a little while; he is so very sure this is not a forever good-bye. He does not believe there is an end to the spirit."

But even so, Pan tucked his nose deeper under his paw, and Kit laid her face against him. Wilma said, "Misto has known other lives. I believe him," she said softly. "He will be bright-eyed when he speaks of waking in vast eternity again, of finding himself once more approaching a new life." She paused at a stop sign, then turned onto the Firettis' street, passing the softly lit dome of the clinic, approaching the lighted cottage that sat deep in Mary's garden.

"Grieving would only make him sad," Wilma said. "Let him tell you of the wonders, of how his released spirit will see the vastness of the earth, see the sweep of centuries again as no living creature can see them. Let him tell you more of his earlier lives, of the wonders that await us all, of how we will all be together again. Don't spoil that for him."

Parking in the Firettis' drive, she picked up Dulcie and stroked Pan. "Misto's vision is so clear, so real, it *must* be true. His view of what lies in the past is too detailed to be only an old cat's dreams. Let him tell you with happiness. Love him, Pan. Tell him you know you will be together again. Don't spoil his parting, don't hurt him with your own sadness."

17

THE FOUR CATS padded quietly into the Firettis' cottage, where Mary stood in the open doorway. Ryan, Clyde, and Wilma lingered behind, then silently joined Mary and John where they'd been lounging by the fire, John in tan pajamas and a brown terry-cloth robe, Mary in a velvet housecoat printed with small nasturtiums. As she drew humans and cats to the couch, Pan alone approached the bedroom. The others waited in silence, filled with his grieving.

In the bedroom Pan reared up to look. Misto did not recline now on the Firettis' big double bed; he lay curled up in a roomy retreat of his own. A child's crib lined with soft blankets had been drawn up against the big bed, the bars removed on that side so he could pad back and forth as he pleased. So he could settle alone with no movement to disturb him, or could curl up against Mary and John, warm and close. Now, as Misto lay sleeping, Pan's heart twisted for the big yellow tom. Misto seemed so small suddenly, so frail. Padding across the covers of the big bed, Pan lay down with his front paws just touching Misto's blanket.

They lay thus for a long time, father and son, Pan wrapped in silence and thin, elderly Misto so deeply asleep, his once-golden fur turned straw-colored from his illness. Pan, seeing his father so old and frail, felt his heart nearly break.

He could hear from the living room Dr. Firetti telling Dulcie that she mustn't go traipsing across the rooftops anymore until after the kittens came. As he wondered idly how many times John had repeated his cautions, scolding the pregnant tabby, suddenly Misto's eyes opened. The old cat had awakened to John's voice, perhaps, or maybe to some inner perception—maybe to the sudden scent of his son reaching him through his dreams. Seeing Pan, he rose up out of the blankets, his amber eyes growing as bright as the eyes of a young cat, gleaming with life now, and with joy. Pan moved close to him in a tender feline embrace, father and son reunited, paws and fur all atangle, old cat and young together once more. For a long time neither spoke, the only sound their rumbling purrs. They didn't see Kit, Dulcie, and Joe look in from the door and then turn away again. Kit, leaving the bedroom, stifled her longing to leap up and hold the old cat close, too, and snuggle him. Her own love for him could wait.

But then from the bedroom Misto, scenting her, called out weakly. "Kit? Kit, let me see you. Let me see how the Netherworld has treated you."

Kit came slipping in and up on the bed and into the

blankets of the crib, easing down close to Misto. The old cat looked her over and licked her face. "You look strong and fine, the Netherworld treated you well." Kit smiled and nuzzled him; and there Kit and Pan remained, beside Misto, for the rest of the night.

Joe Grey and Dulcie, Wilma, Ryan, and Clyde soon slipped away home, leaving John and Mary to read by the fire, leaving Kit and Pan and Misto reunited, snuggled in Misto's bed.

The three were quiet for only a little while before Misto stirred again and sat up as if he felt stronger, as if the closeness of Pan and Kit had brought him new life. No one imagined such a strengthening would last, but, "Tell me," the old cat said, "I want to hear your journeys, I want to see that amazing land as you saw it."

Listening to the crackle of the fire from the living room and watching its flickering reflections on the bedroom ceiling, Kit and Pan told Misto the wonders of those green-lit lands and the amazing beasts, the winged dragons, the white-feathered harpy, the dwarves and selkies and all the magical folk.

"We took a wrong turn at first," Pan said, "where the tunnel split into five branches. Three crossed a sunken river on narrow stone bridges. The clowder cats argued; they weren't sure which bridge, which path. We went a long way in the wrong direction and came out into the dark and fallen lands . . ."

"We didn't mean to go there," said Kit, "into that ruined part of the Netherworld. It is moldering and empty except for the grim old castles with their haughty rulers. The cruel royalty keep armies close around them, they are whip-masters over the peasants. The poor have nothing, nor do they care anymore. Why should they work when all they grow and any sheep or goats they raise are taken by the kings and they are left to starve?"

"They have turned to crime," Pan said. "They think they have no choice, but they are courting even more evil. We moved through peasant villages where we saw no one, the cottages all collapsed, pasture walls fallen, fields fallow and untended. Not even a starving chicken remained, only mice and rats, scavenging. We hunted those, as did the peasants themselves; how thin were those poor folk, all weak and listless."

"The magic is dead," Kit told him. "We didn't want to be there." She tucked her bushy tail tight around her, her ears down as sadness filled her. "Dark spells rule them now. Greed rules that land."

"We headed away," Pan said, "seeking the one lone land that, the clowder cats said, had survived in brightness. Kate told us that, too. But she had approached on her own journey from another direction. We asked, from those who dared speak to us, which path, which tunnel. We asked from those brave enough to approach us."

"We found the way at last," Kit said, "beyond the Hell Pit and up the mountains. It was a hard journey—until the Harpy found us," she said with a little smile. "The brash and loving Harpy. Oh, my," Kit said. "A great, tall woman with a bird's head, with bird's legs and white-feathered wings, and she is all covered with white feathers. *She* is strong, *she* dines on the kings' flying lizards. She took us on her back, all of us at once, our claws deep in her feathers to hang on, and she rose up to the stone sky on those great wings. She sailed up and up the mountains and over and down again in the green light, winging down into that clear, free land, into Zzadarray.

"She carried us down among the happy, smiling peasants," Kit said, "to the only land still free, down among the strong selkies and the sturdy dwarves, and all of them welcomed us and their fields were green and rich and their animals are sleek . . ."

Misto sighed, seeing that land, seeing wonders he'd never known.

"No king," Pan said, "rules that land. No bejeweled queen dictates tithes and taxes nor enslaves the villagers, demanding all their harvest. All farmers are master of their own fields and of what they wrest from them. All farmers own their land; they guard their small, free world fiercely against royalty's cold sword.

"Those peasant armies," Pan said, "with the help of the magical beasts, have gained the love and protection of the fiery dragons, too, the dragons who can be conquered by no man.

"One day," Pan said, "that small country will take back the dark lands, you'll see. Those who live in freedom will make the dark lands free again. Nothing of the Netherworld, then, will be ruled by avarice and greed. All rule will be born of love and caring—and of strength."

"It is their strength in battle," Kit said, "their fierce will to protect, that has kept alive Zzadarray's magic."

Misto rumbled a contented purr; Kit's and Pan's words brought strength to his thin face. The promise of freedom spreading from that one small land of Zzadarray lit his eyes, made the old cat smile. "I have lived many lives, but never in such a world as that magical place. Maybe one day fate will send me there, to that land."

The three cats thought of that, and together they dozed and dreamed; it was not until they heard John bank the fire, to come to bed, that Misto said, "There is one more pleasure I crave, before my time is gone. Just one more visit to the sea, to say good-bye to the great and gleaming sea."

John had come into the bedroom, Mary behind him. "In the morning, early," he told Misto. He looked at Kit and Pan. "Will you come?"

"Oh, yes," Kit said.

"Of course," said Pan. "Where else would we be?"

"Early," John said, "at low tide, when Mary and I feed the ferals. Misto, you can sit on the dock in your blanket as the wild ones share their breakfast. You can enjoy the beginning of their day with them, just as you like to do."

"We will watch the sun rise," Mary said, "red above the far hills, watch its reflection cross the sky and reach down to touch the sea."

"We will watch the waves brighten," Kit said, and as John and Mary climbed into bed, the three cats snuggled close together, yawning and safe. Kit and Pan were still tired from their journey, Misto bone tired from his lifelong journey, though it had been a rich passage. The old cat would soon be ready to leap up into the vast weightlessness beyond all barriers, to drift once again beyond mortal time, assured that one day he would return, to the finite world.

But never would Misto's spirit, in life or in eternity, never would he abandon those he loved. All he had ever touched would remain close, forever would they be close, those spirits whom he treasured.

18

 **MAX HARPER'S OFFICE** smelled of overcooked coffee, cinnamon rolls, and gun oil. The sweet-scented bakery box stood on the credenza just above Joe as he strolled in, his coat damp from the early fog. He shivered once, glanced up with interest at the bakery treats but padded on past. Behind Max's desk he leaped up into the bookcase. Max glanced around at him, broke off a piece of his own cinnamon bun, and laid it on the edge of the shelf. Handily Joe licked it up, every crumb, then lay down against an untidy stack of pamphlets, DOJ reports, and government busywork. Detectives Garza and Davis were settled at either end of the couch with their coffee and snacks. Both looked unusually pleased. They paid little attention to Joe, and that was the way he liked it. He'd worked long and hard to become no more remarkable than the tattered volumes on the shelf behind him.

Juana's uniform was dark against the leather couch, a Glock automatic holstered at her side, along with handcuffs, cell phone, and radio. Dallas's pale jeans were neatly creased, his black polo shirt and tan corduroy blazer soft and well-worn, as were his leather boots. He set his coffee cup on the corner of the oversize coffee table, which was covered with files and binders. And, holding Joe's attention, two batches of photographs were aligned atop the other papers.

The pictures in one set were as ragged as jigsaw puzzles: color photos formed of tiny, chewed fragments pieced together and glued to sheets of white paper—images of shoes, or of shoeprints with fancy treads. Juana hadn't wasted any time. Joe imagined her moving Ben's bed away from the wall, kneeling in her black skirt trying to favor her painful knee, fishing out pieces of the mouse nest a few at a time. He wondered if the mouse was watching. He tried not to picture it attacking Juana, but he had to turn away to hide a smile.

He thought of Juana sitting up late last night in her second-floor condo just across the street from the station, sorting through the torn fragments, carefully fitting them together piece by tedious piece. In one photo of shoes he could see part of what might be the porch of the remodel. In another, a waffle shoeprint gleamed at the edge of what could be the wooden ramp. That pasteup showed a fragment of running pants, too, with a black satin stripe down the side just like a pair Tekla wore—though, since he'd become alert to that pattern, he'd noticed a number of runners in the village with the exact same kind of pants.

Lined up with the fragmented pictures lay whole, untorn photographs taken at various crime scenes. The shoe patterns matched in both sets of pictures—but manufacturers turned out thousands of each model, Molena Point shops probably sold hundreds. Had Ben taken these shots because he thought Tekla might be the mugger, following a guess, laying out a possible scenario to see where it led?

But now, though the pictures could be a great breakthrough, the department still didn't have the shoes to match them. Even what *looked* like Tekla's shoe next to what *looked* like the remodel property was in fact circumstantial.

They needed the shoes themselves. Shoes might give them fingerprints and maybe DNA, evidence far more conclusive than a photograph. And still the officers were ahead of Joe. They knew which San Francisco trial was involved, they knew who had been convicted and with what sentence and would be looking for connections. But now suddenly, as Joe pretended to nap on the shelf, watching the chief shift a pile of papers and pull out his yellow notepad, there it was.

The answer. The missing piece of information for which he had hurried out of the house this morning after gulping breakfast, scorching away over the foggy roofs, never pausing at Dulcie's cottage, making straight for the station. There on the yellow pad was the answer, neatly set down in Max's angular handwriting, the information Joe had missed when he arrived at Celeste Reece's house too late to hear all the facts.

12 November, San Francisco County Court: Trial of Herbert Gardner. Rape and murder of a minor. Guilty, all counts. Death penalty. Incarcerated San Quentin awaiting execution.

A list of the twelve jurors followed. Bonnie Rivers's name was at the top. Max's notation indicated that Bonnie's husband, Gresham, had died when their car was forced off the road and down a cliff north of the Golden Gate, that Bonnie had been hospitalized with severe leg injuries.

The second name was a Jimmie Delgado. Joe scanned the attached newspaper clipping. Delgado was killed riding his bicycle at night on a slick San Francisco street during a heavy rain. The time was just past midnight. Delgado worked as a waiter. The bike was his only transportation. The driver was never found, there were no witnesses, no clue to the make or model of the car that caused his death. Rain washed away any skid marks. Dark blue paint streaks were found on the bike. The car, if it was ever found, might yield more evidence. Or not, Joe thought, aware of San Francisco PD's heavy workload. If they'd found no viable suspect yet, they might soon file the case away among hundreds of others that remained unsolved. He read the list trying not to stretch up and peer over Max's shoulder. What he wanted to do was drop down to the desk beside the chief where he could see clearly Max's jotted notes.

The next two jurors were the Molena Point victims who had died, James Allen and Ogden Welder. Max noted that Merle Rodin had died but had not been a member of the jury, that Rodin had not been in San Francisco during the trial, and according to his wife, knew only what they saw on the news, to which Merle had paid little attention.

The next juror, the third Molena Point murder victim, was Ben Stonewell.

Of the last seven jurors, three were still in the city. Citizens, Max had noted, too well known, of sufficient standing that the killer might have backed off, might be reluctant to attack them. Four jurors had moved away, two to the East Coast, one to Mexico, the other an uncertain destination. The moves had all occurred after the two "accidental" San Francisco deaths. Below the jury list were the names of Molina Point's other four victims, who were not jury members, with a note: *"Shills?"* Attacks that had been set up to put MPPD off the trail? Most of them were elderly—was that choice meant to further mislead the purpose of the assaults?

Joe eased back on the shelf. Now they knew the *why* of the killings, to vindicate the convicted rapist. The murder victims had all been jurors, all but Merle Rodin. Maybe the guy hadn't meant to kill Rodin, maybe Rodin did simply fall on that brick when he was attacked, a minor slip in the killer's plan.

But Ben's murder was no accident. Now the department had the motive for the killings, and the list of further possible victims. But did they have any suspect who might want vindication? Anyone connected to murderer Herbert Gardner?

"Gardner had no family," Max said, startling Joe, answering almost as if Joe had asked. "No siblings, not one relative that the investigating officers found, not even a close friend. No one he ran with, no drinking buddy. No women he dated, which is strange. Except the young woman he killed," Max added. "And nothing in the presentence report, either."

But how good were *those investigations?* Joe wondered. *How thorough was that particular assistant district attorney, how good are these new, young probation officers?* He'd heard too many stories of sloppy work by young, newly hired government employees. *How dedicated* was *the PO who did the presentence? Had he just jumped through the usual hoops and gone no further, had he not really cared?*

Settling more comfortably on the bookshelf, tucking his paws under his chest, Joe thought about someone out there, still on the loose, eaten up with rage over the conviction of Herbert Gardner, someone who loved Gardner well. A girlfriend whom investigators had missed, a sibling or parent that the law hadn't found? Sure as hell Gardner hadn't committed those murders himself, locked up in Quentin waiting to die.

When Max's private line buzzed, he ignored it as he and the two detectives laid out plans for a deeper investigation into Gardner's background, a more thorough search than SFPD, the CBI, or the parole office had made—but a search to be conducted in cooperation with those departments. When the line buzzed again, again Max ignored it. He had finished giving the two detectives instructions when a faint sound beyond the closed door brought Joe alert.

No one else heard the brush of a soft sole on the hard linoleum. Joe stood up rigid, listening. Max was saying, " . . . send Mike Flannery up to the city as soon as he gets home from Alaska, he can do some of the legwork, he's a hell of a better investigator than . . ."

The sound came again, the presence had not moved away: someone was standing close against the door, listening. Silently Joe dropped from the bookshelf to the desk and down to the rug. He approached the closed door, ears back, his walk stiff, his growl rising. Behind him he could feel Max and the detectives watching him. Silently Dallas rose, his hand relaxed beside his holstered weapon; he jerked the door open.

Evijean Simpson stumbled and nearly fell. She caught herself against the doorjamb, her right fist lifted as if she'd been ready to knock. "There's an urgent call from Detective Ray. Chief, can you pick up?"

Max glanced at the phone he'd ignored, nodded to her, and turned to answer. Evijean left, heading back to the front desk. Joe Grey leaped innocently onto Max's desk and curled down yawning beside him, his head on the notepad as close to the phone as he could get. But Kathleen's voice was too low; without the speaker on, he couldn't hear much.

"He did?" Max was saying. "Where? I'll be damned. Yes, get on over and pick him up."

There was a murmur from Kathleen. Joe wanted to reach out a paw and turn on the speaker. Max said, "Retrieve what pictures you can, print them, too, then get both items to the lab. Ask them to move on it. As soon as you're done, let's see what you have." He listened, then, "You bet," he said, grinning. Hanging up, Max looked across at the detectives.

"The cell phone and notebook the snitch called about? Billy found them, near where Ben died."

Joe felt his claws dig into the blotter, and quickly

sheathed them. *Billy found them?* He'd searched all over hell for that phone and notebook. *And Billy Young found them?* he thought, half annoyed, half smiling.

"He was cleaning the dryer vent in the remodel," Max said, "where it dumps out into the yard. They were stuffed back inside, behind the flap."

Joe wanted to yowl. Why hadn't he *looked* there? He'd passed that vent a dozen times, had smelled nothing but the lingering scent of dried blood from where the body had lain, and the mixed, personal odors of the medics and coroner. He'd been so sure about the roof shingles—a bad guess—but not the vent, had passed the vent and hadn't even thought to lift the flap and look behind it!

"Vent's right below where Ben was shot," Max said. "Just beside the marks in the grass where the ladder had been propped against the house. Blood on both the phone and on the notebook." Max was quiet, then, "That was Ben's last act, after he was shot? Hide evidence he thought was important, that he hoped we'd find?"

"Shoe photos?" Juana said. "The same photos I pieced together?"

"Apparently," Max said. "Ben must have thought we'd find the *shoes*, find a match to the crime scene photos. Fingerprint the shoes, and we'd have our killer."

Juana shook her head. "We've *been* checking the trash pickups, the Dumpsters, the landfill. Those two rookies weren't happy, digging through landfill. We've *got* shoes, cartons of running shoes. I went over them again this morning. Not one of them matches the crime scene photos or the shots I pieced together."

19

Earlier that morning as Joe Grey had headed for MPPD, in the chill fog Kit and Pan sat with Misto on the dock, tucked up beside Mary in a warm blanket. The three cats watched John put out food and water for the ferals, watched the wild band approach warily the heap of blanket. But when they caught Mary's scent and the scent of the cats they knew, they relaxed and rubbed against the pilings and approached their food bowls greedily.

Misto, warm and purring, looked out at the incoming tide. In all his travels, he had followed, fascinated, the earth's waters. He had lived on the rough wharves among the commercial fishermen, had once gone to sea with a fishing crew, had watched the hungry waves climb the sides of the keeling boat. Had crouched belowdecks when waves crashed over the bridge, wanting to wash him away, wanting hungrily to drown them all, man and cat alike. He had wandered the land where small blue lakes gleamed among pine forests, had seen the giant osprey dive into diamond-bright water and rise again, clutching silver trout in their talons. But best of all was right here, right now. The shore where, as a tiny kitten, he had waded in the white sand sinking deep, laughing at the incoming tide. He was once again where he was born, returned to this one perfect embrace of land and sea. Curled up between his son and Pan's lady, the old cat was content. This was the place of his birth, this was where he had been set down by eternity, and this was where he would enter up into that realm once again.

The three cats and Mary lingered for some time as John moved among the feral cats, petting those who were tame enough, talking to them all, making sure none was hurt or sick. The little party left the shore, heading home, in time for John's first clinic appointment.

In the bedroom Mary tucked the frail cat up among his blankets and again Kit and Pan settled beside him. As Misto drifted off into a nap, Pan dozed, too, content to be close. But Kit was content for only a little while. Soon she began to feel squirmy. She wanted to roll over but didn't want to wake anyone. She needed to move; she ached from doing nothing, from being still too long; she needed to run. At last, losing patience, she slipped silently out of the blankets and left the bedroom. She crossed the empty living room, swung on the knob of the front door, and kicked it open.

Outside in the fog she raced across the garden to the

next cottage, scrambled up a vine, hit the roofs, and galloped north, bridging between cottages on twisted oak branches. She came down only to cross Ocean Avenue among the feet of wandering tourists, and then up again, up and down the peaks racing, working off steam. Part of her wildness was her very pain for Misto. Part was an explosion of longing for Lucinda and Pedric because she missed them terribly. Having talked with them on Wilma's phone she knew they were safe, but she wanted them *home*. Running in wild circles and from peak to peak, she wanted Dulcie beside her, too, but Dulcie wasn't up to chasing, not now. Leaping and gamboling and too full of herself, and then thinking again about the street attacks and wondering if there was new evidence and what Joe Grey might be finding, she headed for Molena Point PD.

DETECTIVE RAY'S OFFICE was small, just space for Kathleen's desk, a visitor's chair, a tall and crowded bookshelf. Her desk faced the door, as an officer's desk always does. The walls were hung with groups of miniature paintings, sunny and unassuming. Watercolors were Kathleen's one quiet diversion from the pressure of the job. Billy Young, entering with the detective, moved away from the entrance, looking at the miniatures, enjoying the small, bright details of Molena Point's hills and woods and rocky shore.

Painting had eased Kathleen's stress as she worked as a model, too, before she left that world for the more honest company of cops in the small-town department. Kathleen was dressed this morning in slim jeans and a faded tan sweatshirt, her dark hair tied back casually. Billy thought she would be beautiful even in rags. She was kind, too. Kind to Billy, to animals, to everyone. He stood beside her desk watching her lay out her equipment, watched her begin to lift fingerprints from Ben's cell phone and then from Ben's small, spiral-bound notebook.

"Looks like only Ben's," she said at last, glancing up at him. He was pleased that she'd allowed him to come on back and witness the procedure. "These will go on to the county lab, they might be able to bring up prints I can't, they have more sophisticated techniques."

Billy nodded, he knew that. Once she'd lifted the prints, he watched her plug a USB connection into the cell phone and into her computer and download Ben's pictures. He bent over the screen beside her, looking. Most of the shots were of construction jobs, details of the Bleak cottage and of other projects before it. But some were of shoes, photos angled at the ground as if secretly and hastily captured. Kathleen paused over each of these, and enlarged and printed it. She lingered longest over those that showed a bit of tread mark in the earth beside the shoe itself. One grid in particular, with a scar across the waffle pattern, made her smile.

"This could get us somewhere," she said happily, her smile eager and pleased.

Once she'd finished the photos and had fingerprinted the notebook, too, she leafed slowly through its pages, touching only the edges with her thin cotton gloves.

"Notes and sketches of building details. Hardware, light fixtures. Make and model numbers." Not until the back pages did she turn to the copy machine and make two sets of duplicates, five pages each. When Billy stepped up to look, she shook her head.

"I can't officially share these. You know that. Maybe later," she said, "maybe the chief will. You *are* like his own kid." And that made Billy blush.

Dropping the notebook and phone into evidence bags, she packed them up to be sent to the county lab. "The fingerprints, if they can sort out any others besides Ben's, those will go to IAFIS."

"The digital database," Billy said. Cop work was interesting. This last year was the first time in his life he'd thought about some kind of profession. As a little kid and before Gram died, he'd been too busy working to put food on the table, too busy taking care of his drunken grandmother to think of much else. Any job was welcome. He concentrated on doing things right, on keeping the animals well and happy and safe, and didn't think about his own future.

But now he was not only learning the building trade. Max had urged him into firearms training and self-defense, too, into the police cadet class the department had started for a few of the village boys. The precision, the quick thinking and keen analysis of police work interested him a lot.

"Come on," Kathleen said, slipping the phone's photo prints and her copies of the notebook pages into a file folder. "Let's take these into the conference room, lay the photos out where we can compare them." Reaching for her desk phone she punched in the key to call Max.

KIT CAUGHT JOE Grey's scent on the walk of MPPD. Peering through the glass door, she slipped in on the heels of three young officers—she slid into the holding cell as another officer came in and two left walking with a clean-shaven civilian in a suit and tie. A lawyer? Yes, he had that cool, superior look. Beyond the counter Evijean's faded hairdo was just visible beside the copy machine. Now, with the lobby empty, Kit flew to the base of the reception desk, slunk along beside it, and fled down the hall, keeping to the shadows, pressing against the molding where the chief's door stood cracked open.

His office was empty. She could smell where Joe Grey had rubbed against the woodwork, and could detect the horsey scent of the chief's boots, and the scents of Detectives Garza and Davis, but there was no one here now. When she heard voices across the hall she peered out; she watched Kathleen and Billy move up the hall to the conference room and inside, Kathleen carrying a brown envelope and some file folders. Padding in behind them, she watched Max and the three detectives and Billy folding the metal chairs and stacking them against the wall so they could move freely around the conference table. Dallas had shrugged off his corduroy jacket and laid it on the counter. Davis was making a pot of coffee. Joe Grey sat on the counter beside her. Joe was about to lie down on the folded corduroy coat when, catching Dallas's look, he changed his mind and turned away. When he saw Kit he flicked an ear, watched her slip into the shadows behind the trash bin.

From there, she leaped to the counter beside him. She stopped, startled, almost mewled with surprise. She studied the photos laid out on the table, shots of crime scenes, of the victims lying on the ground, an overturned wheelchair. And footprints. Pasted-up pictures of part of a shoe, or part of a print. Kathleen was saying, " . . . not one discarded shoe we collected matches up with the crime scene shots, and doesn't match with any of these that Ben took."

Shoes! Kit thought. *They've been collecting . . . thrown-away shoes? Oh, my! The shoes that woman dropped in the Dumpster right by my house the night Pan and I got home! Does the department have those shoes?*

Max had picked up two photographs and stood comparing them. These might be of the same shoe, one at an attack scene where an elderly woman sat leaning against a stone wall, the other just a fragment, beside a wooden porch. Might or might not be the same.

Kit stared at Max, curious and excited, then dropped from the counter and bolted out of the conference room. Racing past Evijean she barely skinned out the glass door as a civilian came in wheeling a baby. *Shoes. Thrown in a Dumpster. Shoes . . .*

With all those photographs, with all four officers looking at footprints, she only prayed those thrown-away shoes were still there, that the Dumpster had not been hauled away, that full-to-overflowing Dumpster full of dead leaves and branches—and shoes.

20

KIT'S RACING DEPARTURE from the conference room startled the four officers and Billy, and badly unsettled Joe Grey, who wondered why she would make such a scene. But Kit was Kit, addlebrained and flighty. The chief had turned back to the table, to the machine copies of Ben's notebook pages, to Ben's comments about the San Francisco trial. The court would frown on a written personal record by a juror. But no court official was present, the trial was over, and in Harper's view, this was police business now. As Juana stepped to the conference room door and firmly closed it, Kathleen read the pages aloud.

Most of Ben's entries regarded individual jurors, his personal observations of their attitudes and their perceptions: a diary such as one might make on an interesting journey. No one was identified by name. Ben had given each juror a nickname, some amusing, all to retain individual privacy.

> *Pink Lady thinks Gardner can be rehabilitated? He raped and killed this young woman and who knows how many others? Now, all he needs is a few months' therapy and he'll be cured?*
>
> *Big Ears thinks Gardner's suffered enough at his own cruelty, that he is filled with remorse, that now he needs our compassion.*

Besides his wry comments about the jurors, Ben had made observations about others in the courtroom: the attorneys and those regulars who returned several times to the visitors' gallery. For such a quiet young man, Ben had had his sharp side. One entry that drew Max and the detectives, and drew Joe Grey, regarded a woman who sat in the back row of the gallery. "*Day four: She's here again, here every day. Always so bundled up. Well, the courtroom is cold. Strange hair, you'd call it blond, I guess. Cheap dye job. But something more about her. Something odd and unnatural. Maybe just too much makeup, along with the dowdy clothes. She—*"

Kathleen stopped reading when Max's cell phone buzzed. At the same moment Kathleen's radio crackled, but the wail of a medics' van passing nearly drowned Officer Crowley's canned radio voice.

"Another assault," Crowley said as the emergency van headed north, then soon went silent, reaching its destination. "Man in a wheelchair overturned," Crowley said, "medics just arrived."

Kathleen turned off her radio and Max switched on

the speaker of his cell phone. They could hear garbled conversation in the background, could hear arguing, then Crowley came on the line. "It's Sam Bleak, Chief. Dark-hooded guy knocked him over and ran. Bleak says he doesn't want to go to the hospital, says he's only bruised."

"Did he see the man? Did anyone?"

"Says he was alone, attacked from behind. But yes," Crowley growled, "he says yes, he did see his face."

"You got a description."

"Yes," Crowley said embarrassedly.

Max looked puzzled. "Does he know him? You get a name?"

"He doesn't . . . he seems reluctant." Crowley sounded both angry and uncertain. As if he didn't want to give information even on the phone. Again there was discussion in the background, then Crowley came back on.

"He refuses to come in, Chief. Says *he's* done nothing, why should *he* come into the station like a common criminal?"

"Just hold him," Max said, frowning. "I'm on my way." And he was out the door, double-timing through the lobby. He didn't see Joe Grey slip out behind him and leap into the truck bed. The chief swung away from the station unaware of the extra pair of eyes and ears that rode with him beneath a folded tarp.

KIT, RACING UP across the rooftops to the vacant lot, looked down on the Dumpster parked in front, and swallowed back a yowl of dismay. They were finishing up, were about to haul out of there. The lot had been cleaned off. No more dead trees, only stumps. No long, heavy tree trunks. They had been cut up and hauled away, probably on a big flatbed. At the curb, the Dumpster stood overloaded with rubble and branches, waiting to be hitched up and pulled off. Were the shoes still there, maybe way down, underneath?

Angled behind the Dumpster, three workmen sat in their pickup eating lunch—as if, having wrapped up the job, they meant to leave when they'd finished their noon meal. Maybe they were waiting for the tractor that would retrieve the Dumpster?

She had to get the shoes out before any tractor or heavy truck made an appearance and the shoes would be gone forever.

Maybe she'd better call the chief. Get the cops out here to stop them.

But in the time it took to gallop home, even if it was only half a block, the tractor might arrive, hitch up, and move out.

No, she had to do this now. Scrambling down an oak tree, she slipped across the street beneath the pickup, then under the Dumpster on the far side. Nearly hidden from the men, she leaped up, hung from the Dumpster by her front paws, then scrambled up on the thin metal rim.

The piled-up branches were thick with twigs and leaves crisscrossed and tangled together. Carefully poking in between them she could see, deep down, the toe of a tan running shoe. The whole load smelled of pine and willow sap. She didn't want sap in her fur, she'd have to chew it out. Easing down between the branches, willing them not to slip and fall on her, she reached deep with a careful paw. She stretched farther down and down until she snagged the shoe with two claws.

Gingerly she hauled it out. Sliding it up between the branches, hoping she wasn't smearing fingerprints, she pulled it onto the edge of the Dumpster. Balancing it there she took it in her mouth, her teeth clamped on the very edge. *Don't smear the prints*, she kept telling herself. She glanced up to the pickup, praying no one would notice her.

She saw no movement in the truck, just the dark silhouettes of the three men, two of them wearing baseball caps. Dropping down with the shoe, holding her head high, she hauled it across the street beneath tree shadows. There she laid it under the lacy leaves of a low-hanging pepper tree and went back for the next one.

It took her a long time to find five shoes among the tangled branches, to back out hauling each one, without toppling limbs on herself. She dug and wriggled, searching, but couldn't find any more. The sun was well past noon. Watching the three men, she thought, *Eat slow, eat more! Talk and laugh, take your time!*

Did the shoes hold fingerprints? Maybe not the canvas, but the plastic or leather parts? She prayed they did, and hoped again that she hadn't smeared them. And what about DNA? Could that be inside a shoe, or would sport socks have soaked it all up?

Not that it made much difference. The county lab was so far behind it would take maybe a year to get DNA evidence back to the department. By then, who knew what else might happen?

When she had the five shoes hidden under the pepper tree, she hauled them one at a time across the neighbors' yards, staying to the shadows and beneath bushes. She dragged each one to her own yard, four houses down from the Dumpster, and nosed it under the front steps. When at last she'd hidden them all, she scrambled up the oak to her tree house. She lay down for a little rest, and to work the sawdust and leaves out of her long coat. There *was* tree sap; she'd deal with that later. She rested only a few moments, then crossed the oak branch to her cat door and slipped inside.

Max Harper's cell phone number was on the Greenlaws' speed dial. She hit the single digit, listened to the ring, was coughing from sawdust when Max answered.

"Shoes," she said, swallowing. "Are you looking for shoes, maybe evidence to the assaults?"

"Yes," Max said. "What have you got?" He didn't ask who this was. Those days were long past when anyone in the department, except Evijean, would be so gauche as to question one of their prime snitches.

"Shoes thrown away in a Dumpster," Kit said.

"Recently?"

"Yes. While they were clearing this lot. Looks like they're all done, like maybe they're just ready to leave now, but I have the shoes."

"Yes, we'd like a look," Max said. "The Dumpster's where? Can you identify the person who dropped them?"

"No. I saw only their backs for a minute." She didn't want to say *when* she learned the shoes were of value, or when she saw them dumped. "I hauled five shoes out, hid them under a porch across the street." She gave him the address where the Dumpster stood. Then, shivering, she gave him the address where the shoes were hidden, the address of her own house.

"Under that front porch," she said. "That tall house with the children's tree house in the back."

She felt sick, taking a more than foolish chance, leading him to a hiding place so close to the truth. But her own front porch was the only one near that had a hollow beneath it; all the others were just a couple of concrete steps, solid and impenetrable. And if she hid the shoes among scattered bushes, neighbors' dogs might find and chew up the evidence.

No, her porch was the safest. No neighbors' kids poked around there, and it had been a long time since any unruly dog, facing her own claws and teeth, had invaded her yard.

"I know the house," Max said uneasily. "Why that house?"

"It's the nearest one to the Dumpster that has a good place to hide them," she said coolly. "And that house looks empty, not a soul around. I pass that place every day on my way to work. There's no car in the drive and never a newspaper and the shades always the same, half drawn, like they're on vacation."

She hoped she sounded businesslike and detached when in fact she was shaking with guilt. "Will you send someone for them?" she said innocently.

"We will, pronto. And thanks for the help."

Smiling, Kit hit the button that ended the call—and prayed that Lucinda and Pedric's ID blocking was working. With a nationwide phone company, one never knew. She shivered at having put the snitch in her own neighborhood. *I pass that place every day on my way to work.* That did scare her, to draw Max's attention there—but it made her laugh, too. A cat going to work every day?

And how could she implicate Lucinda and Pedric, when they were far away in Alaska?

MAX HARPER REACHED the attack scene as the caller hung up. He pulled to the curb in front of the western shop where the little alley ran back, flanking the bakery. The street was blocked by the medics' van and two squad cars. Parking beside the white van, but before stepping out, he called Dallas, sent Dallas over to retrieve the snitch's evidence.

"*Shoes?*" Dallas said. "Under the *Greenlaws'* porch? How come, after all these weeks, the snitch just now finds discarded shoes in a Dumpster? And near the Greenlaws'?"

"Hell, I don't know. I don't think they've been working long up there, clearing out those dying pines. Just go get the shoes," Max said. "And get shots of any footprints the snitch left," though of course Dallas would.

He sat a minute in his truck watching the four medics crowded around Sam Bleak, a woman medic taking his blood pressure, Sam huddled in his wheelchair looking pale and frightened. Tekla stood beside him, her hand protectively on his shoulder. Her stance was stiff and military, her face filled with anger as she raged loudly at Officer Crowley. The six-foot-six officer looked silently down at her, no smile, no frown, his face as still as stone. Max stepped out of the truck, approached the medics and three officers. Watching Tekla scolding, he took a second look at her black jogging pants, at the smear of dirt on the cuff.

He moved closer. Was that *not* a smear, but a small tear? He thought about Ben's photographs, the one that showed a tiny rip in the cuff of black jogging pants, pants with the same satin stripe as these. Stepping away, he dialed Dallas again. "You still there?"

"Just out the door."

"Before you leave," he said softly, "send Kathleen over here with the big camera for some detail shots."

Hanging up, he headed across to sort out the Bleak couple, Tekla's angry diatribe filling his ears like swarming bees. Trying to hold his temper, he didn't see Joe Grey peering out from the truck bed, didn't see Joe's smile as the tomcat thought about the phone call from Kit, about Kit leading Max to what? New evidence? Or only more useless shoes?

When, in the truck, Max's phone had buzzed and, answering, the chief had straightened up in the seat keenly alert to the caller, Joe had slid out from under the tarp and pressed against the back of the cab, listening.

Shoes? Joe had come sharply alert. From Max's end of the conversation, from the fact that Max didn't cross-examine the caller or ask his or her name—and from the way Kit had raced out of the conference room earlier, she had to be the snitch.

Having been gone so long from the village, having just gotten home and most of her thoughts on Misto, she hadn't realized shoes might be important until this morning. In the conference room piled with shoes and photographs of shoes, listening to Max and the detectives, she'd raced off alone to fetch what she hoped would be evidence. She'd retrieved the shoes, she'd hidden them where they'd be safe, and then she'd called Max, and that made Joe smile. Kit, their scatterbrained Kit, was indeed growing up.

21

IN THE BACK of Max's pickup, parked in the shadows of a cypress tree, Joe Grey reared up to peer over the side of the truck bed. He watched one of the four medics, a woman, tenderly clean up Sam Bleak's forehead and his upper arm, cutting loose his torn shirt, wiping away blood from both injuries. Officer Crowley was present with two other uniforms, talking with the chief. Sam's wheelchair lay fallen across a flower bed that edged a narrow brick walk. Sam sat on a carved wooden bench at the edge of the walk, which ran back between the buildings past the western shop, a boutique, a toy shop. A matching bench could be seen farther in between the windowed stores. Little lanes and half-hidden courtyards could be found all over the village, pleasing the locals and offering a longed-for charm to eager tourists. When Sam's forehead and arm had been bandaged, a second medic, a slim young man, handed him a clipboard and pen.

"This is your release, Mr. Bleak, if you're sure you don't want to go to Emergency."

Sam said he'd see his own doctor. Tekla leaned over, took the board from him, and began to read it out loud to him. As if he were too injured and unsteady—or too senile—to read the form himself.

When she had finished reciting the dull paragraphs, she handed it back for Sam to sign: a release of liability, to protect the medics and police. These days a human could hardly breathe without removing responsibility from everyone in sight. *The day will come*, Joe thought, *when Clyde and Ryan have to sign a waiver so the garbageman can pick up our trash.*

When the medics had finished with Sam and turned away, Joe dropped out of the truck into shadow and slipped beneath the shrubs at the curb. Hunkering there out of sight, he watched the three men and the woman gather their equipment back into the van, their blankets and oxygen tank and masks, their various black leather cases with the big syringes, packaged needles, and who knew what other kind of torture. As the van pulled away, Max began to question Sam, nodding to Officer Crowley to take notes.

"He ran right up behind me," Sam was saying. "Tekla wasn't here, she—"

"I'd left him for just a few minutes," Tekla snapped, "left him here in what I thought was a safe place while I ran into the bakery. Does a person have to be on guard every minute in this village? Isn't there a street patrol? I would think . . ."

Max stared at her with that dry, patient look. The same look as when he was about to strong-arm a drunk.

Joe looked up when Kathleen arrived. Stepping out of her car, she stood a moment taking in the situation; then she adjusted her camera and began to shoot the scene and the surround. Kneeling, the tall, slim detective photographed marks on the sidewalk the wheelchair had gone over, and close-ups of the area of broken flowers in the narrow strip of garden. She took time to lift latent fingerprints from the wheelchair, then photographed Sam and the chair at different angles; she included in her camera range several shots of Tekla's pant legs. She was fast but careful and precise, covering the area thoroughly.

When Tekla started berating the chief again, Max asked her to step on over with Officer Ray. "She's nearly finished photographing," Max said. "She'll want to interview you. You can wait on that other bench, back along the walk there."

Tekla looked as if she'd refuse. Scowling, she moved closer to Sam as if to remain protective of him—as if Max or one of the officers might do him bodily harm. Max looked over at Kathleen and nodded.

Turning, Kathleen headed for her car, locked the big camera safely in the trunk. She hung the smaller camera over her shoulder, took Tekla by the arm, and gently ushered the shorter woman back along the walk to the bench. She sat Tekla down with just enough force to prevent her from striking out as she seemed inclined to do. Quickly Joe moved to the back of the cypress tree out of sight and scrambled up. Hidden in the heavy foliage, he slipped out along a branch that arched over the sidewalk nearer to Tekla and Kathleen, where he could listen.

And where, within seconds, Kit came slipping along behind him as if out of nowhere. Feeling the sway of the branch, he glanced back; she peered out at him half hidden, her mottled black-and-brown coat blending into the shaggy cypress. With a flick of her ears, she looked over.

Max was kneeling beside the wheelchair where he could look Sam in the face. "I know you're shaken, Sam, but can you tell me what happened? Just take your time," he said gently.

"He hit me so hard. I was sprawled on the ground before I knew what happened," Sam's voice was unsteady. "Like Tekla said, she'd gone on a quick errand, left me parked right here in the lane, said she'd only be gone a minute to the bakery. I was looking in the window at those fancy western boots, in plain sight of the busy street, when I was struck so hard from behind I thought a truck hit me." Sam rubbed at the bandage on his forehead.

"I went sprawling, my wheelchair slid away, I heard someone running. I saw a dark figure running, but I was so dizzy . . ." He looked pitifully at Max, pale and shaken—but anger burned, too, deep in Sam's eyes, and that shocked Joe. Sam Bleak, so mild and docile, suddenly burned with a cold rage that the tomcat had not seen before.

Max studied Sam with interest. "Did you hear anything before he hit your wheelchair?"

Sam shook his head. "Nothing. Nothing at all, the street was quiet. Then that terrible blow and I went over, I had no way to stop, no way to catch myself."

"Can you describe the person? Do you remember his clothes? His height? Some idea of age? Was it a man, a boy?"

"A boy," Sam said, looking directly at Harper. "Tan Windbreaker, I remember that. Old, worn jeans and scuffed leather boots. Running away, running from me so I didn't see his face but . . . but I know him," Sam said.

Sam Bleak was silent, looking at Harper. His next words shocked Joe and Kit right down to their paws, made Joe want to leap down and claw Sam's lying face.

"The boy . . ." Sam said, "the boy . . . was Billy Young."

Max stood up, narrowly watching Sam. "Are you sure of that?"

"He looked exactly like Billy, and dressed the same. I swear it was Billy Young."

Max was silent, his look cold and hard. Joe wanted to shout, *That's a lie! What the hell are you up to?*

"The boy who flipped me over," Sam said, "it was Billy Young. That boy who works for Ryan Flannery—that boy who's too young to be working in a construction crew. Who thinks he's so smart because he has a grown-up job."

Joe and Kit looked at each other, fear for Billy sparking between them, fear of what they didn't understand. Max stood rigid and withdrawn. Maybe only the cats and his fellow cops saw that twitch at the side of his mouth, that quick inner fire that some humans wouldn't notice. To the cats, even Max's scent changed, had gone sharp with fury.

Sam felt tenderly at his bandaged forehead. "Same jacket, same clothes," he repeated. "Running away. I shouted at him to stop, shouted his name."

Again he was quiet, fingering his bandaged arm. Then,

"Why would that boy do such a thing? What did he want? It was then, as I fell, that Tekla came around the corner, saw me tipped over. *Tekla* saw him, too, Captain Harper." Sam's fists clenched in anger. "Tekla knew him. He raced away—up the brick alley and into the next street. Tekla started to pick me up, to pick up the wheelchair, but I told her to go on, try to catch him.

"But he was gone," Sam said shakily. "Just like those other attacks." He put his head down on his hands as if he felt dizzy or was still very frightened.

Max glanced at his watch. "And then what happened?"

"I told Tekla to leave me be, in case anything was broken, and she called 911." He did look pale. But, in truth, this was no more than a hoax, no more than a vicious lie.

"The siren came right away," Sam said, "the medics' van. Then more cops while the medics were looking me over, poking and prodding, and one of the cops—that tall one, the first one here, he started taking pictures. The medics kept arguing with me to let them put me in the van, but I didn't want to go to a hospital, I've had enough of *that*. And then," Sam said, "you got here, your pickup pulled in to the curb."

"You're sure it was Billy Young," Max said coldly.

"Looked exactly like him. I only glimpsed the side of his face—high, thin cheekbones, brown hair, tan Windbreaker. Same clothes he usually wears," Sam said, "same Windbreaker, same old, battered boots."

"I'd like you to come into the station, you'll need to fill out a report."

Sam's frown turned uncertain. He glanced across to where Tekla was deep in conversation with Kathleen Ray, as the detective recorded Tekla's version on her phone, so the two interviews could be compared.

"If you file a complaint," Max told Sam, "if you can identify him clearly, you can bring charges. If the boy has attacked others, it's your responsibility to tell us what you can."

Above in the cypress tree, Joe and Kit smiled at how cool Max was. The Bleaks had to know that Billy was the chief's ward, or at least that he lived with the Harpers. So why would they set Billy up? For what possible reason? Simply because Tekla didn't like Ryan, to get at Ryan through Billy, make them both look bad to Harper?

That didn't make any sense. And now, as Max pushed Sam with questions, was Sam indeed getting nervous?

Could this all be Tekla's setup? Had she forced Sam along with it, and now he was losing his resolve?

But then, what was Sam's anger about? Was that all fake, too?

Whatever the answer, Joe thought, *the Bleaks will find out soon enough what the chief already knows.* This was a crime Billy couldn't have committed, Billy was safe at the station when Sam was mugged; a dozen cops had seen him, including Max and all three detectives. The Bleaks, in a moment of misguided inspiration, had backed themselves into a corner, and didn't that make Joe and Kit smile.

Most likely Tekla had tipped over the wheelchair herself, maybe eased it over gently so Sam wouldn't in fact break any bones and create a real problem.

But they did manage to scrape his forehead and arm, Joe thought. *Maybe they didn't mean to do that, maybe* that *part was an accident as they performed their little charade.* And that made him smile all the more.

The question is, why would they go to such lengths to get Billy in trouble? Oh, but Tekla would, Joe thought, *just out of meanness. Or,* he wondered, *did they do this as some sort of diversion?*

"Did you and Tekla walk down from your apartment?" Max said, glancing back along the street. "From the little guesthouse you're renting?"

"Yes," Tekla said coolly. "So that Sam could get some air. It isn't good to always be riding around in the van."

Kathleen said, "I can give you a ride to the station, if you like. So you can file your complaint."

Tekla drew herself up. She said nothing. Sam smiled weakly. Kathleen and the chief stood over them waiting for a response, both officers so stern and severe that the Bleaks might find it hard to refuse. At last Sam allowed Kathleen to help him into the wheelchair, careful of his painful arm, and she wheeled him to her squad car, Tekla walking like an angry guard dog beside him. Kathleen settled them in the backseat and folded Sam's chair into the trunk.

As they pulled away, leaving Max talking with Officer Crowley, Joe and Kit left the cypress tree praying Billy was still at the station. They didn't want to miss this confrontation. Joe wished Dulcie were there. He'd give her a blow-by-blow account, just as he would lay it all out later for Misto and for Pan. Misto needed to be kept in the loop; the old cat needed to see and feel as much as he could of these last, waning days, Joe thought sadly.

But as he and Kit galloped away across the roofs toward the station, he looked slyly at her. "You found shoes! Did Dallas get them?"

Kit smiled. "I watched him fish them out from under my porch. He lifted each one with a stick inside so he didn't smear any prints. I hope I didn't smear any."

"*Your* porch?" He stopped and looked at her, and was getting ready to scold her. But she looked at him so contritely that he swallowed back his words.

What the hell, she'd gotten the shoes, hadn't she? That could be the key, if they could find a matching shoe, one with a good set of fingerprints. That could be the evidence they needed; and he looked at Kit and didn't criticize—he wasn't going to trash her bright-eyed joy in finding them.

As they leaped to the roof of the courthouse and raced its length, Kathleen's squad car pulled up to the red zone below. Dallas's Blazer was already there. He was just disappearing through the glass door carrying a cardboard box. It was filled with evidence bags, each the size and the shape of a shoe. Kit stared down at it with triumph, her ears up, the tip of her tail twitching.

Joe just hoped they'd turn out to be the right ones, belonging to the perp, not just someone's worn-out footwear. Backing down the oak tree, they crouched in the bushes by the front entry watching Kathleen remove Sam's wheelchair from the trunk and unfold it. As she held the glass door so Tekla could roll him through into the lobby, Joe and Kit slipped behind them into the smelly retreat of the holding cell—their retreat for as long as Evijean remained on duty. He thought of Dulcie resting at home as she'd been told, and wished she were there to enjoy the coming performance.

22

THOUGH IT WAS just mid-morning, a warming fire burned on the Firettis' hearth, its blaze reflected in the fog-frosted windows. Firelight brightened the flowered couch where Misto lay tucked up in a quilt between Dulcie and Pan. Mary Firetti and Wilma sat on the matching couch sipping coffee. Wilma had brought a gift for Misto, a big tray of custards. The three cats had promptly lapped up three small bowls before they snuggled close.

At home earlier, Dulcie had paced from room to room wanting to be outside, wanting to roam but having promised to stay in, not to run the roofs but to rest. She had paced and glared at Wilma, who sat at her desk paying bills. She'd wanted to be at the station, wanted to find Joe Grey, wanted in on the action. Whenever she'd trotted out into the garden for a few minutes she felt Wilma at the window watching her. It was all very well to be quiet and protect the kittens, but she'd begun to feel like a caged wildcat. But when the custards were ready to take to Misto, getting in the car, Wilma said, "You need only be idle for a little while, the kittens will arrive soon. I don't need to tell you how important this is, these are the most precious of babies."

Dulcie knew that! She tried not to snap at Wilma. She tried not to sound sulky. But even a trip in the car was a treat, just to get out. Trotting up the Firetti walk through the last of Mary's cyclamens as bright as new crayons, she had raced into the cottage to nearly pounce on Misto and Pan, she was so glad to see them—though it had only been a few hours.

Pan said, "Kit slipped away early. Restless, so restless."

Dulcie snuggled closer and looked tenderly at Pan. "You miss Kit this morning," she said, licking his ear. *Kit might have been restless*, she thought, *but maybe that* was *a loving gesture, too, to slip away at dawn, to leave father and son alone together, just the two of them.*

Mary had set Wilma's dozen little bowls in the refrigerator to keep cool. "Misto does so love your custards. I make little stews, I make soups, but your custards are the real treat." She looked at Misto, then back at Wilma. "We talked about Ben," she said softly. "I told him about Ben."

Misto lowered his ears and put out a paw to Wilma. But as she reached to stroke him she saw behind his grieving look that staunch certainty, too, in his golden eyes. "Where Ben is now," the old cat said, "he is safe, he is beyond human cruelty." He licked Wilma's hand. "Ben is

214

loved with a strength the living cannot imagine, he is free in joy now, he flies weightless."

They talked about Ben and about the attacks, Misto stoic, in his own way removed from the deepest pain. It was nearly noon when Wilma and Dulcie left the Firetti cottage, Misto napping again, and Pan still close beside him. Riding home, Dulcie thought about the street crimes, about new police reports, new intelligence coming in, about Joe at the station, and she looked up forlornly at Wilma.

Wilma sighed. She hadn't worked in corrections for all her career without knowing how these present crimes drew Dulcie. "You want to be with Joe, putting the pieces together."

Dulcie sighed.

"I'll take you to the PD if you'll promise to wait there. To let me pick you up later, not come galloping home alone over the rooftops. You might not go full term, Dulcie, you might . . ."

"I promise," Dulcie said.

Reluctantly Wilma dropped her off in front of the courthouse, watched her disappear into the bushes to wait for a chance to slip inside the station. Wilma lingered for a few minutes, and then a few minutes more, but no one came or went through the glass door. She could see action inside, could see Max and Detective Kathleen Ray; she could just see Joe Grey in a corner of the holding cell, and she glimpsed a fluff of tortoiseshell fur; Kit was there with him. She could see that brittle temporary clerk, Evijean, behind the counter. And was that the Bleak couple in there? That was curious, what was that about?

She watched Dulcie peering out, watching intently from the bushes. She watched the tabby move beneath a camellia, closer to the glass door where she could see in better. Wilma waited a few minutes more, got an angry scowl when the tabby reared up to look back at her. Whatever was happening had Dulcie's full attention. At last Wilma left her. Joe Grey and Kit were there if the tabby needed someone. Dulcie had a loud yowl if she found herself in trouble. *As many times as I've worried over her, I have learned to trust her. I'm not going to rein her in completely, even now.*

IT WAS EARLIER, just after Sam Bleak's fake attack, that Joe and Kit slipped into MPPD behind Kathleen Ray and Sam and Tekla, the two cats sliding into the shadows of the holding cell. Surely Evijean hadn't seen them, there had been no cry of outrage. Beyond the reception counter among the computers, radios, and office machines they couldn't see even the top of Evijean's head. When Joe reared up for a better look, he was sure no one was minding the counter—though the clerk's area was never left unmanned.

As he watched, Detective Ray moved toward the counter, alert and wary. She had switched on her radio when Max pulled up outside, swung out of his truck and in through the glass door—and as Evijean emerged from the conference room, slipping out with a guilty look.

Max watched Evijean, frowning because she'd left her station. He looked down the hall at the door she had closed. "Are you keeping that room locked?"

Evijean set a cup of coffee on her desk. "Detective Davis moved those . . ." She glanced at the Bleaks. "That material that was on the table. She moved it to her office," she said with more finesse than Joe would expect. "Detective Garza is with her and the boy." Joe thought she might have the courtesy to call Billy by name.

Max looked at the Bleaks, then back at Evijean. "How long has Billy been here?"

She looked confused.

"How long has he been in the station this morning? Since what time?"

"Maybe two hours," Evijean said. "Since Detective Ray brought him in with . . . Since around nine when she brought him back to your office." She watched the chief, frowning. Her finesse just went so far. Over in the waiting area, Tekla and Sam had come to full attention. Both had begun to fidget.

"Evijean," Max said, "ask Detective Davis, Detective Garza, and Billy to come up front. And hand me two complaint forms."

Evijean frowned uncertainly and looked down into the shelves beneath the counter.

"Those forms in the box at the end," Max said impatiently. Joe knew what he meant. These were the sheets the chief had made up for previous incidents where he wanted the complainants' statements in their own handwriting; they were not the usual documents that an officer himself filled out. Evijean found them, inserted the forms in two clipboards, and handed them to him. Even she knew this was unorthodox, that a complaint was filed verbally to an officer and the complainant only signed the paperwork.

When Evijean had called back to Juana's office and relayed the chief's message, Max said, "Has Billy left the station since Kathleen brought him in this morning?"

"No, sir."

"Not at all, for any reason? Are you sure?"

"Yes, sir, I'm sure." Her look was sharp, keenly puzzled.

In the waiting area, Tekla had risen and stood scowling at the chief. "You *would* stand up for that boy. Isn't he your ward or something? Of course you'd say he was here, you wouldn't want—"

Max looked hard at her. "Mrs. Bleak, there's a law against false accusation." Whether he meant false accusation of Billy as the attacker, or false accusation of Max himself for lying to cover for Billy, his words made Tekla back off, and made Joe and Kit exchange a whiskery grin.

Max had turned to Sam. "You can have a good look at Billy Young now. If you're sure it was Billy who attacked you, you can file the complaint and we can move on with the matter. Maybe we can put him in juvenile hall until we get this sorted out."

Beneath the bunk, Kit's yellow eyes widened but Joe Grey only smiled. There was no way in hell Max would do that. They heard a door open down the hall, footsteps approaching, and Billy and the two detectives came up to the front. At the sight of Billy, Tekla moved behind Sam's wheelchair as if to remain in control, to wheel Sam on out of there to safety. Billy, looking puzzled, came to stand beside the chief. Max put his arm around him and turned him to face Sam.

"Is this the boy who attacked you, who tipped over your wheelchair?"

Billy stared at up at Max and then at Sam, uncomprehending.

Sam wouldn't look at Billy. Nor did he look at Max Harper. "Maybe . . ." he began, "Maybe . . . maybe that boy's jacket was gray, not tan. Maybe . . ." He frowned at Billy as if seeing him for the first time, this boy he saw nearly every day working on the remodel.

"I think," Sam said, "I think that boy's hair was darker. Yes, a darker brown, and longer, down around his neck. Hard to remember," he said, "when I was sprawled there dizzy and hurt, and he was running away . . ." He looked down at his hands, at the scuff marks that the medics had bandaged.

"I guess," Sam said lamely, "I guess I could be wrong. I was so frightened and confused when I was knocked over, the sidewalk seemed to be whirling under me, so dizzy . . ."

Max and the detectives watched him with interest. Had the Bleaks thought, with the crime scene cleared at the remodel and the yellow tape removed, Billy would be cleaning up there now as Tekla had demanded? Had they, this morning, seen Scotty, or maybe Ryan or both off in the village running errands, maybe picking up material? Assuming Billy was working alone as he sometimes did, thinking there would be no witness to the boy's whereabouts, had they jumped at the chance to stage their little ruse, to lay the crime on Billy? A spark of inspiration that went bad? Joe and Kit, looking hard at them, wished they could stare the truth right out of that pair of liars.

"Even if you're not sure of the identity," Max was saying, "if you file a complaint describing the attack, that will help us. That would be considerable assistance in finding whoever did attack you. You needn't mention Billy at all, if you're not sure he was involved."

He handed Sam a clipboard with a complaint form. Sam took it with his right hand, laid it carefully against his hurt left arm. The chief handed a second form to Tekla. Joe watched Max pick up one of the folding chairs and settle Tekla across the room. "You need to each do your form separately, without discussion," he told her.

The chief and Kathleen had already taken their statements, that *was* the complaint. Now Max was poker-faced. Joe had seen him at the card table with that look, running a bluff.

"Describe only what you remember," the chief told Sam. "Tell what happened as best you can, just as you told it to me and Detective Ray. You're the only witnesses we have. Your statement is of great value." Max's demeanor was smooth as silk. As Sam filled out the form, bent earnestly over the clipboard, Evijean came out from behind the counter carrying her purse. One of the rookies came down the hall to take her place, relieving her for an early lunch, a blond young man brushing a speck of lint from his uniform. Evijean had hardly left when Kit stiffened, peering out the glass door.

Joe barely caught sight of Dulcie as she slid past the station following Evijean. The next minute, as two civilians came in, Kit slipped out and fled down the sidewalk, to follow Dulcie. Why was Dulcie out of the house where Wilma had meant for her to rest and act matronly? And what the hell was she up to? Joe remained still, his ears back, watching them. He wanted to follow her, too, but his questions swung so sharply back to the Bleaks that he stayed put.

The couple had finished up their complaint forms, signed them, and were handing them to Captain Harper. Something about the look they exchanged as they headed for the door held Joe.

They left the station quickly, Tekla determinedly pushing Sam's wheelchair as if wanting to be swiftly away from MPPD and Max Harper. As Max turned to the desk with the forms, Joe leaped up beside him, rubbing chummily against his arm.

Max looked down, laughing at him. Joe was happy to lighten the chief's mood, and as Max stroked him, he got a look at the forms with the Bleaks' rental address.

Molena Point did not have house numbers. Sam identified the street and cross streets in the usual way, then the name of the house, Daffodil Walk, with an added note, "the guesthouse in the back." Joe knew the house, a two-story frame painted butter yellow. Joe had never seen a daffodil in the yard. Giving Max a nudge and a purr, Joe dropped down from the counter, galloped to the glass door, and yowled stridently for the chief to let him out.

"Spoiled, worthless tomcat," Max said, sounding too much like Clyde.

Smiling, Joe slipped through the open door, skinned up the oak tree as Max turned back inside, and scorched away over the rooftops. He wanted to arrive at Tekla and Sam's rental before they did. He wanted to slip into the apartment behind them and hastily conceal himself.

23

DULCIE WAS ALREADY gone from in front of the PD when Joe Grey went racing out, headed for the Bleaks' rental. Watching the busy lobby, she had drawn back when Evijean came out and headed along the street. A few doors down stood Effie Hoop in her red sweatshirt, smiling, waiting for Evijean. What was this? Did these two know each other? Curious, Dulcie followed, slipping along in the shadow of the building. She watched the two women hug in greeting. They glanced toward the police station, then quickly entered the new little tearoom that stood between two larger shops.

The leaded front windows were low to the ground, looking out on a row of ceramic pots planted with red geraniums. Dulcie stood half hidden among these, looking in. The tiny restaurant was charming, was most attractive to tourists. It was handy to the department, too, for a quick snack. But a cop wouldn't be caught there with its fluffy flowered curtains, its décor as overdone as a dollhouse. It was perfect, however, for lunch for the two ladies. Dulcie wondered where Effie had left her husband, Howard. This was sure not his kind of place. And how *did* they know each other, Effie, with her strange remarks about San Francisco, and sour, bad-tempered Evijean? They looked as easy together as old, dear friends as they were led, laughing and talking, to a frilly corner table, its ruffled cloth printed with a tangle of daisies.

When Kit appeared suddenly pushing in beside her, Dulcie nuzzled her in greeting; both cats were so focused on Evijean and Effie that when another two ladies entered they slid inside at once and under a padded window seat.

The tearoom was small, its decorative windows framed by ruffled curtains. Though the day was warm, a tiny stone fireplace sheltered an equally tiny but welcoming flame of miniature logs. The women, only glancing at their menus, were already deep into a discussion. Dulcie crouched, listening. Hadn't Effie Hoop or Howard mentioned a sister, that morning in the café patio over breakfast? But Effie was saying, "It doesn't make sense. Seven attacks, three of them jurors. Those jurors dead, plus the two killed in the city. But what about the others, those here in the village that had no connection to the trial?"

She went quiet as the waitress came to take their order, setting down a pot of hot water and a selection of teas. Both women ordered a small salad and scones.

"Those other attacks," Evijean said, "may be a diversion. The department thinks that's what it was."

"I suppose that's possible. What did you find out this morning?"

"They have more photographs. They took shots this morning, too. And they have some kind of new evidence, Detective Garza came in with a box full of evidence bags. I didn't get a look, he took them on back to his office. As for Herbert Gardner," Evijean said, "as far as anyone knows he didn't have any connections. No family anywhere.

"But someone's out to get the jury that convicted him."

"Maybe some slimy friend of his," Effie said, "that the investigators didn't find."

"Whatever," Evijean said, "Marilain's dead, that can't be undone. It's not surprising," she added. "The girl was no better than a streetwalker."

"No matter what she was, she *was* our niece! Our own brother's child. It's not his fault she went bad."

Dulcie and Kit glanced at each other. The two women, despite their difference in size and bulk, did look alike, their pale coloring, their long noses. Effie's brown hair had started to go gray. Evijean was some years younger, but her hair was so faded that, under the strange blond coloring, it must be graying, too.

Evijean stirred sugar into her tea. "Well, she had a poor start, fell into bad ways herself."

"Don't you *care* that she's dead?"

Evijean shrugged. "Gardner will die for it. However this turns out, that's the consolation."

Effie looked at her sister, her round face disapproving. "You dated him once, didn't you? Before Marilain met him, when you lived in the city?"

"Not dated, he was a generation too young," Evijean

said sourly. "Marilain was only seventeen, a child. I just had dinner with Gardner a couple of times, after work. Then when he met Marilain, of course he had no time for anyone else, even a friend. I think he hung out with me to meet her. I *thought* he was a friend. I had no idea what he was, what he might do," she said bitterly.

"Well," she said, "that was a long time ago, before I worked for the sheriff's department and then moved down here. I might never have gotten this temp job if I hadn't been cleared, back then, for the sheriff's office.

"But now . . . it's the jurors," she said, "*they* had no need to die. How did the killer get their names? All that is sealed. But you were there in the courtroom, in the gallery. Did you notice anything strange, or anyone you knew? Did you know any of the victims?"

"The only victim I know is Betty Porter, and she wasn't *on* the jury. I know her from earlier visits, from talking with her in the drugstore.

"Well, in the courtroom, I did see that other woman, Bonnie, who was nearly mugged right here in front of the station. *She* was on the jury—but it was her husband who was killed. I recognized her from the San Francisco paper. *She* was the juror, and he died for it." She paused as the waitress brought their order.

Evijean said, "So strange that the San Francisco investigators, the county attorney, knew so little about Gardner's background."

"They found enough to prosecute him," Effie said. "They didn't need to know his life story. That defense attorney," she said with a smile, "his heart wasn't in saving Gardner."

"You have to give him that," Evijean said. "No one wanted Gardner to go free."

"Except the stalker," Effie said. "Didn't Gardner ever say anything to you about his background, his family?"

"Nothing. He was so closemouthed. That in itself should have alerted me. Marilain never said anything about his past, either, and by that time, I didn't care. And then I moved down here and didn't see her anymore. She might have been our niece, but I didn't like her much. She wasn't much good," Evijean said.

Effie poured more tea for herself. "Well, someone was close to him, cared about him. Someone is killing innocent jurors because they did their job." She set down the teapot. "Marilain did come to see us a time or two when we lived on Grant Street—wanting to borrow money. She said Gardner had no family, that his mother would have nothing to do with him, that he hadn't seen her in years, that she'd moved to the East Coast somewhere—maybe as far away from him as she could get."

"Well, it couldn't have been her," Evijean said. "If his mother hated him for how he'd turned out, maybe knew about earlier crimes, why would she come back here and go after innocent jurors for convicting him? She should celebrate."

Effie shrugged. "Some women are like that. Hate their kids when they turn bad, but then they go all defensive when the kid gets caught and has to pay for his sins." She settled heavily back in her chair, buttering a scone. "And the police here, they don't have any background on Gardner? *They* don't know who might be connected to him?"

"Not that I can find," Evijean said. "But now, this morning, they're working on new evidence, something's going on in there." She sipped her tea, looked up at Effie; she went quiet as the waitress brought their check.

When Dulcie looked at Kit, Kit looked sly and smug. A look of triumph, as if she had her paws in the cream. "What?" Dulcie whispered. But the women had paid the bill and risen. With no more useful information forthcoming, and with not much traffic in and out of the tearoom, the two cats hurried out the door behind them.

Evijean went on into the station. Dulcie and Kit waited in the bushes until they could duck through, unseen. "What?" Dulcie said again. "What did you do?"

"The shoes," Kit whispered. "I found thrown-away shoes. Dallas has them." Quickly Kit told her about Sam's "accident," about the Bleaks' charges against Billy. "And Joe," Kit said, "Joe was mad enough to . . . I didn't know what he'd do." She peered in through the glass door. "Looks like the Bleaks are gone. They . . ." She hushed as Officer McFarland pulled up in his squad car. As he got out, they slipped up to the door behind him. Seeing them, McFarland grinned, his boyish brown hair mussed under his cap, and he held the door for them. They trotted through, glanced up at him with a flick of their tails, and hurried past the counter out of Evijean's sight, quickly down the hall, to the safety of Max Harper's door.

His office was empty, the door cracked open but no one there. They could hear voices from Juana Davis's office. They crossed the hall and slid inside, halting inches behind Detective Davis's black shoes and the chief's western boots where they stood at a long, folding table. Kit slid in first. She knew at once by the smell that the shoes were there, the shoes she'd found in the Dumpster; the smell of pine pitch was so strong that she had to hide a grin.

24

JUANA DAVIS'S USUALLY neat office looked like a jumble sale. A long table stood in the middle of the room, her furniture pushed against the wall, the credenza, bookcase, and desk shoved together. Davis, Max Harper, and Billy stood at the table absorbed as Dulcie and Kit slipped into the room. Silently they hopped up onto the desk and to the top of the bookcase where they could look down.

Besides the shoes there were photos again: crime scene photos crowded the table. A set of pictures neatly arranged by each shoe. Now they had a match, the corresponding color shots marked with time, date, name of the victim. Kit looked smugly at Dulcie. She was so proud she could hardly help lashing her tail and grinning.

But Dulcie was looking for Joe Grey. Why wasn't he

in here scanning the evidence? She couldn't even catch his scent.

She thought about the Bleaks' scam, how they'd tried to incriminate Billy, how angry Joe had been—Kit said she didn't know what he'd do. *Oh*, she thought, *he hasn't followed them, he hasn't followed the Bleaks home?*

But that's just what Joe *would* do.

Stay outside, she thought. *Just watch the house, see if they try to run, see if they try to get away from Harper.* Then *call the station. Oh, don't go in there.* She moved to drop down to the desk, to head for the door and follow him—but now even Dulcie herself was too wary, thinking of the kittens. She *was* feeling heavier, clumsier. She thought of running over the rooftops, maybe getting into a tight squeeze inside the Bleak rental . . . If anything happened to the kittens, to Joe's kittens . . .

And somehow, looking at Kit, at the flighty tortoiseshell, she didn't want to ask Kit to follow him. *When he's alone, he's extra careful. Alone, he can sometimes plan his moves better, he's not distracted.* No, this time she would put her trust in Joe, in Joe Grey's strength and macho intelligence. Creeping closer to Kit, snuggled against her, she watched Billy Young, standing at the long table beside Juana, answering her occasional questions. She was comparing the crime scene shots and their matching shoes with a handful of the pasted-up photos.

"Yes," Billy was saying, "that's just behind the remodel, under the bedroom window. Those two pieces of two-by-four? I tossed them there a week ago, and forgot them. Same shoe, though. Same torn pant cuff."

Was this why Billy was here, a civilian looking at police evidence to verify the locations of certain photos? But these locations could be verified by police photos of the larger surround, they didn't need a witness. Dulcie and Kit looked at each other. Was this an added experience for Billy? Max's ongoing introduction to see if the boy was truly interested in police work? Billy said, "How long will the lab take?"

"Hopefully, a week or two," Max said.

"*That's* wishful thinking," Juana said, laughing.

"If they're as backed up as usual," Max told Billy, "could take a month or more."

"While the killer," Billy said, "could be long gone."

Neither Max nor Juana replied.

Near the shoes lay machine copies from a small, spiral-bound notebook. Though only the top, lined page was visible. Ben's note was short, but was carefully dated.

> *Monday, November 4. Ten A.M. Blonde in back of gallery again, back row but different seat. No hat today, dressed kind of fluffy, full skirt and a blousy shawl. Nothing like that leather cap and bulky jacket. I guess she's hiding her extra weight, she could stand to lose a few pounds. It's the same woman. She walks the same, kind of slow and like maybe she has arthritis. Same blond hair . . .*

That was all the cats saw before Max glanced up at them and they turned to wash their paws.

Near the notebook pages, three photos had been set aside. Each showed a running shoe with the bottom of a pant leg, a black satin stripe down the outside seam and a small tear at the bottom. One showed the print of the shoe's tread on the concrete, a waffle pattern with stars in it. The second photo showed only the footprint, but it was the same odd pattern. Neat handwriting in the white margin at the top of each photo gave the date and identified the attack. The third photo was of the same jogging pants with the black satin stripe, the tear, but with different shoes. It was dated this morning, and in different handwriting, and marked with a file number and the name "Sam Bleak."

Max was saying, "This is enough to bring them back in for questioning."

"Enough to file charges?" Juana said doubtfully.

"No. Only as persons of interest," he said. "We're not filing charges on a dead man's notes and photos, even our own crime scene photos. We wait for the lab, hope they come up with prints. And Sam's false accusation of Billy isn't much of a case against them. You read their statements, how they backed down."

"But they're tied into this," Juana said. "You want to try for a search warrant? Before they try to skip?"

"With Judge Manderson? You know he wants hard evidence before we do a search."

Juana sighed. "Wish we had the gun that killed Ben. And what *was* that about, that fake attack this morning, throwing themselves right in our faces?"

Max shrugged. "No one said criminals were smart."

Billy said, "Did they think if Sam was mugged, that you'd see them as helpless victims? And I guess," he said, grinning, "I guess they don't like me much. But," he continued, "even when they left the station, they looked nervous."

Juana turned when her desk phone rang, and flipped on the speaker.

Evijean said, "I just took an anonymous call. A message for Captain Harper. The man wouldn't give his name."

"I'm here," Max said.

"He wouldn't wait. He said to tell the captain that the convicted rapist, the one in San Francisco? . . . Gardner? That he has a mother somewhere, that they are estranged. The last he'd heard, she was living somewhere on the East Coast. He said you were looking for a connection, for family."

"Why didn't you switch him directly to me?"

"He didn't *want* me to transfer the call, he said he was in a hurry. He told me to pass it on promptly . . . A very curt man," she said. "He gave me the information and hung up."

"No caller ID?"

"No, sir. Maybe an old cell phone with no GPS?"

Dulcie looked at Kit; they both watched Harper. The way Evijean described the call, that didn't sound much like Joe Grey. Dulcie thought about the conversation in the tearoom. Could Evijean have made up that call, to pass her own information to the captain? And, when she glanced at Kit, she knew the tortoiseshell was thinking the same. So what was Evijean's interest in this? Besides that it was her niece that Gardner raped and murdered. Maybe just a nosy clerk wanting in on the action, sharing information in her own ego trip?

Yet even as Dulcie puzzled over the phone call she began to feel edgy. Not uneasy about the Bleaks now, or the street prowler, or even about Joe Grey. She had every confidence in Joe, in his instincts to come out on top. Something else was bothering her. Rising, she began to pace the top of the bookshelf.

Is it the kittens? she thought nervously. *Is it time?* She felt no pain, there were no contractions, though the little mites were, as usual, squirmy and restless. Kit watched her with alarm, her yellow eyes wide.

Below them, Max was on the phone again when the cats heard Charlie's voice in the hall. They watched Charlie and Ryan squeeze into the room, both dressed in jeans and T-shirts. Watched them move out of the way among the crowded furniture, looking with interest at the evidence, the shoes and photos and Ben's notes—though most of their attention was on Dulcie. Charlie, taller than Ryan, reached up to pet her.

Dulcie stiffened when Charlie scooped her up; she glared at Charlie indignantly. Charlie lifted her gently down and cuddled her—imprisoned her—in her arms. Securely gripping the nape of Dulcie's neck so she couldn't leap away. Holding her *captive.* Shocked, she hissed at Charlie. When Ryan reached over to gently stroke her, she growled and hissed at Ryan, too. What *was* this? Neither Charlie nor Ryan had ever manhandled her. Captive, incensed, she wanted to snag her claws in Charlie's red hair and pull hard. She was mad as hell and she couldn't say a word. Couldn't swear. Couldn't scream for help. She could only snarl and growl.

"What the hell?" Max said. "What's the matter with her? You only picked her up." Putting his arm around

Charlie, he reached out his hand to see if Dulcie would strike at him, too.

She didn't, she drew back. She *could not* bloody the chief, that was unthinkable.

But even so, Max's hand paused in midair. "What . . . ?" He looked hard at Dulcie, and then at Charlie. "This cat's pregnant, no wonder she's cranky. Didn't you know she's pregnant? Does Wilma know? She shouldn't be out on the streets like this, look at her." Max might be a tough cop, but he had a tenderness for Dulcie and Joe and Kit, just as he did for all animals.

But now Charlie and Ryan looked at him with cool female tolerance. "Yes, pregnant," Charlie said, "waiting for kittens. We came to get her."

Juana watched the scene with amusement. Davis had cats, too, but neither one was in danger of getting pregnant. Billy, stepping up beside Max, stroked Dulcie's ears and face. Then, taking liberties Dulcie would allow to only a few, he felt her belly knowingly.

"Pretty soon," Billy said, looking up at Charlie. "Less than two weeks?" Billy had taken in rescue cats since he was a small boy; in the last few years he had helped birth more kittens than he could count, strays that came to him half starved when he'd lived in the shack down by the riverbed, strays more prevalent before CatFriends got to work saving lost and abandoned cats and ferals.

Max said, "Wilma can't want her running the village when her time is so close. Why did she let her out? If the kittens come early on some rooftop, in some out-of-the-way place . . ."

"Dulcie's supposed to be locked up," Charlie said innocently. "Wilma called, she's frantic and is out looking for her. Somehow Dulcie managed to slip out through her cat door. I'll take her home," she said, keeping a strong grip on the nape of Dulcie's neck.

Beside them, Ryan put her arm around Billy. "And you and I need to get back to work, finish cleaning up until we know what the Bleaks intend to do. Keep on building, or scrap the job?" she said with irritation. "Charlie can drive us over. I left my truck there."

"Don't leave Billy there alone," Max said, "until we have this sorted out. Are you carrying?"

"In my truck," Ryan said.

"Wear it," Max said.

Charlie's eyes widened. She nodded, gave Max a kiss, careful not to squash Dulcie between them, and they left.

In the SUV Dulcie didn't need to be held captive. She snuggled on Charlie's lap obedient and silent—worrying again about Joe Grey. *Had* he followed the Bleaks when they left the station, was he watching their apartment? Was he *in* the apartment? Was that why she felt so nervous? If he had followed them, he'd be sure to find a way inside. She didn't want to think of him shut in alone, with those two. Maybe she and Charlie should swing by the Bleaks' rental, after they'd dropped off Ryan and Billy.

And maybe not. Maybe that would make things worse, would really alarm the Bleaks, would make them run or would put Joe in jeopardy.

She didn't know what to do; she was in a quandary and that wasn't like her. She wanted to race over there herself, but when she felt the kittens squirming she knew she wouldn't.

Charlie pulled up in front of the remodel beside Ryan's truck, and Ryan and Billy got out. As Charlie headed away again, she gently stroked Dulcie. "I'm sorry I manhandled you. You looked determined to take off. Tell me about the photos and shoes, and what happened with Billy? Those Bleaks didn't really accuse him!"

"They did," Dulcie said. "Kit told me, blow by blow." She passed on to Charlie everything she knew, from Sam's fake attack and the Bleaks' accusation of Billy, to the conversation in the tearoom, to Evijean's strange phone message. Charlie was silent as she pulled up in front of the stone cottage, putting the details together. Wilma came hurrying out, scowling at Dulcie and ready to scold her. But instead Wilma gathered her up in a hug of relief, and Dulcie relaxed against her. Purring, she patted a soft paw against Wilma's cheek—and she could smell a pot roast cooking. Yawning against Wilma, suddenly drained of all her cat energy, she wanted only to eat and then sleep warm in Wilma's arms.

25

WHEN JOE HAD left the station, he'd had every intention of tossing the Bleaks' apartment for evidence; surveillance was not enough. Racing the length of the courthouse roof, he hit the peaks above Jane's Knitting, Matelle Bakery, and three upscale clothing stores. On the roof of a small motel he galloped past second-floor windows, surprising a little child looking out. From a patio café across the street, the smell of frying onions followed him as he headed a block north to the tall, two-story frame on the corner, the butter-yellow house named Daffodil Walk. There were no daffodils in the scruffy fenced yard.

The small rental cottage at the back might once have been brown. It was not fenced, as was the big house. A narrow, cracked drive led from the side street to the cottage's attached one-car garage that jutted out in front.

The Bleaks' white van stood to the right of the drive on a patch of grass, handy to the front steps. Oak trees shaded both yards.

Dropping into a tangle of twisted branches, Joe made his way to the back. In the yard of the big house a heavy-shouldered Rottweiler stopped chewing on a fallen branch and stared up at him, his yellow eyes small and mean, his growl a low rumble. He glared unblinking as Joe slipped over the hip of the cottage roof out of sight. The beast knew he was still there, could surely smell him; but, not seeing the invading feline, he might be less likely to bark and draw attention.

Stepping stones led from the street along the drive to the front door of the cottage. Over in the fenced yard the dog rumbled once more, leaped at the closed gate, then returned to maul his oak branch. Joe could see a kennel at the back near the big house.

Padding on across the cottage's ragged shingles, he backed down the last gnarled tree into the sweet smell of mock orange bushes shedding their wilted flowers. A temporary wooden ramp led up beside the three steps to the small porch. The front door stood open.

The van's passenger door was wide open, too, revealing Tekla's black-clad backside where she leaned in. Her posterior and thighs looked narrow as a boy's. She backed out, carrying a crookedly folded blanket, a six-pack of bottled water, and a handful of road maps. Before she could turn toward the house Joe was inside and under the first shelter he came to: a padded bench against a short wall that faced the front door. Diving under, he glimpsed the small, crowded living room beyond.

To the left of the front door in a narrow alcove hung two Windbreakers and a yellow raincoat on wooden hooks. The front door itself was flanked by tall panes on either side, swirly glass so you could see only a person's shape and what color he was wearing. The glass panes were the perfect arrangement for a thief. Only a moment to break the window, reach through and turn the key; unless, of course, one had had the foresight to remove the key.

To the right of the front door a narrower, closed door probably led to the garage, Joe could smell the oil-rubber-tire-mildew scent common to most village garages. To the right of that door was the kitchen alcove with a small breakfast table. The cramped living room behind him held a faded couch, a fake leather easy chair, a TV on a rolling stand, a depressing tableau for the desperate renter.

Two hard-sided suitcases stood beneath the hanging coats beside the front door. From the shadows beneath the bench, he watched Tekla lay the blanket on the larger one, set the maps and the bottled water on the blanket. As she shut the front door the hinge gave a little squeak. Her black jogging shoes were inches from his nose as she headed down a short hall to his left past a tiny bedroom to a larger one at the back. He followed her, praying she wouldn't glance around. At the sound of Sam's muffled voice from the back room, Joe froze. "You want *all* these clothes?" He didn't sound happy.

"Just the front ones," Tekla snapped. She moved on to the larger bedroom, Joe following; even this room was minuscule. Just space for a double bed partly blocking a glass door with the draperies drawn, a dresser, a small armoire that would hold a TV. Tekla entered the small walk-in closet, its door standing wide, Sam's wheelchair parked beside it. Joe waited in the shadows, watching.

Inside the closet Sam was standing up, supporting himself by gripping the overhead rod. As Tekla lifted off the first few hangers, Joe slipped across behind them to the unmade bed and underneath to the far side.

Rearing up between bed and draperies, he considered the suitcase that lay open atop the tangled sheets and blankets. He was poised to disappear again if they turned. The suitcase was packed with Spandex pants and shirts, most of them black. On top of a folded black tank top lay a handgun, a dark automatic. The clip was in, and he assumed that was loaded. Another clip lay beside it, and two boxes of ammunition marked *.32 caliber brass jacketed hollow point*, a hundred rounds each. The same caliber bullets as the one that killed Ben.

If he could get out of here with the gun, that would be all ballistics needed—compare these riflings to the bullet that murdered Ben.

Why had he been so sure he'd *find* a gun? The *right* gun? *And, what am I doing shut in this house within grabbing distance of these people?* They'd seen him at the remodel; they knew him, if they'd paid any attention. Whatever, they'd have to wonder what a cat was doing in here.

So they wonder. So, what are they going to think? That I'm tossing the place?

But even so, Sam and Tekla gave him the creeps. In the closet, Sam was saying, " . . . was a stupid thing to do, a cockamamie idea. You only set the cops onto us."

"They were *already* onto us, poking around like they were."

"That's your imagination."

"That boy was right there in the house that morning, he could have seen everything."

"Then why didn't he tell the cops?"

"*I* don't know, Sam. But I don't trust him. And it was too good an opportunity to miss, you falling like that on the edge of the walk, wrenching your arm and crying out. There was no one around to say you weren't pushed and that it wasn't the boy did it. I *thought* he was alone this morning, we *saw* the contractor and that red-bearded carpenter in the village, I *thought* he'd be alone in the remodel and no one to say where he really was . . . Put him in as bad a light as possible in case he did tell what he saw that morning. Maybe he saw nothing, maybe he heard the shot, but make a liar of him right off, *before* he started talking. It was just too good *not* to say it was him. How was I to know he was with the damn cops?"

"You blew it, Tekla. And you made me lie for you. Again," he said darkly.

"I never made you lie for me. You could have—"

Sam laughed, a bitter, small sound. "What was I supposed to do? Call you a liar, in front of the cops?

"As it is," he said, easing out of the closet and into his wheelchair, "they're suspicious now, all right. Hurry it up, let's get moving. They might have already put a watch on this place."

He was silent a moment, getting settled properly in the wheelchair. "I want out, Tekla. I want out of this now, I want done with this even if Herbert was—is—my son."

As Sam turned the chair to wheel toward the bed, Joe slid to the floor and behind the draperies. Looking out through the small space where the two drapes met, he watched Tekla turn to the suitcase carrying a plastic grocery bag. "And what about the house?" Sam was saying. "All that work—and money."

"Have we ever worried about money? I have my ways. When we get where we're going, we contact the Realtor, sell the house in the name of Bleak." She turned to look at him. "There was a good chance no one would ever find out, that we could have stayed right here, live rich in this village for a while. Rub elbows with the movie stars," she said, laughing.

"It didn't work out, did it, Tekla?"

"No matter. Everything's set up for the sale, escrow and bank accounts in the Bleak name, fix it like we always do. Sell the place from a distance and move on." Reaching deep in the suitcase beneath the folded black spandex, she pulled out four rust-colored folders, the kind of heavy envelopes that a bank might use. Fanning them out, she chose one. "This will do."

Putting the other three back beneath the clothes, she shoved the one envelope in her purse. She removed a golf cap from the plastic bag, wadded the bag inside to keep the cap from wrinkling, and tucked it down in the side of the suitcase. The plain beige cap had a ponytail attached to the back, a dark auburn hairpiece—stirring a perfect picture of early mornings when the cats would see a lone runner on the beach, her auburn ponytail bouncing in the dawn light.

Though sometimes they would see a blonde running, equally petite, loose blond hair streaming out the back, and sometimes running with a young boy. Or sometimes it was two boys, both wearing baseball caps.

Tekla picked up the gun, checked what Joe assumed was the safety. She fished a soft, pistol-shaped gun case from a side pocket of the suitcase, slipped the gun and the extra clip into it, zipped it up, and slid it back into the slim pocket.

"Aren't you going to . . . ?"

"I don't want to be caught with the guns. Not until we're out of California. Unsecured, loaded guns on us, and an underage kid in the same car?" She looked at Sam, scowling. "I don't think so."

"What *about* Arnold?"

"I called the school, he's on his way. I said his daddy was hurt bad, had been assaulted like those others. He . . ." They heard the front door slam, and Arnold called out.

"In here," Tekla answered as Joe drew deeper behind the drapery. Adult eyes, even Tekla's, might miss him. But kids were so nosy, and Arnold made him nervous. And what did she mean, guns? Where were the rest? How many guns? What did they have, a whole arsenal?

"What are you doing?" Arnold said, stomping in.

"Get packed," Tekla said.

He kicked at the corner of the bed. "Why are we leaving this time? What's happened now?"

"Just get packed. Make it snappy."

Arnold stomped out. Joe listened to him banging around in the other bedroom as if heaving his possessions into a suitcase. But Joe had to smile. They might think they were hauling out of there, but Harper's patrol would have a tail on them, pronto. What made them imagine they could dodge the cops in that big white van?

When Sam retreated to the closet again, and Tekla

followed him, reaching to sort through another load of clothes, Joe slid up into the suitcase. Feeling carefully along the sides and between the folded layers, he searched for other guns. He shocked himself, quickly drew his paw back, when he uncovered the cold stainless steel of a big, heavy revolver.

It was twice the size of the automatic, smooth and slick to the paw, not holstered, not encased in anything he could carry.

But the one he wanted was the automatic, the gun that could have killed Ben. Feeling into the narrow pocket where he'd seen her stash the padded gun case, he took it in his teeth. Praying the safety was indeed on and that there was no shell in the chamber, gingerly he hauled it out. Easing it to the floor, he half carried, half slid it across to the armoire, guiding the muzzle away from him, all the while keeping an eye on the closet and listening to Arnold banging around; he didn't want to hear silence from the boy, see him slipping back into the bedroom.

With a careful paw he pushed the gun case under the armoire as far back as he could reach. If she missed this gun and went looking for it, maybe she wouldn't look here.

The banging from the next room stopped. When Arnold's footsteps started down the hall Joe slid fast under the armoire, flat on his belly beside the gun case, flat as a sardine mashed in a can.

At the bedroom door, Arnold paused. "You want the suitcases in the van?"

"Leave them by the front door," Tekla said.

Arnold turned, his footsteps scuffing away down the hall. Joe heard him drop his suitcase by the door. Tekla swung over to the bed, stood a moment as if arranging clothes in the open suitcase, then a thump and click as she closed and latched it. The space beneath the armoire smelled of dust, dust clung to his whiskers, and, peering out, he could see dust under the bed and along the edge of the fallen blankets. He hoped to hell he wasn't going to sneeze. Across the dusty floor he could clearly see drag marks where he'd moved the gun and that made his heart pound.

Tekla, busy hauling the suitcase out to the entry, barely noticed Sam grappling with his own, smaller suitcase and the wheelchair. He finally got the suitcase aboard, and the chair turned around in the tight space. Tekla was much more helpful in public. At the front of the house Joe heard a door open, but not the front door with its squeaky hinge. The other bedroom door *was* open. Only the garage had been closed.

Could they have another car? He'd never seen them in anything but the van. Could they have kept a car hidden, ready to travel? They meant to leave the van so it would look like they were still home? If they left in a different car, without a description, they'd be hell to find once they got out on the freeways. A cop would have to spot the Bleaks themselves, and because of Tekla's little tricks with hairstyles, even that could be iffy.

26

JOE HEARD TEKLA drag a suitcase across the entry, heard it clunk down a couple of steps into the garage and the door slam. He heard a click and then a thunk, as if the tailgate of a hatchback or SUV had been opened Skinning out from beneath the armoire, he slipped down the hall, leaving the gun hidden. Halfway down, he froze. The door to the garage opened and Arnold clumped in—but he turned away to the kitchen. Joe heard the refrigerator open. While the kid was occupied, Joe hit for the bench and under it.

Tekla's purse stood on top. He longed to claw it open and drag out that narrow brown envelope. He pulled deeper into the shadows as Arnold came back munching, smelling of peanut butter. The boy, turning back into the garage, let the door slam behind him: one of those spring-hinged jobs as lethal as a spring-loaded rat trap. Before the door slammed shut Joe tried to see in, see what kind of car, but he got only a glimpse. The space was dim, the big garage door still closed. With Arnold blocking the view, he could see only a dull brown, dirt-encrusted rear fender and open tailgate where the car had been backed in, perhaps for faster loading. Now, with the inner door to the house shut again, he heard the faint sounds of suitcases thumping into the back and the mumble of their voices, could make out only a few scattered words. Behind him Sam was coming down the hall, sounded as if he were pushing his wheelchair, leaning on it in an uneven walk. The garage door opened again and Tekla came into the entry. "Leave the chair, Arnold will bring it. Arnold, help your father get in the car."

Arnold appeared, shoving the last of his sandwich in his mouth. In that moment, as he clumsily handed his father down the two steps into the garage, Joe saw the SUV more clearly, but it didn't help much. Faded brown in color and far from new, but he didn't recognize the make, nor could he see a logo. Creeping out straining to see the license, he sucked back fast as Tekla turned.

Picking up her coat and purse from atop the bench above him, and Sam's and Arnold's jackets, she hauled them into the garage, letting the door slam closed. This time Joe heard the dead bolt turn. In a moment the car started, the garage door rumbled up, he heard them pull out and the door rattled down again.

He leaped at the knob, swinging and kicking—but the dead bolt held tight. They were gone, gone before he'd seen much of the car, and sure as hell they were headed for the freeway.

The van still stood in the narrow drive, the van the police would be watching. Paws sweating in his haste, he searched the house for a phone. He looked everywhere, every room, but found only empty jacks. They must have used only their cell phones. Half their belongings were still scattered about. In Arnold's room, wrinkled clothes, school papers, empty drink cans strewn everywhere. By the front door, the three coats still hung abandoned. But they'd taken the front-door key.

They couldn't have left it unlocked? *Were* they gone for good and didn't care if someone came in? Maybe they had simply left what they didn't want? Leaping, he swung on the knob until he'd turned it. Holding it, kicking hard against the molding, he fought until he was out of breath but he couldn't force it open.

He wanted out of there, wanted to get to a phone. Turning, he surveyed the small crowded rooms.

He seldom saw a house he couldn't break into or out of. Always he and Dulcie were able to jimmy a window or a lock somewhere. But as he made the rounds of the small cottage, leaping up to each sill, he found himself fighting uselessly. The metal bolt locks were driven down hard into the molding; all were so old they maybe wouldn't slide at all. Didn't these people ever open a window? The old house had settled, too, making everything even harder to operate. Maybe the bedroom slider would work better; he had seen a narrow patio beyond. Maybe in spite of the position of the bed, they might have used that opening on warm nights.

Slipping in behind the bedroom draperies, he peered at the slim crack where the moldings met. He could glimpse the engaged dead bolt, the door securely locked. When he leaped for the lever that would unlock it, it flipped right down. Scrambling up again he gripped the handle with both paws and kicked against the wall. Kicked again and again. The door remained solidly closed, stuck tight. Or was it screwed close? Yes, when he examined the bottom molding, there were four big screws embedded.

When he checked the bathroom window, it was frozen in place. They sure as hell didn't believe in fresh air. Or the landlord didn't. Doubling back through the house, he peered up at the ceiling-high heat vents, their grids secured with rusted screws. Even if he could climb on the bookcase in the boy's room—which was crowded with junk and sports equipment, not books—even if he could somehow get into the vent, where would that lead him?

Inside the heater, that's where.

By the time he reached the kitchen, one bruised paw was bleeding and he felt as mean as the Rottweiler. By this time the Bleaks would be well out of town on one of the freeways, headed who knew where? And the van still in the drive to keep Harper's patrol complacent. Springing to the counter beside the sink, he peered out the kitchen window.

The main house was just to his left. Straight ahead across the narrow, scrubby yard and just inside the woven fence, the Rottweiler was demolishing the last of the oak branch. Joe envisioned a huge lump of splinters in the dog's stomach. Despite his distaste for the mean-tempered animal, Joe didn't envy him that misery.

A light was on in the yellow house, in what looked like the kitchen. Behind the thin curtains he could see a figure moving about, maybe fixing a bite of lunch. Stepping onto the sill Joe tried the window lock, but this, too, was totally stuck. One of those ancient curved jobs that would have to be turned with pliers. Maybe even pliers couldn't budge it—the device was thick with coats of old paint. Watching through the window as the Rottweiler pursued his frenzied chewing, Joe reared up against the glass.

The moment the dog paused to get his breath Joe let out a bloodcurdling yowl and raked his claws down the pane. The scritching sound put even Joe's teeth on edge. The Rottweiler paused, looking up. Joe stretched taller and gave another howl. The dog stared at him, roared, and charged the fence hard enough to break through—but the fence held. When Joe yowled and clawed again, the Rottweiler's barking frenzy brought the back door crashing open. A broad-shouldered, bearded man stepped out clutching a leash in one hand, a cell phone in the other, holding the phone to his ear—talking, and watching the cottage.

Joe couldn't hear a word with the dog roaring. Twice the man stopped talking to shout at the dog, but it kept on barking and lunging. Still talking on the phone, the guy came down off the porch and headed for the cottage. He paused once, looked back uncertainly at the dog, glanced down at the leash, and turned back toward the closed gate.

Don't bring him. Leave him be, he'll only complicate matters, don't bring the damned dog.

The man opened the gate, shouting to quiet the animal. When he leashed the Rottweiler, the dog settled down. Together man and beast headed for the cottage.

Joe heard them walking around the yard, circling the

house, the dog huffing and snarling. When Joe heard the man's step on the porch and the click of doggy toenails he fled past the front door to the open alcove where the coats were left hanging. He leaped, hung with his paws on the shelf above the hooks. With his hind feet he kicked down the wrinkled jackets, dropped on top of them and pawed them into a heap. They smelled of the boy and of Tekla. Outside the glass, the man had paused, still talking on the phone. Yes, he was talking with the dispatcher. Joe waited, listening.

"No, I'll stay on the line," the man said irritably. He spoke again to the dog, to quiet him, then he knocked and called out to Tekla. His shadow shone through the obscure glass, waiting, listening, the dog a dark mass moving restlessly against his knee.

When no one answered, he knocked harder and called out again. He waited, then, "They're not home," he told the dispatcher. "But my dog don't bark for nothing. *Yes*, send the patrol. My dog don't bark for no reason." When Joe heard keys jingle, he raced halfway down the hall. There, Joe Grey did the unthinkable.

He backed up against the wall and sprayed.

Streaking to the bedroom, he did the same on the bedroom door and then hastily sprayed the bed. Storming back to the entry, he heard the key turn in the lock. Diving beneath the jackets, Joe was out of sight when the door edged open. The Rottweiler, pressing his face at the crack, got a good whiff of tomcat and let out an echoing roar. Joe was peering out, ready to leap up for the closet shelf, when the Rottweiler lunged through, exploded into the entry as black and huge as a rodeo bull, jerking the leash so hard the big man could barely hold him. Charging toward the hall, he bolted for the smell of Joe's markings, the man double-timing behind him, leaving the door wide.

And Joe was out of there.

Leaping from beneath the jackets, he flew out through the open door as two cops answered the landlord's call, pulling in behind the van.

Parking their police unit, Officers Brennan and Crowley got out and approached the open door, their hands poised near their holstered weapons. Joe watched from the bushes for only a moment and then he was off, scrambling up the oak to the roofs, streaking away home. Racing for a phone, to get the message to Brennan and Crowley before they cleared the house and left again. He wanted them to find the gun, not leave it there unguarded. He wanted them, in proper police procedure, to bag it at once, fresh with Tekla's prints.

27

 DULCIE, HAVING BEEN chauffeured home by Charlie—like an invalid, she thought irritably—woke much later warm and cozy curled in Wilma's lap.

It was late afternoon, the westering sun slanting in through the living room windows across Wilma's cherry desk. How *hard* she had slept. She woke filled with strange dreams, though already they were fading. She tried to bring them back, but they had flown apart, vanishing into fragments. Why did dreams *do* that?

All that remained was the sense of danger, of Joe Grey's fear. But now even that was fading—and as fear vanished, she was filled with Joe's wild amusement. She could hear faintly from the dream the roar of a barking dog. She sat up, puzzled, kneading Wilma's leg, pushing Wilma's book aside.

Wilma stroked her, watching her. "What?" she said softly.

"A dog, a huge dog threatening Joe. A gun. And . . . Tekla. Tekla Bleak," she said, hissing. "But now . . . Joe's all right, it's all right. He's all right," she said, purring. She looked into the fire that burned on the hearth, trying to sort out what she'd seen, what exactly had happened. As she reached for the dream again, trying to slip back into its shadows, faces and action overlapped into softer visions, and soon she dozed once more and Wilma returned to her book.

But then as she fell into sleep a brighter vision touched Dulcie, not a dream at all but something more alive and urgent shaking her awake, her heart pounding.

"It's time," she said, leaping down from Wilma's lap. "Something's happening, it's time."

"The kittens!" Wilma said, shoving her book aside and getting up.

"No," Dulcie said, "not the kittens. It's Misto." She shivered, staring at Wilma. "It's time to go to Misto."

Wilma grabbed her purse, smothered the fire with ashes, found a jacket on the hook in the kitchen. She never questioned Dulcie's perception. She picked Dulcie up gently and they were out the kitchen door into the bright afternoon, into the car, backing out. "What did you see? What did you dream?"

Dulcie snuggled close against her. "I was with Misto in another place, not Molena Point, not this world but a place so bright, larger than our world could ever be, the sky stretching away more huge than *our* sky and millions of miles of green hills rolling on and on and up into endlessness . . . And yet," Dulcie said, "at the same moment we were in our own village, so tiny in those vast spaces. I can't explain how that could be, we floated in eternity but still were in our own tiny village, and then . . . And then Misto and I were in the village library but the room, the book stacks, were dwarfed like a tiny jewel in endless space. We were looking through old, old books at pictures of my little calico, the way I dream of her, the way Misto describes her. We were looking at our girl kitten over the centuries. The same sweet face, sly and clever, the same faded calico markings and dark swirling stripes, and her little soft paws.

"There she was in those ancient tapestries and books, in lives so many generations gone. There, in one century and then another, born to different times, though Misto said she will remember little of those lives. But now," she said, "he has shown her to me for the last time. Now Misto himself is going home. My dream of Courtney is his parting gift."

Slowing the car, Wilma turned onto the Firettis' street. She felt cold, her hands shaking. Parking before the cottage, she lifted Dulcie as if, Dulcie thought, she were as frail as porcelain. Contritely Dulcie leaped from Wilma's arms into the fern bed by the Firettis' front door, the fronds soft beneath her tummy and paws. She waited as Wilma knocked, both strung tight with heartbreak—but both would smile and comfort Misto. They would offer only brightness to the old cat, would lay only love before the venerable cat they so treasured.

IN MUCH THE same way that Dulcie knew Misto needed her, Kit looked up suddenly from hunting gophers in Lucinda's garden. She had come home from MPPD alone, abandoned by Joe, left on her own by Dulcie and Ryan and Charlie; had padded home feeling lonely and not sufficiently praised for finding and retrieving the evidence of shoes; had padded home to her empty house, to hunt alone in her empty garden. But now suddenly she turned from the gopher hole, startled. She listened. She sat very still looking away across the village, hearing in her thoughts a bright whisper. She felt awash suddenly in brilliance. Joy filled her, a need filled her, the old cat was calling to her . . .

She was distracted suddenly as the gopher stuck his head out. She grabbed and killed it all in a second, in a fast reflex, and then she bolted away, left the dead gopher lying limp and forgotten. The old cat was calling her. She raced away through neighbors' gardens and up to the roofs and down and down across the shingles and peaks of cottages and shops, hurrying, sprinting for the Firettis' cottage.

BUT JOE GREY, bolting home from the Bleaks' empty rental, was driven by another mission. Still smiling at his well-timed escape from the Rottweiler, he leaped into his tower and through it onto the high rafter and dropped down onto Clyde's desk. From the love seat Snowball looked up at him sleepily. She was alone; likely Rock was with Ryan. The little white cat yawned, watching him paw at a pile of papers. Finding his cell phone he punched in the one digit for Max Harper. He waited only two rings.

"Harper," the chief said shortly.

"The Bleaks have skipped. Left town in another car, a small brown SUV. Clothes, suitcases, maps, like they're set to travel. I didn't get a good look at the car, can't tell you the make, couldn't see the license. It was in that little garage where they were renting, it was gone when your officers got there. If they're still there," Joe said, "there's a gun in the bedroom, under the armoire. A loaded automatic, in a gun case. Get it out before the damned dog—"

"They have the gun," Max said, amused. "The dog did find it, but he couldn't get his nose under." Max was silent, then, "We lifted a couple of pretty good prints, good match for Tekla's. We've sent the gun to the lab."

Once again Joe smiled to hear that Max was confiding in him. This whole situation was different from past cases. But there was something else that he hadn't yet told Max. "There's a second gun in Tekla's suitcase. A big, stainless steel revolver. I couldn't get a good look to tell what make."

But it was the automatic that was the real evidence. If the riflings on it matched the bullet that killed Ben, they'd have the Bleaks cold. Have evidence far more telling than a notebook and phone and torn pieces from a mouse nest.

And yet now, even after Max had thanked him and they'd ended the call, Joe had an edgy, "something waiting in the background" feeling, as if something were yet to happen. He looked down at Snowball, who was deeply asleep again. He listened to the hollowness of the empty house. He stared away to the east of the village where Ocean Avenue met Highway One, where the Bleaks would have escaped—and suddenly he was out of there, leaping nervously from the desk to the rafter.

With a sudden sure sense of what *was* wrong, he was through his tower onto the shingles, streaking away across the roofs of the village plaza and the cottages and shops beyond. Heading not toward the tangle of highways where the Bleaks would be speeding, where no cat could ever catch them. Heading for Firetti's Veterinary Clinic, led strongly now by the same urgency that had called Dulcie and had summoned Kit.

IN THE FIRETTI bedroom, the old cat didn't sleep. He was not, this day, feeling exhausted; he was not drugged by medication. He had had no pain shots since the night before, nor did he want them. His body was in a transition that he knew well.

Though he was weak, he had put his failing aside, had found a new temporary strength. He sat tall on the bed, snuggled all around by his furry entourage, by Kit and Pan and Dulcie, and now Joe Grey as the tomcat slipped in across the room and up on the bed to join them. In Joe's eyes there was sadness, there was hurt at what was to come.

The cats heard Wilma's and Mary's voices from the living room, but the two women didn't enter. They heard the fire crackle to life and sensed its warmth. The old cat looked at each of them and smiled. He put a paw on the paw of his son Pan, his constant companion these last days. He looked at Kit. "You found shoes," he said, smiling. "You hauled all that evidence across the yards and hid it for Captain Harper to find."

Kit beamed.

He looked at Joe and the old cat shook his head. "That Rottweiler could have eaten you in one gulp, tomcat."

Joe's eyes widened. The venerable cat's omniscience unnerved him.

"You did well, Joe Grey. But you'll soon be a father." He gave Joe a stern look but said no more. Smiling at Joe, he turned to Dulcie.

"You have another poem in your head, my dear. So much goes on, within. Even as you nurture your kittens, that clear voice nudges you. Those words want life, too. Your verses want to take *their* place in this world. Will you tell us this one?"

"A little of it," Dulcie shyly. "Just a little . . ."

> *Duchess of the garbage can*
> *Queen of the alley*
> *Lolling under dustbins*
> *Rolling fat and jolly*
> *No thin beggar, never shy*
> *This lady dines most royally*
> *Fine salami, leftover Brie*
> *Scraps of salmon from the sea*
> *She is beautifully obese*
> *Who feasts on kippers and roast geese*
> *Queen of the garbage can*
> *Duchess of the alley*
> *Accepting largesse with greed*
> *Rolling fat and jolly.*

Her words made Misto laugh. "Your children will grow up on poetry," he told her. "Poetry and," he said, looking at Joe Grey, "maybe on cop work, too."

The old cat settled back, and he told them a final tale. He held close his guardians of love. They waited together for his final moment, for the instant when he would step away from them into his next great journey. Misto painted for them, now, realms he would again travel; he gave them views down upon the earth, deep into ancient lands as if those times were again alive. He showed Joe and Dulcie moments from their kittens' own pasts, each experience a tangle of puzzles.

Slyly Misto showed Joe Grey the tomcat's past lives that Joe did not remember and didn't want to remember. At Joe's dismay, Misto laughed.

To Joe, those faraway moments, if they had ever really existed, were gone and done, not part of life here and now. Life was in the moment and that was as it should be.

But for Dulcie and Kit and Pan, the glimpses Misto gave them into kinder realms beyond earthly evil, that promise was a valued gift, and the cats reached their paws close around him. They held Misto, snuggled with him as he dozed in a light and easy sleep. It was later in the small hours of morning that they woke.

28

Misto died before dawn. It was
just after four, the witching hour, the
hour when restless human sleepers
wake filled with unsettling thoughts,
when restless felines rise and stretch
bright eyed and hit the bedroom floor or the cold ground,
ready to prowl, that secret and exciting hour that all cats
welcome, knowing adventure waits.

Misto woke fully from last night's gentle sleep. Beside him, Pan and Kit and Joe and Dulcie still slept, deep
under, curled close around him. Misto smiled at the dear
cats, guardians of his frail body and of his restless spirit.
John and Mary lay on the bed dozing near them, but when
Misto woke, they woke. All four cats woke, startled.

It was time.

Misto lifted his head and looked at John; his look said

the pain had returned and it was very bad. His look said that now he wanted help. It was time.

John Firetti rose, and with care and tenderness he prepared the shot that would bring a cessation of pain, that would bring peace. Tenderly he administered the medication and, leaning down, he kissed Misto's forehead and ears. Mary leaned close over the other cats, kissing Misto's face.

In seconds he was gone.

Now, in this world, Misto slept deep and forever, but beyond this world a brightness glowed. They all could see it, they watched Misto's spirit rise up, they could feel his passing, they saw his golden form as delicate as gauze above them. He was, for a moment, a clear light above them, and then he was gone. To another place.

They sat with him for some time. No one moved or spoke. From far away they felt his spirit caress them, and an echo of his thoughts drifted back to them: *Do not grieve, I am with you. You have lives to live, wrongs to right before you complete your journey. You have kittens to raise,* his voice said with a smile, *before you move on to the next adventure.*

As dawn began to color the sky, John and Mary rose. They fetched the little casket that John had prepared, with its carved designs of flowers and trees and its silk liner. They laid Misto within, and John said a prayer for him.

In the living room Wilma rose from the couch where she had dozed. They carried Misto in his small casket to his resting place, which Mary had prepared in the garden. The morning was chill, barely light, the sky streaked with trails of dark clouds and the first hints of sunrise shining through; it was the kind of morning Misto liked best.

The humans knelt. John uncovered the grave he had dug, set among its five granite boulders. The cats crept close and sat quietly. It was then that Kate appeared and, behind her, silent and close together, came Ryan and Clyde, and Charlie. Ryan took Wilma's hand. Both wiped away tears.

John laid Misto's casket in the flower-lined grave between the granite boulders. They patted the earth down, each hand and each paw adding a benediction.

When the grave was covered, each mourner said a few words, then Mary planted primroses over the little mound. As they turned away, weeping, in Dulcie's head the words of a poem began. The first few words of an ode to Misto, a bright caress that would be a long time in the making, but would speak for all of them.

> *Golden spirit, you reach down*
> *Your ghostly paw to touch the earth you love*
> *To touch the sea*
> *To stroke the lakes and rivers . . .*

29

I<small>T WAS LATER</small> that morning that Max Harper received a third call on the BOL for Tekla and Sam Bleak. All three reports were from California Highway Patrol. Max hadn't had much description to put out, no make or model, no year, no license number. Just an older brown SUV, faded and dirty. One responder thought it might be an older Chevy. None caught the license number, the plates were smeared with dirt. In one response the car carried three occupants. In the others, only two people were visible. It annoyed him that the snitch hadn't gotten a better handle on the car, hadn't found a way to follow it. But then, Max hadn't been there to witness the action; maybe the car *had* vanished too fast. The positive part was, in all three calls the car was moving east, heading now through Nevada.

This same morning, in Anchorage, the Greenlaws

parted from Mike and Lindsey Flannery, watched them take off in a light plane for a few more days of fishing north of Anchorage. The Greenlaws spent the morning comfortably before the Inn's fireplace. Their flexible schedule and their several side trips aboard small ferries had been exciting, but they were tired out, they missed Kit, they worried about her—it was time to go home.

And it was much earlier that morning that, up at the new shelter construction, Kate Osborne ended up crying in the arms of Ryan's uncle Scott, her tears drenching Scotty's red beard. Kate wasn't sure how this had happened. Scotty wasn't sure what Kate was crying about. He knew she was grieving for Ben. He knew that the Firettis' old yellow cat had died, that Ryan and Billy were sad about him, too.

But no one could tell Scotty how deep the grieving went, no one could tell him Misto's story. In Scotty's arms, she didn't try to stop the tears; she just let herself weep.

She was well aware that Joe Grey and Ryan were glancing in their direction, trying not to show their interest in this sudden tenderness—but did they have to stare?

When she had arrived at the shelter site, parking beside Ryan's red king cab, Scotty had looked up from where he was installing a window. He had paused in his work, watching her approach, had looked hard at her, at her tear-blotched face. She had headed on back into the building, but he'd stopped her.

"Kate?"

She'd turned, looking at him in spite of her tears. He'd switched off the drill, laid it down and, as natural as the shining of the sun, he'd put his arms around her, had held her, let her cry against him. Across the yard Joe Grey, draped over Ryan's shoulder, watched the couple until Ryan politely walked away to disappear behind the building.

"When did this start?" she asked the tomcat. "It's just this week that I've noticed."

Joe shrugged. "How do I know when it started? You put Scotty up here working on the shelter, and Kate is here all the time. How can he work around Kate Osborne and not be aware of her, she's a knockout."

Ryan looked at him. She said nothing. She moved farther back among the raw wooden beams and posts behind the main building. Sunlight warmed the plastered block walls of the shelter and warmed the three outdoor enclosures—these open-air spaces would be living quarters for dozens of feral cats who would not want to be shut inside. Wild-living cats that CatFriends would neuter, give their shots, and turn loose again in their own colonies.

Ryan said, "If Scotty and Kate get serious, that does present problems."

Joe agreed. Scotty and Kate would be another couple where one partner knew the cats' secret and one didn't. Scotty had no notion the cats could speak. Not an easy way to live, where one member of a happy couple had to harbor lies, as did Charlie Harper. No happily wed couple wanted the dark specter of deception shadowing their honesty with each other. And in Kate's case, the stress could be worse.

Kate, who had divorced a philandering husband long ago, said she'd never trust another man. Scotty, the loner, dated casually but had never found a woman he loved—he said he wouldn't marry for less than a deep, true commitment. How would Kate hide the truth from him, when she herself had such a close connection to speaking cats?

Joe looked around for Billy, wondering if he, too, had been watching Kate and Scotty, but then he remembered this was a full school day in the work/school schedule that had been set up for the boy. Joe had turned on Ryan's shoulder so he could look behind them when Ryan spoke softly. "Look," she whispered, facing away toward the tree-sheltered Pamillon mansion that stood beyond the rise.

Across the hilly meadow, on the remains of a fallen stone wall, a brown tabby crouched. "One of the clowder cats?" Kate said. "Oh, have they come back from the Netherworld, too? But Kit and Pan can't know, they didn't say anything."

Joe stretched up from her shoulder to look. The tabby was gone, but a white face peered out from the shadows; he could barely see her pale calico against the light stone wall. "Willow," he said. "That's Willow! I don't see the tabby, but Willow's back! They're back!" He leaped down to join the clowder cats, racing away.

Ryan stood looking after him. What would this mean? Were the ferals still fine with her building the shelter here? They'd better be, at this late stage. They'd known about it before they descended down the tunnels to that other world. She would not have begun the project without Joe and Dulcie and Kit and Pan seeking out the wild clowder and telling them. *Asking them*, she thought, smiling.

The ferals had seemed all right with the plan, had seemed comfortable with the close proximity to the rescues. They were pleased with this caring human help for cats in need. Though no one had been sure, in fact, that the little group of feral cats *would* return from the Netherworld; there were charms and wonders in both lands.

Kate had situated the shelter, and the road that approached it, nearly half a mile from the mansion, away from the ferals' preferred hunting grounds, from the overgrown rose gardens and the woods beyond. Ryan and Kate hoped, as the shelter was populated, as volunteers came and went, they wouldn't drive the shy little band away. They would never want to do that. They had already posted small signs around the mansion grounds marking that area dangerous and off-limits.

When Ryan heard the sound of the drill once more and saw Scotty back at work, she found Kate inside the main building in a large communal room, busy with her drawing pad. Planning the cat perches, the overhead walks, the lofts and hiding places to entice the resident cats. Laying down her drawing pad, Kate handed Ryan one end of her tape measure. Neither spoke of Scotty. Kate smiled and hugged Ryan, showed her what she wanted to measure, and said nothing more.

JOE GREY GALLOPED across the wide, hilly berm and through scattered trees into the weedy grounds of the stone mansion, searching for Willow and the ferals. There, by the stone wall: Willow came out, stepping delicately, smiling, then rubbing whiskers with Joe. One by one the ferals appeared to greet him. Soon he was surrounded by seven cats all talking at once. He followed them deep behind the big house where no human would see or hear them. Their eyes were bright with a secret, their tails lashing. There was no small talk, not even tales of their return up the tunnels. What were they so eager to tell him? He had no notion that their message would send him racing away again for a phone.

The ferals greeted him with nose touches and rollovers and a little crazy chasing, then they led him to a narrow dirt road back in the trees beyond the mansion. "You'll want to see this," pale-coated Sage said. "This might be for the police. These people that were here made our fur bristle. Those humans coming here into the ruins, they were scum."

The cats led him down the old sunken road, hidden deep in the woods, where he and Dulcie had sometimes wandered. It was hardly wide enough for a car, so cars never came there. But now a car had come, its tire marks fresh and deep in the mud where a small rivulet crossed. Joe could see where the vehicle had parked and where it had turned around, making several passes, its bumpers and fenders biting into the earthen berm. The feral cats crowded around him, dark tabby Coyote, creamy Tansy, light tabby Sage, and Willow of the pale calico coat, all seven of the small band of ferals that had ventured down to the Netherworld. Willow said, "This is your kind of hunting, Joe Grey. Hunting humans. Those people smelled of evil."

"The car nearly got stuck," Coyote said, the long-eared tabby smiling with pleasure. "They came here in daylight yesterday. The first thing they did was turn the car around. Took them a long time, big clumsy wheels spinning in the mud," and that made Coyote laugh. "Way too big for this narrow road. They waited until dark to leave. Hiding," the dark tabby said. "Hiding from what?"

"Did they see you?" Joe said.

"Not us," said Sage, glancing at Tansy. "They had a boy, a big, rude boy, he got out and stamped around in the woods and broke branches and threw them. We made ourselves scarce."

"What kind of car?" Joe said, not expecting them to remember. "What make?" The ferals didn't pay much attention to man's noisy machines, except usually to avoid them.

"Brown," Willow said. "Like a station wagon."

"An SUV?"

"I think so. It opened in the back so you could see through to the front. There were suitcases, blankets, as if for traveling. We could see the mark that said Ford. The license was all mud, caked and dry. But close up, you could read it. We thought you might want to know what that was?"

Joe Grey smiled. "Of course I do." Well, the ferals did know, from past encounters, what police work was about. When Willow told him the number he said it over twice, committing it to memory. Now he burned to get to a phone. He said his hasty good-byes, nudged each cat gently and touched noses and promised to return soon.

"Most likely," Joe said, "a detective will be out to look the scene over, to photograph the tire marks and those footprints back and forth into the woods."

"What about our pawprints?" Willow said.

Joe thought about that. "They know there are feral cats up here, they think you are one of the wild bands that CatFriends feeds. Charlie has made it clear you are to be left alone, to be protected. They won't be surprised to see pawprints." He gave Willow a final friendly nudge, spun around and raced back through the woods and across the berm to Ryan, praying she hadn't left.

He found her in the car, sitting quietly. He leaped in. "Thank God you waited."

"What else would I do? You take off like gangbusters, all riled up. I knew I'd better wait."

Standing in her lap he snatched up her cell phone and hit the button for the station—hoping he wouldn't get Evijean.

Of course he got Evijean. "Captain Harper is not . . ." she began with her delaying routine.

"Evijean," Joe said coldly, "I have the license number the chief is waiting for. If he doesn't get it *now*, *pronto*, you'll *never* get a recommendation for another job, no matter where you look—and believe me, you'll be looking."

Evijean put him through.

The conversation was brief. Max said, "I'm putting the information out as we speak. We'll see what this gets. Again, many thanks. This could reel in our fish." And he hung up.

When Joe ended the call Ryan grinned and caught him up in a hug that, as usual, deeply embarrassed him.

When he explained what the ferals had found, she hugged him again, and he felt her tear dampen his cheek. "Those dear clowder cats. I can't believe they've grown so close to humans—to care about human problems, to get that information to you."

She looked at him, frowning. "If you hadn't been here, do you think one of them would have come down into the village to find you? The village, the streets and buildings, seem so threatening to them."

"You and Kate were here, you're here every day. And Charlie. It was Charlie who sprung that trap for them when one of them was captured, sprung it and crushed it." Joe looked at her coolly. "They would have come to you," he said with assurance.

She nodded. "They've helped us, helped the law before. They *do* trust humans. When Sage was so badly hurt by that killer—when he was so scared—he put all his trust in John Firetti to help him—and that was hard," she said. "Sage was scared to death. But now," she said, "what made Tekla and Sam turn up in the hills onto that narrow little road instead of hitting the freeway?"

"When they left the rental," Joe said, "did they see an unmarked surveillance car? Or *thought* they saw one? Or they passed a black-and-white cruising, maybe it slowed to watch them?"

She smiled. "Whatever happened, they got nervous. Found a place to hole up until dark, *then* they doubled back to the freeway." She started the car, glancing down at Joe. "I guess you'll want a ride down to the station, to see how this falls out?"

"I guess I'd like that," Joe Grey said, twitching a whisker.

"The law will find them now, Joe, with this information. They're sure to stay on the freeways if they want to make any distance."

"Right. But which freeway?" He thought of the tangle of highways that led out of Molena Point. "Which freeway, Ryan? And heading where?"

30

ALONE IN HER tree house Kit huddled among her cushions sad and grieving, still licking away tears for Misto. Joe was with Ryan, up at the shelter. Dulcie would be cuddled close to Wilma. And Kit had parted from Pan at the Firettis': *Mary and John need him, they need Misto's son close. I need him, too, but they need him more. And I need Lucinda and Pedric, I need my dear humans. I need not to be alone just now.*

Why had the three of them ever parted? What if something happened to her old couple before they could return from that huge, cold land? *But what if something bad had happened in the Netherworld? How would that be any different? How would Lucinda and Pedric feel if Pan and I hadn't returned?*

Besides, she thought sensibly, *you could get hit by a truck right here in the village. Life is never certain, no one said it was*

*all neatly laid out and safe. No one said life comes with a guar-
antee. Pedric always tells Lucinda that. You have to walk quick,
watch quicker, and take your chances.*

But still she grieved. She napped, and when, waking,
still she felt lonely, she left her tree house and went down
into the gardens and wild fields to hunt.

It was late that evening that she slipped into Kate's
basement apartment, where Kate had installed a cat door.
Having feasted on mice, she licked all the blood off her
paws and whiskers to make herself presentable if she were
to sleep in Kate's bed. The cat door made her feel so welcome that she slept there with Kate that night, the next
night, and the next; in fact she moved right in. Missing
Lucinda and Pedric, she took solace in Kate's gentle ways
and in their small suppers together that were indeed more
companionable than any lone hunt. In bed at night they
talked about the Netherworld and about Kate's own adventures there in the darker realms that Kit and Pan had
avoided.

"The magic is all but gone," Kate said. "As the magic
dies, fewer and fewer children are born. Without the
magic that includes love, those babies who do live are pale
and weak. Even the shape-shifters' skills are fading . . . I
can no longer change," Kate said sadly. "After I decided
not to do that anymore, I tried twice." She looked shyly at
Kit. "I couldn't. I miss looking in the mirror and seeing
that lovely, cream-colored queen looking back at me, my
golden eyes and ivory whiskers, the marmalade streaks in
my fur."

Kate shook her head, embarrassed. "I *was* lovely," she
said longingly. "Though not as beautiful as you." She

stroked Kit's mélange of black, brown, and orange fur, as soft as silk. "I couldn't change," she said again sadly. "My own magic was gone."

Kit felt sad for her. But *she* couldn't change, either, she never had; in the Netherworld she and Pan had tried. But they were happy; they didn't need the complications that came with being a human person. Mortgages, income taxes, stalled cars. Let humans deal with those irritations. Maybe next time around she and Pan would be human, burdened with human responsibilities. But right now they were free spirits.

Each night Kit slept safe and content beside Kate, waiting for her own humans to come home. Each morning, Kate rose early, if only to enjoy the sunrise. She liked to sit on the deck with a cup of coffee, looking down on the village, watching the world come awake. On the fourth morning when Kit woke she heard the glass door slide closed, heard it lock, heard Kate's step up the outside stairs, heard her car start in the drive. Heard her back out and head away. Kit rose, yawning. Sometimes the carpenters came early to the shelter. In the tiny kitchen, leaping to the table, she found the porridge and the fried egg Kate had left for her. Beside them lay a note, held down by the porridge bowl.

Lucinda called my cell. They took a late flight last night, the four of them. I'm picking them up at San Jose. We'll be home before noon.

Kit licked the note, shivering. Lashing her tail, she raced the length of the apartment, leaped from book-shelves, bounced on the unmade bed, flew to the dresser and almost slid off again. She was so excited she thought she couldn't eat, but the next minute she was back in the kitchen devouring the cereal and egg, slurping it up so fast she scattered half of it on the table. Then she was out the cat door, up the hill, up her oak tree, up its rough bark into her tree house, where she could see the approaching street, where she tried to settle down to wait. *Tried* to settle down. Fidgeting and twitching, she knew quite well it would be hours before they got home.

She thought of going to tell Pan, but she didn't want to disturb their grieving household with her own excitement. She could go tell Dulcie and Wilma or she could tell Joe Grey if she could find him. She could *call* anyone, she wanted to tell *someone*.

But Kate would do that, Kate would call their friends from her cell phone; and Kit didn't want to leave home, because what if they caught an earlier flight and got home sooner than Kate said and she wasn't there at all? Sighing, she wriggled deeper into her pillows, put her nose under her paw and tried to be patient. For the flighty tortoiseshell, patience didn't work very well.

31

PICTURES OF SPORTING dogs filled the walls of Dallas Garza's office, a fine succession of bird dogs with whom Dallas had hunted for much of his childhood and most of his adult life; had hunted any time he could, between college, the police academy, and then police work. Dallas's last two, aged pointers had died not long ago. He had not bought another pup, he had little time now to train and work a sporting dog—and he was not a man to replace his respected hunting partners with a little lapdog; that was not his style.

Beneath the handsomely decorated walls, the detective's desk was a tangle of odd papers, handwritten notes, computer printouts, faxes, and bank information from a dozen cities: account numbers, the names of his contact at each bank. Leaning back in his chair, the phone to his ear, Dallas was talking with the manager of a small Kentucky bank. So far this, too, sounded like a dead end. Each account Tekla had opened across the country, each in a different name, had been closed out, the money withdrawn, and all information on the bank records had proved to be counterfeit. False addresses that turned out to be short-sale houses or vacant lots. He had left Juana's office some time ago, where she was tracking the couple through rental agreements.

The Bleaks had apparently lived this lifestyle for several years, under a revolving collection of pseudonyms. Apartments secured with invented information, bogus past employment that no rental office had bothered to check. Or, if the information had been looked into and found wanting, the applicants had simply been sent packing. Tekla and Sam would move on, and no complaint was made. What good was it to have efficient police, if civilians didn't pass on suspicious information when they had the chance?

When he heard Juana's step crossing the hall he motioned her in. She looked frustrated and tired. She poured a cup of coffee, filled Dallas's cup, sat down at one end of the couch, laid a clipboard on her lap, the page covered with neatly inscribed notes. They looked at each other in silence. They looked up when Max appeared, coming from his office, carrying a half cup of coffee. His twisted smile held them both.

"What?" Davis said.

"The Bleaks' brown SUV is a Ford," he said, looking smug. "Don't know what year, but we have the license number, I just put it on the BOL. It's all across the country now."

Davis laughed. Dallas said, "Was that from the snitch?"

Max grinned and nodded, making Dallas smile. The detective said, "I heard Evijean grousing at some phone call. When she shut right up, I assumed she put the call through. Is our snitch getting her trained?"

Max laughed. "Let's hope so." He glanced at Dallas's scattered notes, then at Juana's yellow pad. He sat down at the other end of the couch. "What've you got?"

"I think we know this much," Juana said, "the Bleaks—Gardners—began this marathon in Northern California, when son Herbert was first arrested on suspicion of molestation. As far as I can find, Gardner is their real name; they lived in Seattle for some years. Herbert was twenty-three when the first complaint was filed against him. Without sufficient evidence, Seattle held him only a short time, released him with a warning." She looked across at Max. "There was plenty of evidence, no reason the district attorney shouldn't have pursued the case. Would have saved everyone a lot of trouble—would have saved a life."

"Too busy," Dallas said, shrugging. "Docket too full."

"From that point on," Davis said, "I have twelve charges, all molestation. All insufficient evidence, or so the DA thought. Seattle, Tacoma, Spokane. Tekla and Sam had already distanced themselves from him. They moved to several cities in Southern California, then back up the coast to San Francisco. Herbert tracked them somehow. When he found them, he moved right in.

"Two weeks later he was arrested on a rape charge. A neighbor saw him attack the girl and identified him. Girl was hurt real bad, she filed charges, but then she dropped them, she was too scared. This time Tekla and Sam left the city in a hurry; they must have thought this one could turn really serious and didn't want to be involved. They changed names as usual, closed bank accounts, ended all contact with Herbert. I *think* I've traced them to Denver under one of the names, but that was some time ago. There's no new contact in Denver. I found where her father had left her a sizable amount of cash. She manipulated that very well, both legally and illegally, using a number of names."

Max said, "There's no indication they ever tried to put Herbert into treatment?"

"Not that I can find. As if they just wanted to get away from him." Davis looked up at the chief. "How often does treatment help a rapist?"

"It doesn't," Max said. "But getting him off the street helps. Now that we have some ID on the car, let's see what we can do. They've got Herbert locked down tight, but his murdering folks aren't much better." Max paused as Joe Grey strolled into the office, his ears up, his head high with tomcat bravado.

Leaping to the couch, Joe stretched out between Davis and Max. The chief looked mighty pleased, Joe thought. They all three did, and that made him hide a smile. The ferals had done all right, they'd found what the department needed. Now it was a matter of waiting for the enhanced BOL to pick up more reports—and a matter of Joe catching up on the conversation he'd missed. Rolling over closer to Juana, he leaned against her arm where he could see her notes.

Davis was saying, "After she filed charges, then dropped charges, as soon as she could travel she left the state. Scared, afraid Herbert would find her. Herbert did some jail time, then walked. Surprisingly, he stayed in the city. Found a job of sorts, as an assistant janitor, rented a cheap room.

"It was not until his next arrest, maybe three months later, that the charge stuck. He was found in the storeroom kneeling over the body of Marilain Candler. The head janitor walked in on him, hit him with a shovel. While he was down, janitor made the 911 call.

"Herbert's indicted for rape and murder," Davis said. "He chooses a jury trial. Tekla learns about it, in the papers or on TV, her son on trial for murder. And she has one of those emotional turnarounds. This is *her son*, charged with murder. Suddenly she's as angry as a mother tiger. They can't do this to *her* son. She hikes on out to San Francisco to be there for the trial. What did she think? That she could stand up for Herbert, could defend his character?"

Dallas smiled. "That could be the odd-looking woman in Ben's notes, the woman he watched from the jurors' box."

Davis nodded. "The woman always in the back row. When Herbert's convicted and gets the death sentence, that's the real turning point. She goes hot with rage against the jurors that convicted her boy. Herbert is misunderstood, he's been grossly wronged, and she vows that each and every juror will experience exactly what they dealt out to him."

Dallas finished his coffee. "I've called the lab twice to hurry them up on the ballistics. Maybe, now that we have the license number—if the Bleaks don't switch cars or change plates—someone will pick them up and ship them back to us."

"Let's hope," Juana said. Beside her, Joe Grey tried not to look smug. The license number and make of car were a big plus; he was mighty proud of his feral friends. That timely information from those shy, reclusive cats was one more nail in Tekla's coffin.

32

IN HER TREE house Kit turned round and round among her pillows. She curled up and dozed for a little while. She fidgeted and paced, waiting for Lucinda and Pedric to get home. The morning sun rose high and higher, but still it was far too early, it was a long drive from the San Jose airport to Molena Point. Below her, no car came along the street, not even a neighbor going to grocery shop or drop the kids at school. She slept fitfully again and dreamed of her elderly couple surrounded by polar bears. She woke terrified for them, surprised there was no snow.

Crawling out from under the pillows, she climbed up the branches onto the high roof of the tree house. She sat in a patch of sun looking down at the empty street. Where were they now? Still on a plane somewhere in the sky? Or were they already leaving the plane, going with Kate to claim their luggage?

The sun *was* higher, they *could* already be on the highway heading home. They *could* already be turning off Highway One down into the village. She waited. No car appeared. At last she crawled among her pillows again, trying to quiet her restless nerves. This time when she fell asleep she and Pan were safe in the Harpy's arms flying through the green-lit Netherworld over the craggy, dark lands . . .

She woke, startled.

A car was coming up the street. She wished it were Lucinda and Pedric and knew it couldn't be because the sun still wasn't high enough.

But the sound *was* Kate's car. She leaped up to peer over, watched the SUV pull into the drive. Yes, Kate's Lexus, curved bars on top where the Greenlaws' luggage was tied. Kit fled down the oak tree, dropped the last six feet as Lucinda opened the passenger door. She flew into Lucinda's arms. Lucinda's wrinkled cheeks were sunburned; she was dressed in safari pants and a khaki jacket. Pedric stepped out from the backseat dressed in khakis, too. They held her between them, hugging and loving her so hard they nearly squeezed her breath out. Lucinda was crying. Pedric's wrinkled cheeks were wet—but then they were all laughing and Kit thought she'd burst with happiness and they couldn't talk here in the front yard for fear of the neighbors, though they saw no one about. They hurried in the house, leaving the luggage on the car. Inside there was more hugging and Kit scrambled from one to the other and all of them talking at once. They were home, her dear family was home, they were safe, they were all together and safe.

In the living room Kate turned on the gas logs, made sure the tired couple was settled comfortably in their own soft chairs—as if Lucinda and Pedric were guests in their own house—then, in the kitchen, she put the kettle on for tea. As bright flames danced on the hearth, Kate went to bring in the luggage. The Greenlaws had traveled light, just their three canvas duffels. Why had they been tied on top when there was plenty of room in the big Lexus? But then Kit caught a whiff of salmon as Pedric went to help Kate carry in an oversize Styrofoam cooler; she sniffed a stronger scent as they headed for the laundry where the big freezer stood.

In the living room again, Kate told Kit, "At the last minute they changed their flights, decided to all come home together. I dropped Mike and Lindsey off first, so they could get their own salmon in the freezer.

"Lovely salmon," Lucinda said, leaning back in her soft chair. "A lovely trip," she said as Kit leaped into her lap. "But a tiring flight home, we didn't get much sleep last night."

"Tired and hungry," Pedric said. The couple stayed awake long enough to enjoy the hot tea and the quick lunch Kate had put together. Gathered before the fire, they shared a favorite, grilled cream cheese and salami sandwiches on rye; then Lucinda and Pedric headed for the bedroom, yawning. They didn't unpack, but pulled on nightclothes and crawled into bed, where Kit snuggled between them purring a sleepy song. She could hear Kate in the kitchen rinsing the dishes; soon she heard Kate leave, locking the front door behind her, heard her car back out. And Kit snuggled deeper, safe between Lucinda and Pedric—an unaccustomed midday nap for her two humans. Contentedly Kit dozed, drifting on a cloud of happiness that only a little loved cat could truly know.

IT WAS NEARLY a week before Lucinda and Pedric felt up to a party for their homecoming, a simple gathering of friends to celebrate their safe return. It would be two weeks more before MPPD would celebrate the end of another journey: the end of the Bleaks' cross-country escape, the moment when neither of the Bleaks could any longer dodge the law. Much would happen, between.

While Lucinda and Pedric rested at home with Kit, exchanging tales of their adventures, while Dulcie languished in her own house feeling heavy and nervous, Joe Grey prowled the offices of MPPD scanning computers, listening to phone calls, waiting, as Max and the detectives waited, for a positive response to the BOL. A few calls came in where a citizen thought he'd spotted the car speeding by, tried to follow it, lost it, and didn't get the license number. It was raining across several states, and the Bleaks, taking advantage of stormy night travel, managed to slip through. Meanwhile MPPD was busy with the usual shoplifting, car break-ins, and domestic violence cases that, these days, plagued even the tamest of small towns. There were, as well, daily inquiries from concerned citizens asking if there was any line yet on the attacker. The next report on a brown SUV, again with only a partial license number, put the couple somewhere in Alabama, still heading east. Alabama HP put patrols out, but in the heavy storm that had hit the state, the Bleaks had the advantage.

SAM COULD DRIVE only short distances because of his left leg. In Molena Point, he hadn't driven the van at all. Best to let people think he was more crippled than he was, to garner sympathy, make folks feel sorry for him. Now, moving across the country, he did drive, though it made his leg hurt. His increasing crankiness continued to irritate Tekla.

They didn't stop in Atlanta; she wanted to move on through, head north into Georgia's less populated backcountry. Freeway drivers were fast and brutal, so even she got nervous. They gassed up outside Canton, moved away on a narrower road into low hills, thick pine woods, and tacky mom-and-pop farms. "Home places," the gas attendant called them when they asked for directions, *home places*, with an accent that made Arnold smirk. The rain had stopped, the weather hot and humid, further souring Sam's mood.

With a local map they checked out a couple of shabby motels back in the hills at the edge of small manmade lakes. The only motels available in that backcountry, where people went to fish. Following the crooked roads they passed truck gardens and commercial chicken farms, long rows of rusted metal buildings that stunk of burned feathers and burned, dead chickens.

They holed up in a sleazy motel north of Jasper, the hick town where juror Meredith Wilson had moved to take care of her aging father. The weather had turned even more muggy, sticky and overcast with dark clouds hanging low. Sam said it was tornado weather. He was always imagining something, some disaster that never happened. Coming across country he'd grown more and more bad tempered, critical of her and of this whole plan, whining that they were going to get caught.

Well, they hadn't even been stopped. Couple of glances from GHP black-and-whites on the highway, but with Arnold ducked down out of sight, and with her long blond hair, they sailed right on through.

Getting caught hadn't been Sam's complaint earlier, right after the trial. Those first two "accidents," he'd been pretty high, seeing Herbert vindicated. "One more payback," he'd say. Then when she'd pulled off the first Molena Point assaults without a hitch, and then Arnold did one while she watched from the shadows, *then* Sam had been really excited. He'd even got a kick out of the fake attacks. "They probably deserved it, anyway," he'd said. And all along, *he* hadn't had to do one damn bit of the legwork.

But now suddenly, running from the cops, he'd decided, *this* late in the game, that he didn't like the program.

It was half his idea in the first place. More than half. It had been his rage as well as her own, at the twisted law, at the self-righteous courts. It was *Sam's* anger, at that lawyer and the jurors, that's what started them planning. He said, when Herbert was committed to die, "Those twelve lackeys just signed *their* death sentences. No one," Sam said, "has the right to take Herbert's life. Every one of them will pay, and pay hard."

It was later that he started to get shaky. Though not until they were through Texas did he really get cold feet, when that trucker slowed and ran alongside them for half a mile, looking. But by that time they'd changed license plates, and she and Arnold sat in the back, both with long blond wigs; she thought that was funny. Arnold didn't. But it was then that Sam, glancing up at the trucker, began to really whine.

Well, to hell with him. Now they were in Georgia she wasn't stopping, not this late in the game. Now they had a motel just where she wanted it, a place to hole up near to Meredith Wilson, and now it was her turn to pay.

A thin, nervous creature, the Wilson woman, fidgeting in the jury box looking upset every time the coroner up there on the witness stand mentioned some gory aspect of his supposedly unbiased examination—the bastard putting Herbert in the worst light. Deliberately making the weaker jurors, like Wilson, squirm with unease.

She wished she'd taken care of those other three jurors that were still in San Francisco, they'd been just as bad. Once she was done here, maybe they'd go back, see to them, too. By that time, those three would stop jumping at every shadow on the street, would have let their guard down. Meanwhile, the Wilson woman would be a pleasure to terrify before she died.

She didn't need to stage an accident, not back in these Georgia hills. This country was full of pot farmers and no-goods, it was nothing for someone to shoot a prowler. She read the papers, she'd looked at the statistics. People got shot all the time, raped, beat up. Half those guys were never caught, were friends with enough of the deputies to accidentally escape or to wiggle around the law.

Meredith Wilson lived only half a mile up the gravel road from the shoddy motel, and that was handy. Hot, hilly country running along both sides of the valley where the narrow lake lay. Mostly summer shacks down by the water, just the one old motel. It rented fishing poles and rowboats, and when Sam kept at her, whining not to do the Wilson woman but to move on and get away, when he'd *kept* at her, she rented poles for him and Arnold. Bought bait from the motel keeper and sent them out to the end of the dock to fish so maybe she could have a little peace.

Sam didn't like that the sky was so heavy and dark. She told him, there was a little wind, if he'd be patient it would blow the clouds away. Leaving them occupied, she went back to the small, muggy room, pulled the blinds, lay down on the sagging bed, thinking about the moves she still had to make. The shifting of money to a nearby state, calls from the throwaway cell phone, another motel registration, North Carolina maybe, using one of the fake driver's licenses and fake names. She needed to pay attention to the details. Well, she was good at that.

She was dozing off when the room darkened suddenly. The wind rose howling, the blind flapped, and the window glass warped into flashes and shadows. She hurried to look out but didn't understand what she was seeing. The air was full of flying sticks, flying boards. Two windows broke nearly in her face. The wind hit her like a freight train, the force sent her reeling away, covering her eyes. Tree limbs, furniture, pieces of wood and glass hit her as she was flung against the far wall. Behind her another window exploded and the roof was gone: she watched the whole roof lift and drop in the lake. It settled on the water, hung up on the edge of the dock. Where the roof *had* been, dark, roiling sky boiled down. Where she'd glimpsed Arnold racing in, pushing Sam in the wheelchair, now there was only the great slab of roof covering the dock and torn lumber and crashing wind. When she turned, the wall behind her was gone. The motel office and the line of rooms were gone, torn apart into rubble. She ran, falling and stumbling, dodging flying debris.

33

THE DAMENS' PATIO was crowded
with friends gathered belatedly to welcome the wanderers home from Alaska:
the Greenlaws, and Ryan's dad and
Lindsey. The walled garden echoed
softly with talk and laughter. Joe, Kit, and Pan wandered
among the guests begging politely. It took only a soft paw
and a gentle meow to receive an offering of Brie or pâté, as
their human friends, drinks in hand, waited for the main
course.

But soon Joe and Pan, growing impatient, leaped
to the wall beside the barbecue, closer to the broiling
salmon. Below them Kit prowled restlessly, her mind on
Dulcie and Wilma at home alone missing the party in
their patient deference to the unborn kittens. Even Joe
Grey, though he sat greedily licking his whiskers, had not
liked leaving his lady.

The backyard of Clyde's original bachelor cottage had once been a depressing expanse of dry grass and weeds that Clyde had euphemistically called the back lawn. Ryan's description had been less endearing. Under her imaginative design, and with a good crew, she had transformed the half-dead patch into a charming and private retreat. The tall white stucco walls offered privacy from prying neighbors, and cut the sea wind. The brick paving was dappled with leafy shadows from the young maple tree she had planted, and was edged by raised planters now bright with the last of the winter cyclamens. Beneath the trellis that shaded the barbecue, hickory coals glowed where Ryan and her dad stood broiling the big salmon that Mike had split down the center and laid on foil.

Father and daughter did not resemble each other except for their green eyes. Tall, slim Mike Flannery's sandy hair and his light and ruddy complexion spoke clearly of his Scots-Irish heritage, in contrast to Ryan's warmer coloring and dark hair from her Latina mother, who had died of cancer when Ryan and her sisters were small. Ryan was thankful for Lindsey, for her dad's new wife. He had remained single for so many years. Too busy to date, not wanting to date. Too occupied raising three girls, with the help of Scotty and Dallas. Lindsey's dimpled smile and laughing hazel eyes, her fun-loving, easygoing ways, fit exactly Ryan's view of what a stepmother should be.

Lindsey sat now with Charlie Harper and the Greenlaws at a small table, the three voyagers telling Charlie about their cruise. The same unstructured, small-boat cruise that, a few years ago, would have been Charlie and Max's honeymoon trip. If, at the last minute, local crime hadn't gotten in the way when someone blew up the church. Their close call minutes before the wedding still sickened Charlie. That disaster had pulled Max back into the office, unwilling to abandon his men during the continuing alerts and ensuing investigation.

With the money they hadn't spent on their honeymoon they had remodeled the ranch house that Max had owned for years. The handsome addition was a solid and lasting gift to each other, a luxury in which to enjoy their new life. *When Max isn't chasing the bad guys*, Charlie thought, *working long and crazy hours*.

But they had a lot to be grateful for, they *were* blessed, living on their comfortable acreage where they could have horses and the two big dogs, where they could ride over the open country in the evenings. *She* was blessed to have the time now to pursue her own career as an artist and writer. But loving Max, their close and comfortable marriage, that was way at the top of the list.

THE TWO TOMCATS, waiting for supper, watched their gathered human friends, and listened, attuned to every conversation, Joe Grey keen with interest, though Pan was solemn and withdrawn, the red tabby badly missing his father. Joe watched Kit, who had only now settled on Lucinda's lap between Charlie and Lindsey, trying hard to be still.

Kit wanted to ask Lucinda if someone should be with Dulcie and Wilma in case the kittens came, but among this crowd of human friends she could say nothing. She was always having to tell herself to be careful. It was so hard not to blurt out a question, to swallow back her words when so many urgencies railed inside her head, too compelling to *not* talk about.

But Dulcie's all right. What could happen? Wilma has a phone, and John Firetti is right here at the party, he and Mary are only minutes away if the kittens come. And then she worried, *How will the kittens handle their gift of speech? How will they learn that they must not speak in front of most humans? How will Dulcie impress on their young kitten minds that talking is a secret? If they do speak? If they are born with that talent, they will think it as ordinary as sharpening their claws. There's so much Dulcie and Joe will have to teach those tiny mites. How will the new babies ever learn to keep their kitty mouths shut?*

But Lindsey was saying to Charlie, "The new exhibit opens when?"

"Next week," Charlie said. "Two landscape painters, and a woman who does wonderful birds. And my animals." They watched Ryan leave the barbecue, pick up several empty plates from the table, and head into the kitchen.

"I'm coming to see your animal drawings," Lindsey said. She glanced down at Kit, then looked at Lucinda and Pedric. "There's one of your lovely tortoiseshell peering down from an oak branch that I'd like to buy." She smiled. "If you two don't snatch it up first. She's so lovely," she said, reaching to stroke Kit.

Kit gave her a sweet kitty smile and tried not to preen. But then, even with such praise, her attention turned suddenly to Max and Clyde and Scotty, sitting on the low wall of a flower bed; their serious talk, Clyde's sudden frown, drew her curiosity; she dropped to the brick paving and padded across to listen. Hopping up into the flower bed, she stretched out among the blooms.

"I don't like what will happen to the Bleak house," Clyde was saying, "now that they've skipped. Ryan could be stuck with a big loss, though she did, after a couple of weeks of Tekla's crazy changes, demand more money up front."

Scotty laughed. "Tekla wasn't keen on that."

Max said, "Their bank account—the only account we've found so far—shows only forty thousand. I expect the mortgage company will attach that, and look for the rest. I'd guess there'll be a foreclosure, maybe a short sale. If—when—we pick the Bleaks up, bring them in and prosecute, maybe the court will assign what assets they can find to help the victims or their families."

"What I don't get," Scotty said, "is why they ever bought that house, why they ever started on a renovation. If they came here to . . . If their intention was these attacks, they can't have thought they'd be staying permanently.

"Or," he said, "did they really believe they'd get away with this, that everyone would think the assaults were some kind of prank—and that the murders themselves were unfortunate accidents? That's insane thinking. Or," he added, "was that remodel all for show? For distraction, to put you off the track?"

"Pretty expensive cover," Max said, "though they're adept at manipulating money, sliding out from under."

Scotty shrugged. "The woman's crazy as a drunk squirrel." Picking up a canapé, he slipped it down to Rock, who sat watching the three men, the Weimaraner's eager yellow eyes following each morsel from hand to mouth. Clyde gave Scotty a look; Scotty knew Rock wasn't allowed a human diet, but sometimes the Scotsman couldn't resist.

"Well, we've got a line on them," Max said. "That sighting in Arkansas. Too bad the café owner didn't report it sooner. He didn't know about the BOL until a couple days later. A deputy stopped in for coffee, mentioned it and described the Bleaks." Max scratched Rock's ear as the dog nudged him, but he didn't feed Rock. "They were headed toward Georgia, if they kept on in that direction." He sipped his beer. "Maybe we'll pick them up on the East Coast, maybe the odds will turn." He looked up when Ryan caught his eye from the kitchen door, holding up the phone extension.

Max rose and headed for the kitchen, but moved on through toward the guest room, wanting that extension where he could hear above the party noise. The minute Joe Grey heard the guest room door close he dropped down from the wall and slipped away through the crowd. Kit, watching them both, hopped off Lucinda's lap and followed. Pan remained on the wall, stoic and quiet.

Kit, passing the guest room's closed door, paused to hear Max say, "She gave you this number, and not my cell phone?" His irritation told her he was talking about Evijean. She flew up the stairs as, above her on the desk, Joe Grey eased the phone from its cradle. As she landed beside him, he hugged the headset in his paws and eased it down on the blotter. They hoped Max would hear no small electronic click and no thump on the thinly padded surface. Pressing their ears close, Joe and Kit listened.

There was no break in Max's voice as if he'd been alerted that an extension had been picked up. Glancing at each other, they tried not to breathe into the speaker; and they watched the stairs warily in case someone started up to the office and studio—why would the two cats have the phone off the hook, crouched over it?

Mice in the speaker? Kit thought, and had to swallow her laugh.

Max's call was from Georgia, from Sheriff Jimmie Roy Dover. Dover's drawl was deep and heavy. Kit imagined a portly man who enjoyed his native southern cooking.

"So far, this is the way we've put it together," Dover was saying. "The worst of it is, we've got every unit out there looking for wounded, for bodies. And of course evidence is disturbed, stuff flying everywhere.

"Well, when the tornado passed, she *must* have known Sam's and Arnold's bodies were there on the dock, under the fallen roof. Maybe she thinks they're dead, maybe not. Maybe she runs to help them, maybe not. All we've found is a line of muddy footprints where she gets out of her room, where she runs outside—and she doesn't head their way.

"When she's clear of the worst of the debris," Dover said, "she pauses beside the body of a dead woman among the fallen walls. Later, one of our men photographed the body and what may be Tekla's footprints. The dead woman must still have been clutching her purse. Looks like Tekla—if those are her footprints—grabs the purse, you can see where it was dragged out from under the muddy debris. It took us a while to find this much, with the mess, and with victims needing help.

"We figure Tekla now has the woman's car keys, fished

them out of the purse. She steps on out to the parking strip. The first row of cars was smashed. Tornado sheared through the building neat as a Skilsaw, dumped the fallen walls on that row of vehicles. It missed the more distant cars, she must have bleeped the electronic key until she got a response from one of them, an answering bleep or blinking light. Now she has the right car, she gets in and takes off."

Max was silent, listening.

"But Tekla's wounded," Dover said. "She drives about three miles, then starts swerving, tire marks all over the road. Pretty quick she loses it, runs the car into a tree."

"You got her."

"No, we didn't. She must have sat there for a while, but then you could see where she backed the car up. Apparently didn't do too much damage, gas line must have been okay, apparently no tires punctured, and she takes off again."

"Well, hell."

"Rescue units were on their way to the motel, but in the dark and the hard wind they must have sped right by her, didn't ever see her.

"We didn't find the tire marks and the gouge in the tree until the next morning, first light. By that time," Dover said apologetically, "she was long gone."

"And Sam and Arnold?"

"Dead," Dover told him. "Crushed by the fallen roof. GBI has the report. They'll be calling you."

Max was quiet for a long while. Joe and Kit felt a surprising twist of pain for Sam and Arnold Bleak. No matter what they had done, no matter whether they'd been a willing part of Tekla's plan, the two cats didn't like to think of someone being crushed that way, in that terrible storm—and of Tekla not even trying to save them, just leaving them.

Max gave Dover his cell phone number. As the officers ended the call, Joe used both paws to ease the headset back onto the phone. They waited in the shadows at the top of the stairs until Max left the guest room and moved out to the patio again. Only when he'd gone did they wander casually down the empty stairway—but at the bottom Kit paused, startled, the fur along her back lifting. Joe Grey froze.

A faint ripple of tension ran through those gathered, through not everyone seemed aware of it. A subtle glance across the patio between Ryan and Clyde, between Charlie and Kate and the Greenlaws, a look as meaningful as a whisper—and the Firettis were headed for the front door, John fishing his car keys from his pocket.

"The kittens," Kit whispered. "Joe, the kittens are coming." But Joe was gone, racing away, flicking his heels in her face. Clyde bolted across the living room and out of the house, across the yard trying to snatch Joe from the air as the tomcat leaped past John Firetti—and Joe was through the driver's door into the back of the medical van.

Joe Grey glared out at Clyde. *"Leave me alone,"* he hissed softly. "They're *my* kittens!" Clyde stepped back, returning Joe's angry stare.

"Let him come," John said. "Let him be with her."

"But . . ."

"There's not much chance of germs, they're always together. Whatever Joe's been exposed to, so has she."

Silently Clyde stepped back. John closed the door and they were gone, roaring away up the street headed for Wilma's cottage. In the van, Mary reached out to Joe. He crept up between the bucket seats to the front and into her arms. She stroked him but said nothing; the kittens were coming and they were both nervous.

Behind the retreating van Clyde turned back to the house, ignoring questioning stares. Approaching the front door, where Max, Scotty, Mike, and Lindsey stood, he didn't want to talk and didn't want to know what they were thinking. Joe's behavior and his own were too strange. "Cats," Clyde said with disgust, shouldering past them, coming in the house, putting his arm around Ryan.

Ryan smiled, and before anyone could ask questions, she led Clyde away to set out the desserts and make a fresh pot of coffee.

Lucinda and Pedric had risen and headed for the living room behind the Firettis. Kate followed as, behind them, Clyde said casually to those around him, "John's off to deliver Dulcie's kittens. Wilma—Wilma's been a bit nervous."

From the mantel, Pan sat watching the action, cutting his eyes at Kit as she leaped up beside him. Kit wanted to be with Dulcie. Her look at Pan said, *Shall we?* She knew John didn't want a crowd. Birth was a private business. And he didn't want other cats' germs near the kittens. *But we haven't been around other cats— Oh! Except the ferals, up in the hills. And John's ferals at the beach.*

But they've had their shots. And John always changes his shoes when he gets back in the van, changes his lab coat and cleans his hands.

302

She thought about Dulcie in labor and hurting. She told herself they'd keep out of the way, that they'd stay outdoors, she just wanted to *be* there. She looked at Pan, edgy and nervous. The fascination of Dulcie's miracle made her shiver. Pan frowned back at her but then reluctantly he rose. Together they dropped from the mantel and fled out the open door.

34

DULCIE PACED THE living room back and forth, past the flickering hearth, past the couch where Wilma was pretending to read. She could feel Wilma watching her and trying not to worry. She moved from room to room, padded into the kitchen, sniffed at the nice custard Wilma had set out, and turned her face away. She drank from her bowl, but only a few laps. There were no pains yet, but her restlessness was intolerable. She wanted to crawl into her new kittening box, and she didn't want to be confined in there. She wanted to creep into the farthest corner of the house under the darkest bed, but when she did that, she backed out again. She wanted to be near Wilma, but then Wilma's lap was too warm. She wanted Wilma to come to the kittening box with her, but she didn't want anyone there at all. This should be a lonely vigil, only her kittens should share the coming moments, she wanted to be alone to bring them into the world, yet she didn't want to be alone.

The kittening box Wilma had set up in the bedroom, beside her own bed, was sturdy and splendid. It was constructed from a heavy packing carton uncontaminated by grocery store insecticides. Wilma had cut a smooth little door at one corner arranged so a draft wouldn't blow in. She had made a lid for the top, which could be lifted off to clean the box. A nice thick bed of newspapers lined the bottom. Papers that Dulcie wanted to rip up, that she intended soon to tear apart, she could feel the urge itching in her pads; papers that would be thrown away after the birthing and would be replaced by a warm blanket.

There were clean soft towels stacked outside the box, that John Firetti had asked Wilma to provide. Everything was ready. But as perfect as was her nest, Dulcie couldn't stop creeping into dark corners, turning around and around and then hurrying out again into space and light—and then returning to her box. She didn't know what she wanted; she was eager and scared. She felt ravenous, but the sight of food made her ill. She wanted Joe Grey, but she didn't want him until the ordeal was over. Where was he, why wasn't he there with her? She returned to the kitchen, longing to race outside, but Wilma, after futile attempts to reason with her, had fetched the electric drill and screwed her cat door closed.

And now suddenly as she paced and fussed, the front doorbell rang. Wilma picked her up to keep her from running out. She opened the door to the Firettis, they stepped in quickly, and Mary deftly shut the door behind them. Even a sentient, speaking cat could behave foolishly when she was about to give birth. The minute Dulcie saw John, she relaxed. The minute Joe Grey wound in behind John's ankles, Dulcie hissed and spat at him. Why was she behaving like this?

She let John take her from Wilma's arms; as she laid her head against him, trust in the good doctor filled her. She quit spitting at Joe and she felt easier. It was then that Charlie arrived. Dulcie heard the Blazer pulling up, heard the kitchen door open and close. Charlie came through the house, reached gently to stroke Dulcie, then put her arm around Wilma. "I thought you might like a little more moral support?"

Wilma smiled and hugged her niece. At their feet Joe Grey was quiet, watching their friends gathered around Dulcie. Dulcie didn't want to spit at him now. And now, for a moment, a brightness filled the room, glowing around them, and she could hear Misto's whisper, the faintest breath, *You will be all right, the babies are strong, they will be just fine.* The glow hung a moment, then was gone, Misto's warm, familiar voice gone. But his love remained.

IN WILMA'S BEDROOM, John lifted Dulcie down into the kittening box. She settled at once, she didn't fight him, she didn't try to run away now. She put a paw up, she wanted him near, she didn't want him to leave her. John waited, sitting on a low bedroom chair beside the box. She felt restless but then lay quiet. Her purr rumbled stronger, a purr of anticipation and of fear waiting for the pains that would come. She heard from the living room a bold scratching at the door, heard the door open, heard Kit's mewl, Wilma's voice and then Pan's, and she was glad they were there: a loving entourage waiting—filled with kindness but leaving her to her privacy.

It was a long time before the first pain hit her, then soon another, and another. Soon they were coming faster than John had told her they would. She murmured once. Another pain and she strained and mewled softly. She cried loudly only once, pushing hard when the pains were sharpest. The rhythm of the contractions carried her as if on a huge wave, soon so close together she thought she couldn't breathe; this first kitten was eager, was clamoring to get out.

In the living room where Charlie held Joe Grey, he tried to leap away when he heard Dulcie cry, tried to go to her. Charlie grabbed the nape of his neck. "Don't, Joe. Don't go in and upset her, let her be, John is with her." She scowled down at him. "You have to be patient."

He didn't feel *patient*, he wanted to be with Dulcie. He hissed at Charlie and raised a bristling paw. She held him hard, held him until he eased off and settled once more on her lap, only faintly snarling. Dulcie was hurting. His lady was in there crying out and maybe in danger. Birthing kittens was frightening and perilous, why hadn't he realized that? He butted his head against Charlie, shaken with fear.

Across the room Kit and Pan snuggled close to Wilma in her soft chair, Kit shivering but Pan stoic and calm, hoping to calm his own lady. They heard Dulcie's whimpers and her single yowl, they watched Joe Grey flinch and strike at Charlie, saw Charlie's green eyes widen as she settled him once more. They heard the back door open, watched Kate and the Greenlaws slip through. Dulcie's patient but nervous attendants filled the living room, looking quietly at each other, waiting. These were not ordinary kittens, these were miracle kittens, and their friends waited nervously.

Only Ryan and Clyde were absent. How could they leave their guests to attend such an ordinary occurrence as the birth of kittens? So many folks had already rushed out. The Damens didn't need more puzzled questions—but Joe Grey wished they were there. Clyde to bolster his courage, Ryan, like Charlie, to soothe and mother him.

"Sometimes," Charlie said, stroking him, "it's harder on the father."

Joe Grey glared up at her. How could that be true?

"Do you remember," Charlie asked him, "how proud you were when Dulcie told you? Proud and shy and excited?"

Joe remembered. *"Kittens?"* he'd cried. *"Our kittens?"* He remembered backing away from Dulcie, perplexed and amazed, racing away across the rooftops, then flying around her, skidding nose to nose with her. *"Kittens?"*

IT WAS LATE evening. The three kittens had been born safe and strong. Dulcie had cleaned them up and was resting, the tiny little ones nursing against her when Joe Grey slipped into the room. John Firetti, kneeling over the box, looked up and nodded.

"Come, Joe Grey. Come see your babies." John and

Mary and Wilma had just cleaned the kittening box, Mary sliding the soiled newspapers out from under as John and Wilma gently lifted Dulcie and the kittens. Deftly Mary had slipped a thick warm blanket in, and John had settled mother and babies back onto their nest. Joe Grey entered warily, nearly electrified with shyness.

He crept up onto Wilma's bed where he could look down into the box. He crouched there very still, looking at their new family. He was, for an instant, fearful of how he might respond. He was too aware of the ancient instinct of some tomcats to ravage their own young. Would this age-old urge surface in him now, would emotions he detested hit him suddenly? Looking down into the box, he was ready to turn and run before he hurt his tiny, helpless babies.

But no. Watching Dulcie and their three beautiful kittens, Joe Grey knew only wonder.

Only when Dulcie lifted her eyes to him did he see for an instant the female's equally primitive response, the inborn ferocity of a mother cat to protect her young. But then her look softened, her gaze matched his own contentment. They looked at each other and at their babies, and they knew they had made a fine family. Three kittens so beautiful that Joe couldn't resist slipping carefully down next to the box, next to the door where he could reach his nose in, could breathe in their sweet kitten scent.

"Courtney," Dulcie said, licking the swirl-marked calico female. Joe thought about names for the two boys but nothing seemed to fit; the two pale buff kittens were still so small, how could one know what kind of cats they would be?

Lucinda and Pedric and Kate slipped into the bedroom, having removed their shoes. They looked down into the box at the three tiny kittens and pronounced them the most beautiful babies ever born. Charlie was enchanted by them. She came again the next morning wearing freshly laundered jeans and shirt, removing her shoes outside the back door, washing her hands at the kitchen sink. Not until the kittens had their several shots would the "germ vigil," as Wilma called it, ease off and the little family be free from isolation. John Firetti, indeed, worried over the rare little newborns.

Now everyone, humans and cats, would wait impatiently the two weeks or more for the kittens' eyes and ears to open, for their curiosity to brighten. Wait for them to crowd to the door of their kitten box, peering out, for the boy kittens to reach for the wider world. Courtney needed no encouragement; she was already pawing at every new stir of air, mewling at every small change that occurred around her.

The next days, while the friends waited to hear more than kittenish meows, to know if the kittens *would* speak, Joe Grey prowled restlessly between his new family and MPPD: a doting father, but still a nervous hunter, as alert as were the police for some clue to Tekla's next move, for law enforcement somewhere on the East Coast to pick up her trail, to arrest and confine her.

35

TEKLA'S LEFT ARM and side hurt bad from where the car had hit the tree. Maybe she was only bruised, or maybe she'd cracked a rib. Fighting the "borrowed" Honda back to the narrow dirt road, getting it on solid ground again and easing out of there in the wind and blowing rain, she slipped the loaded revolver from her purse into her jacket pocket. She was still nervous over the automatic's disappearing, back in Molena Point. She and Sam had fought all the way across the country about that, too. Either Sam or Arnold was lying, or both were. Why would Sam move the gun? To use it as evidence, to prove that *she'd* killed Ben Stonewell? If the cops picked them up, did he mean to turn it over, with her prints on it, get himself off the hook?

There'd been no one else in the house to take it after she'd put it in her suitcase. Had he stashed it in the garage somewhere? If he had, sure as hell, the cops would find it. She didn't understand what he was up to, and that scared her. She'd wondered if, that night in that first out-of-the-way motel, somehow a maid had slipped in, gone through their bags, and taken the gun. That didn't seem likely; they'd left only long enough for a quick burger, and she'd locked her bag. The other gun, the Magnum that was now in her pocket, hadn't been taken.

But all across the country, Sam had been losing his nerve. Whining, getting cold feet, not wanting to go on with this, wanting to leave the last jurors they *could* reach. Just let them go free, after all his earlier talk about getting even. His malingering had delayed them, too, pulling off the highway early, sleeping in late, not wanting to get started.

After she shot Ben, she'd wiped off her prints, but then she'd handled the gun briefly again when she packed it. That missing gun scared her bad. What the hell had Sam done?

When the tornado hit, she'd been lucky to get out of there, the whole room caved in around her. Lucky to *find* her purse with the Magnum safe inside. The .357 was heavy, but with the automatic gone, it would have to do. With that mess back there, the twisting wind picking up the roof, she knew Sam and Arnold were dead. How could she go to look when the fallen roof covered the entire dock, when everything it had hit was underwater. All she could do was run.

She was terrified when she found their car outside the room smashed beyond use, the wall of the building crushing it. She was lucky to nearly fall over that dead woman, that's what saved her. Rooting around under the woman's body where she could see a leather strap, digging out the woman's purse, that was luck, finding those car keys. Beeping the car, hoping *it* wasn't crushed, she'd found it and gotten out of there fast. You had to live right to have luck like that—but then on the dark dirt road when she hit that tree, skidded off the road, she thought she was done for. Jammed in tight against the steering wheel, she'd hurt bad. Cops with their lights and sirens careening by in the dark never even saw her, not that she wanted to be found.

Strange that once she'd left the destroyed motel, had passed maybe half a mile of wrecked cottages and fallen trees stacked like broken toothpicks, that was the end of the damage. Nothing more had been hit. That's where the road turned away from the lake and climbed. Was that how these tornadoes worked? Ran along between the hills, hit in just the low places?

Now, using the penlight in her purse and the local map, she followed the back roads to the next small town. It hadn't been hit, either, just a little wind damage, an awning torn. Dinky little burg, one dumpy motel right out of some old movie. She checked into a room, she had no choice. She hurt real bad and it was too dark to move on with what she meant to do. She couldn't afford to get stuck on those back roads at night, lost trying to get away afterward.

At the front desk she paid with cash. The bearded fat man didn't blink an eye, just gave her change. The room was ancient. Scarred wood furniture, worn-out bedspread, limp drapes. She finished the bag of chips she'd bought at the last gas station. Her side felt like fire. Was it going to keep getting worse?

She took four Tylenols, didn't undress, just fell into bed. She slept most of the night. She woke before dawn, sick with hurting. When she stripped and looked in the mirror her whole side was purple, a vast, tender bruise. Sure as hell her ribs were cracked, maybe broken. She didn't need this, she didn't want to move on Meredith Wilson in this condition.

Picking up the phone, she cajoled the bearded, overweight rube at the front desk into sending her up some breakfast. What she got was stale cold cereal with milk that was about to go sour, and a cup of lukewarm coffee. She ate, took four more pain pills, crawled back in bed and slept.

She stayed in the fusty room a week, hurting bad, sure her ribs were broken. She didn't want to see some doctor. Toward the end of the week the pain began to ease, and the bruises were fading. She lived on stale cereal and stale cheese sandwiches. On the eighth day she hauled herself out of bed, sick of the place, sick of the food. It was late morning, later than she'd meant to start, but she couldn't stand waiting any longer. Making sure she had the map, she headed out, paid the rest of her bill with cash. She stopped at a burger place for takeout, first hot food she'd had in a week.

None of the narrow back roads were marked, most of them dirt with patches of gravel, walled in by thick timber tangled with bushes and vines. She had to guess which road, none were marked. Only once in a while did a small, faded sign appear, but with names she couldn't find on the local map. Twice she came to dead ends and had to turn around. It was early yet, but the woods were growing dim; this was taking longer than she'd planned. She didn't want to get on toward evening out here, get lost in the pitch-dark. She wanted to find the woman, do what she came for, and get back to civilization.

Meredith Wilson was the first of the jurors who had left the city after the two accidents. She didn't know whether it was because of the accidents. Her friend from the court, who'd gotten the sealed jury list for her, said for sure the Wilson woman was going back to Georgia to be with her sick father; Meredith Wilson had told her all about it. A jury clerk could get real friendly with the jury, bringing them sandwiches and coffee and all. Her friend Denise Ripley, they went way back, they'd been in high school together, in the city. Denise had worked for the Clerk of the Court for years—she had not only given Tekla the jury list and their addresses, she'd passed along other useful information, including several people headed for Molena Point, maybe for a few days' getaway after the stress of the trial.

She'd found out more about those people, first in the city itself, talking to their neighbors, checking mailboxes. That's why it took so long from the time Herbert was sentenced and sent to San Quentin until she went into action. Took time, finding out how best to get at each of those righteous jurors who had sentenced her son to die—die for a pitiful weakness that Herbert himself couldn't help and that no one knew how to cure.

On these narrow dirt roads trying to follow the map, it seemed like she'd been driving forever; and now the road itself was beginning to darken as the sun dropped behind the trees. The sky was clouding over again, too. She didn't like this. But she was too far now to turn back.

When she came to the next fork, she could see a small

sign. When she brightened the headlights, a thrill touched her: the hand-carved letters read WILSON. This was it. She wasn't lost. Far ahead through the pine woods, scruffy open fields still held evening light. She turned off the headlights, moved on up the dirt road. She could smell the stink of chicken houses, smell them before she saw them. Bumping along, she came to the turnoff that led, maybe a quarter mile, to the long rows of corrugated metal buildings rusted and sour with chicken dirt. A cottage stood between the road and the metal structures, its two front windows faintly lit, enough to light her way—a raw wooden shack with a weedy vegetable garden along one side. A wide front porch ran across the front, complete with rocking chairs. She could smell woodsmoke and could smell meat frying. Before turning into the long dirt drive she paused at the mailbox.

The name and numbers were nearly invisible. ROBERT CLIVE WILSON. She pulled along the rutted drive to a small stand of red-leaved trees. She decided the ground was hard enough that she wouldn't get stuck. Carefully she backed into the shadows between the spindly trunks. She didn't get out of the car but sat waiting for full dark. Finding the house cheered her, had put her back in charge again. She sat watching the windows as darkness closed in, feeling the car rock when the wind picked up. She'd say she was looking for a Timmie Lee Baker. Any name would do, she'd say she was lost. She could repeat road names from the map and from the few nearly illegible signs; that was all she needed to get her foot in the door. When it was dark enough and with the wind pushing at her back, she stepped out of the car, the loaded .357 heavy in her jacket pocket as she approached the house.

36

LATE-EVENING SUN SHONE through Wilma's dining room windows into the large new cat cage she had set up there. The bedroom quarters had grown too small for full-time use. Now Dulcie and the kittens, and Joe Grey, too, had room to sprawl for a nap in the sunshine. The ringing phone woke Joe.

The babies didn't stir, they slept deeply, their tummies extended and full. Nor did Dulcie wake, worn out from the kittens crawling over her in their attempts at rough-and-tumble. The babies' eyes were open and their tiny ears unfurled. It was less than two weeks and Joe was proud of them; John Firetti called them precocious and waited eagerly for their first words. They all waited, trying to think how to *keep* them from talking at the wrong time, in front of the wrong people.

Wilma answered the phone on the second ring. Joe heard her desk chair squeak.

"Oh, yes, I'd love that. What can I do?" By the smile in her voice he could tell it was Charlie, she had a special tone for her niece. "Are you sure? Is Max . . . ?" She was quiet, then, "Yes, that sounds fine." Hanging up, she looked across into the dining room. "Charlie's on her way over with a shrimp casserole, a last-minute potluck. Ryan and Clyde are bringing a salad. Max will be along, he's at the station waiting . . ." She paused, watching Joe. "Waiting for a callback from Georgia."

Joe came to full attention.

She said, "Looks like they've got Tekla!"

He leaped out of the pen and headed for the cat door. Wilma watched him disappear. She couldn't *not* have told him, nor would she have stopped him.

Joe, racing from peak to peak, was hardly aware of clouds darkening toward evening. Almost thundering over the roofs, he hit the courthouse tiles, raced their length and dropped down the oak tree to the station. He slid in through the glass door behind a pair of teenage girls. Across the lobby, Detective Davis was headed down the hall toward Max's office. Joe fled past the counter, hoping to avoid Evijean, but a familiar voice stopped him.

"Yes, sir, Captain. I'm still waiting, I'll put it straight through." Mabel Farthy's voice—Mabel was back. There she was, his blond, pillow-soft friend standing at the counter beside sour-faced Evijean Simpson, a stack of papers and files between them. Was Mabel catching up on the cases at hand? Was this Evijean's last day? He was torn between racing to Max's office or leaping to the counter.

He leaped—Mabel grabbed him up in a warm and smothering hug. "Oh, my. Look at you. Where's Dulcie?

But Davis said she had kittens? Oh, *my*! Imagine. Kittens! You're a father, Joe Grey, and don't you look proud."

He tried not to look too proud. He rubbed his face against her shoulder; he nuzzled her face and smiled. She petted him until Evijean cleared her throat loudly. When Mabel turned to frown at Evijean, Joe slipped from her arms, dropped from the counter and fled. He didn't want to get Mabel in an argument with Evijean on her first day back.

Life was good, leave it that way. Evijean would soon be history.

Slipping into Max's office, he hoped that somewhere on the East Coast, Tekla was resting her heels in the cooler, and that would top off the day.

Juana and Dallas sat on the leather couch, sipping fresh coffee and looking pleased. Max lounged behind his desk, his feet up on the blotter, waiting for Mabel to put his call through. Whatever was coming down, all three were smiling. Joe flopped down on the deep Persian rug and tried not to look curious. He rolled luxuriously, then had a little wash. Nothing so distracted a human from a cat's true intention as to watch the cat bathe. A little cat spit, a busy tongue licking across sleek fur, and most people would relax as if hypnotized. Maybe they could feel the comforting massage in their own being, a kind of reflex contentment. He looked at Max, at ease behind the desk, and a sense filled Joe that indeed all was right with the world. Slipping up on the couch beside Juana, he waited, as the officers waited, until the phone's open speaker came to life—until Mabel said, "Sheriff Dover is on, Captain Harper." The call from Georgia law enforcement was not from the GBI as Joe had expected, but the deep, slow voice of Pickens County Sheriff Jimmie Roy Dover.

When Max answered, Dover said simply, "We lost her."

"Lost her?" Max barked, envisioning as Joe did that again Tekla had given them the slip.

But Dover didn't sound dismayed. In fact there was a smile in his voice.

"When she disappeared, and every deputy out helping the rescue crews, the best we could do at the moment was put out another BOL and alert Meredith Wilson. This wasn't one big tornado, Max. Narrow, slicing ones hit all over the state, scoured the low places between the hills. At the lake here, wiped out nine cabins and the motel. That low wind roaring along the cleft between the hills, screaming like a banshee, struck through half a dozen of these valleys, uprooted trees like mown hay, flattened buildings. Couldn't tell where it would hit next, never seen anything like it. Local police and highway patrol and us, we had every man out looking for the dead and injured.

"Twenty-four hours, the storm began to ease up. No word on Tekla. Phone lines were down, but we got Meredith Wilson on her cell. All was quiet at their place. We sent two deputies out there as soon as we could spare them, but no sign of Tekla.

"About then, GHP got a call from a citizen with a police band, said he'd spotted the car Tekla was driving, just north of Waycross. Blue Honda Civic, he didn't get the plate. Headed for Florida. Lone woman driving, blond hair that looked like a wig, he said, kind of crooked on her head. County sheriff deputy made her and pulled her over.

"It wasn't Tekla," Dover said. "This woman checked

out, she had family in Florida. Officer fingerprinted her but no match, and sent her on her way."

On the couch beside Davis, Joe had to hide a smile. These law enforcement guys from the South, they were talkers, they liked to string it out. Well, that was okay, southerners were storytellers, it was in their blood. Wilma said some of the best writers came from the South. She had described for him and Dulcie southern families sitting on their deep, covered porch in the warm evenings, rocking away, watching the fireflies, weaving family stories and ghost stories and their traditional tales.

"We had two other reports," Dover said. "Blue Hondas, lone women, but both turned out duds. Until tonight, nearly a week later," the sheriff said.

"Weather blowing in again, but it wasn't here yet, just heavy clouds, when Meredith Wilson called us. Said a blue four-door, she couldn't tell the make, had stopped on the road in front of their mailbox, then turned in, pulled in among a stand of young sourwood trees.

"I sent two deputies. Takes about twenty minutes from the station, and called in four more as backup. Our first car gets there and turns in, the storm is gearing up. Enough wind to cover sound and movement. Meredith and her father could still see Tekla's car. We told them to stay inside, don't answer the door, stay away from the windows.

"First patrol car checks in, approaching the house. Next thing, we hear gunfire. Second car pulls up and we get an Officer Down call. We radioed for the medics. Two more cars arrive, deputies surround the place. The officer is lying in the doorway shot in the leg and a wound in his side, his partner kneeling over him applying tourniquets to stop the blood. And Tekla's sprawled on the steps," Dover said. "She's dead, shot through the chest—but not by our men."

There was a little pause. Dover said, "Meredith Wilson killed her, with her daddy's favorite handgun."

They were all silent. Then, "It was later we found the scar on Tekla's revolver where one of my deputies shot it from her hand. She could well have kept firing, have hit more of us if she'd had the chance.

"So I guess," Dover said dryly, "besides saving lives, Meredith Wilson saved the California courts some money. Maybe," he said, "the good Lord handled this one."

And Joe Grey, face hidden from the chief and the detectives, couldn't stop smiling.

IN WILMA'S LIVING room before the fire, Max and Charlie sat close together on the couch, Ryan and Clyde on cushions before the hearth. Joe and Dulcie lay on Wilma's lap, in her easy chair. The kittens, for the moment, were blessedly asleep in their pen. The house smelled deliciously of shrimp casserole set in the oven to keep warm. Ryan's big salad bowl and a basket of French bread waited on the table. Impromptu meals, Wilma thought, were the best. The Greenlaws had brought a berry shortcake; Lucinda sat near Charlie and Max, at the other end of the couch; Pedric chose the padded desk chair, Kit stretched out on the blotter beside him. Pan was home with the Firettis. Kate and Scotty had opted out for their own impromptu supper, they didn't say where.

Just this morning John Firetti had examined the kittens again, had pronounced them fine and healthy and had doted over the babies. Talking to the kittens and stroking them, he had called the lighter buff boy Buffin, then had looked up guiltily at Dulcie. "It's just a nickname, it's not for me to name them."

Dulcie smiled. "Why shouldn't you name them? You helped them into the world. Buffin? I like that. Buffin," she said, "as golden pale as the sea sand. The name has a gentle sound." She looked up at John. "Misto named Courtney, and he would like this name, too." She laid a paw on John's hand and looked down at the tiny baby. "Hello, Buffin."

"And this other little fellow," John said, "with the dark shadow on his pale coat? Does he yet have a name?"

"Not yet," Dulcie said. "I guess Joe and I are waiting . . . for our friends to help. Or maybe," she said, "maybe we're waiting for this little boy to name himself."

And now this evening, this was how it happened when, the friends all moving to the dining table, paused around the cage looking down at the kittens.

"You don't want common names," Max said, startling Dulcie—as if they had been talking about just that. She watched the chief nervously.

"They're Joe's kittens," he said, "Joe Grey's and Dulcie's."

Everyone was quiet. What was Max saying, what was he thinking? That the kittens were far more than *just* special? In the silent room Charlie glanced at Ryan and Clyde, and at Wilma.

But maybe, Dulcie thought, Max meant nothing—his expression was bland, maybe he was just taken with her babies. He had grown to enjoy Joe's bold and purring interruptions in the office. Now he admired Joe's kittens; surely that was all he had meant.

Charlie said, "Wilma has already named the girl kitten, she is Courtney."

"And this morning," Wilma said, "John Firretti gave me another name . . . maybe not so original, but it fits." She bent down to stroke the paler boy kitten. "Buffin," she said. "This is Buffin."

Charlie said, "I like it, it's a sturdy name. He *is* sturdy, look at him." She leaned down to pet the sand-colored baby. But when she picked up the other kitten, with the gray cloud marking his pale coat, he immediately nipped her and dug his claws in, making her laugh. "This one's a little wildcat, he's going to be a handful." She glanced down at Dulcie and Joe, then at Wilma.

"Striker," she said. "What about Striker? But Striker as in to protect, not to threaten."

Behind Max's back, Dulcie and Joe looked at each other, amused. Yes, a strong name. And a strong, determined kitten. And Joe thought, *A good name for a young cop kitten—if that's what Striker turns out to be.*

Wilma looked into Dulcie's green eyes, then into Joe's level gaze. "Striker. I like that," she told Charlie. When she took the kitten from Charlie she received a sharp scratch of her own. She set him down in the pen, tapped him gently on the nose when he tried for another swat. When he drew back, she gently stroked him. He looked up at her uncertainly.

"Hello, Striker," she said, laughing, and she removed her hand before he thought to lunge again.

When Ryan brought the casserole to the table and everyone gathered, Courtney and her brothers, smelling the warm shrimp, let out lusty mewls. Even kittens with full tummies could bellow demanding cries; but a look and a soft mumble from Dulcie, and soon they quieted.

As they all took their seats, Ryan was saying, "What I don't get is how Tekla got the jurors' names. Doesn't the court seal those, so no one can influence the jurors during the trial or do them harm afterward?"

"It was the jury clerk," Max said, "a Denise Ripley, she passed the names and addresses to Tekla. They went through high school together. Maybe buddies, maybe not, but Tekla paid her well. Ripley spilled when the chief judge called her in. He got her story—I'm not sure how. Maybe she thought he would only fire her and not prosecute, though I'm sure he didn't promise that." Max smiled. "Ripley's in jail now, under indictment."

"She got what she deserved," Charlie said, "and so did Tekla. Meredith Wilson is alive, unharmed. Because of Meredith, maybe so are a couple of deputies. And maybe those jurors, too, who were lucky enough to escape the Bleaks."

"What would the world be like," Ryan wondered, "if all the vindictive, blood-hungry people suddenly went up in smoke, vanished into nothing?"

"I'd be out of a job," Max said, laughing. "I'd be spending my time with Charlie, in a long and satisfying retirement."

"And pretty soon," Wilma said, "with no more evil in the world for us to stand against, people would become as weak and ineffective as garden slugs."

Dulcie thought about that. But in her mind, at that moment, the prospect of an innocent world, of a safe life for her kittens, such a dream would offer more than a few virtues.

It was later in the evening when, yawning, Dulcie watched their friends depart, that she thought a little prayer for them all, for cats, kittens, and humans. Her purr was deep, she was content with life as she and Wilma moved the kittens into their nighttime pen beside Wilma's bed. Dulcie settled down among them, inundated by pummeling babies who did not want to go to sleep. Soothing her lively youngsters with a gentle paw, she willed herself to forget the last lingering images of Tekla's brutal assaults, of the suffering that woman had caused.

She thanked the greater powers for all their good fortune, despite the ugliness. She thought of Pan tucked up with the Firettis, the three friends comforting one another. She thought lovingly of Joe Grey stretched out in his tower staring out at the sky and she thought, *Good night, Joe, dream well*—and in his tower at the same moment Joe Grey bade happy dreams to Dulcie and their three babies. The late spring night tucked warmly around humans and cats, and the kittens beneath Dulcie's restraining paw drifted into sleep, safe and loved. Dulcie, looking out the bedroom windows to the night, hoped that Misto could hear the kittens' purrs and could hear her own contented rumble. And they all slept, cats and humans.

It was only much later that Dulcie woke again and rose, that she trotted out into the dark living room, leaped onto Wilma's desk, and with a quick paw she turned on the computer. She sat in its soft light thinking about Misto,

thinking about the poem in her head that had been forming ever since the old cat died, the verses that wouldn't
leave her, and slowly, with her forepaws squeezed small,
she shared her words on the screen, her ode to Misto.

> *Golden spirit, you reach down*
> *Your ghostly paw to touch the earth you love*
> *To touch the sea*
> *To stroke the lakes and rivers*
> *To caress green hills and forests*
> *To bless this mortal land you left behind.*
>
> *Though you are gone,*
> *Your spirit dances now*
> *In bright eternity.*
> *You are young again and strong*
> *You whisper, "I am with you,*
> *I am with you, still."*
>
> *You whisper,*
> *"When your spirits join me,*
> *You will know all secrets.*
> *You will then fly free,*
> *Fly paw to paw with me.*
> *Our spirits sailing free."*